T0146431

SHADOW
OF THE
FALL

Other titles by Aaron T. Brownell

Reflection
Contention; a Sara Grey Tale
The Long Path
Progression; a Sara Grey Tale

SHADOW
OF THE
FALL

A Novel

AARON T. BROWNELL

SHADOW OF THE FALL
A NOVEL

iUniverse books may be ordered through booksellers or by contacting:

iUniverse
1663 Liberty Drive
Bloomington, IN 47403
www.iuniverse.com
1-800-Authors (1-800-288-4677)

ISBN: 978-1-5320-5072-5 (sc)
ISBN: 978-1-5320-5071-8 (e)

Library of Congress Control Number: 2018906838

Print information available on the last page.

iUniverse rev. date: 07/31/2018

Thank you:

Once again I would like to thank my good friend Jeffery for correcting and massaging my horrendous use of the English language. I owe him beers.

CONTENTS

CHAPTER 1

Lieutenant Colonel Pickard watched the young woman tap the eraser end of a pencil on the casing of the device. Each time the eraser tip struck the weapon he could feel his blood pressure rise. He could not for the life of himself figure out how he had come to be sequestered in an ammunition bunker with a live nuclear device and a seemingly crazy woman, but he now just hoped he made it out in one piece. He also couldn't quite figure out how the flash traffic communications from the base weapons team had landed the young woman at his doorstep, but he was sure it would all end badly.

The young woman leaning over the open bomb casing, wearing beach shorts and blue bikini top, could not be any more than in her mid-20s. Her hair pulled back into a loose blond ponytail made her look ever younger than that. The thick black plastic rimmed glasses she was wearing just made her look strange.

"Hmm, that's odd. Not bad odd, but just odd."

"What's odd?" The military officer didn't really want to ask the question, it was reflex.

"Every time I tap the outer casing, the elevational-timer jumps down a number. The actual clockwork isn't really moving, as much as the analog display is. I was hoping it was going to be a mechanical problem. It's usually a straight up mechanical problem when they've been in the crate as long as this fellow has. This, however, is definitely an electrical problem. That's odd."

What does odd mean, exactly?"

"Well, the same way a plane's control surfaces are basically electric-over-hydraulic, and a computer actually flies the plane –"

"You mean, fly-by-wire?"

"Exactly. You can think of a nuclear bomb the same way. Just here, it's electric-over-mechanical. Normally, when a mechanical problem appears, you unplug the electronics and fix the mechanics."

"But, you don't when it's electronic?"

"It's certainly not recommended. With the electronics being on the top end, they can act as a mask. The problem could be an electronics component issue, or they could be masking some mechanical problem downstream of the trigger assembly. Masking in such a way as to make it appear upstream, follow? If you just unplug it, it could go boom."

The lieutenant colonel visibly blanched. Kristin smiled at the man softly and looked back down at the device, which she had disassembled as far as she was comfortable.

Dr. Kristin Marie Hughes, twenty nine years old and leading field operative for the Nuclear Emergency Search Team (NEST), was nobody's idea of your typical weapon's specialist. At 5 feet 6 inches tall, crystal clear blue eyes, and a beach-caliber body that tipped the scales at about 120 pounds, she was much more surfer girl than scientist. This was especially true considering her current state of dress. Sadly, her b-cup bikini seemed to always make more of an impression on people than her PhD in Nuclear Physics or her expertise with weapons.

In a funny way, her toned physique had nothing to do with her All-American beach girl persona. Living in Henderson, Nevada, outside Las Vegas, she spent her off time rock climbing, or mountain biking. She was a naturally outdoorsy girl and it showed in her attributes.

Why was she currently in Italy? Well, she wasn't. Not really. She had been on a beach in Croatia when the problem with the nuke had first started. A phone call, a helo ride, and a Mach 2.0 fighter jet flight had put her down in Camp Darby, Italy, in record time. The base's bomb handling unit, currently standing outside the ammunition bunker, was not happy when she appeared and universally took control of the situation. The base commander, Lt. Col. Pickard, was equally unhappy when he was locked in the ammunition bunker with her. Such is the way, some days.

"So colonel, married? Any kids? Most base commanders have families. They must love it in Italy?"

"Ah – yes. I have a wife, and a daughter in high school."

"What's her name?"

"My daughter? It's Sam. That's short for Samantha. And yes, she really likes Italy. She goes to the local high school. Why do you ask?"

"Talking about familiar topics tends to calm people. You were starting to look freaked out."

"We're locked in an ammunition bunker with an activated 20-kiloton nuclear bomb. Shouldn't I be freaked out?"

Kristin laughed quietly and smiled at the colonel.

"You have no idea how many times I've been in this situation. It's really not that crazy a scenario. Besides, there's lots of elevation left on the altimeter. We'll get this old boy calmed down, long before it gets upset."

The color started to creep back into colonel Pickard's face. While what she said was true, and they most-likely would fix the nuke with no issues, activated nuclear weapons were notoriously touchy creatures. It really could all end badly.

Kristin turned her attention back to the ticking time bomb in front of her. This early-era Cold War bomb was a predecessor to the current era of sophisticated nuclear warheads. Where today's generation of weapons were warheads on missiles, this beauty was a big drop bomb with an altimeter for a trigger. It was certainly something built before the doctor was born. It would be like working on her grandmother's tube radio without any instructions or proper tools. But sometimes, like today, the coolest part was just figuring it all out as you went along.

"What do you say we get about fixing this thing, colonel?"

The colonel nodded enthusiastically and Kristin gave him a warm smile. Her All-American smile had a way of making men calm.

"Could you please hand me that No. 12 Torx driver? It's the blue handle, third from the left."

The colonel picked up the tool and handed it over to her, grip first. Kristin tried the tool on the exposed screw head and then sat it on the ground next to her leg.

"Okay, let's try the No. 13. That one was a tad too small."

3

The colonel handed over the next tool and leaned slightly forward to watch the crazy woman work. Kristin checked the driver on the screw head and then sat it on the ground next to her other leg. Feeling semi-good about her path forward, she picked up a No. 7 Phillips head screwdriver and removed the screws holding the adjacent exterior panel. She stopped for a moment as she placed the panel on the ground next to the others and took stock of the sheer number of pieces. Modern nuclear weapons were a study in simplicity. This bomb had more pieces than a child's erector set. They really didn't make them like this one anymore. It was the Urban Dictionary definition of Old School.

Bending all the way over the device, Kristin shoved her head as far inside the device as it would physically fit. Several grunts and hmms emanated from inside the casing before her face reemerged. She picked up the pencil and gave the casing a quick tap, tap, tap, before straightening up. As expected, the altimeter jumped three times in corresponding to the taps.

Kristin leaned back and returned to her original cross-legged sitting position. She pushed the black framed glasses up on top of her temples and her glacier-blue eyes sparkled in the dim light. A mild look of bemusement ate at the edges of her neutral expression.

"Sir? Could you hand me that can of diet Mountain Dew, please?"

The base commander handed over the room-temperature canned soft drink and watched the crazy bomb technician down about half of its contents with a large gulping sound. Kristin returned the can to the colonel and cracked her knuckles in a pre-fight sort of way.

"You can have the rest of it if you want. It's kind of muggy in here. I just needed to run a little liquid down my throat. This next part tends to make my mouth dry."

The base commander blanched and swallowed audibly. He looked down at the young scientist with a kind of fatherly disbelief.

"Before you take the next big leap, may I ask you a question?"

"Yes, sir. Fire away."

"What do your parents think about you running around the globe, defusing nuclear bombs, at your age?"

Kristin looked down at the clockwork laid out before her and was momentarily sad. It had been some time since she had thought about her parents. It usually only hit home around the holidays. The old soldier looked down at her and could tell that he had unintentionally penetrated her well-worn armor. He instantly regretted having asked the question, but the damage had been done. And, as quick as it had appeared, the melancholy was gone, and a smile once-again covered the young doctor's face. Kristin looked back at Pickard with her usual exuberant optimism.

"My mom was a medical doctor. She had a family practice, mostly kids and older people. She was beautiful and very kind. My dad was an Army Ranger. He had a CIB, Bronze Star, and a fist-full of other ribbons. He was sturdy, and so gentle you couldn't believe he was a soldier. He used to let me blow things up out on the demolitions range at Fort Benning when I was little. It was great fun. Some of the other operators would let me play in the MOUT Village. Blanks only, but it was still loads of crazy.

They both died in a car accident, when I was twelve. I was at a friend's house for a sleep over. They were out to dinner. The roads were awful. A big truck came around a corner and hit them head-on. I ended up finishing out school at Benning. I got custodied over to the unit commander, like a ruck full of old gear. It was cool, I spent most of my time at his house anyway. He had two daughters that were my age."

The colonel looked down at the floor and moved some dust around with the toe of his spit-shined combat boot.

"The 75th Ranger Regiment. I know some operators from the 75th. They are world-class soldiers. I'm sorry. I didn't mean to open old wounds."

"No worries, colonel. It was long, long ago. In a galaxy far, far away. I take what was given me, and I do what I can with it. It's Okay."

"Do you see your foster father anymore?"

"Dave? Yes. I make sure I track him down every Father's Day. He's retired now. The family is scattered all about, but he and his wife are usually bombing around the Southwest in a big RV. Dave's great! He never tried to be my dad. Not one time. He just was there for me, you know? He and June are good people."

"Well, that's good to hear that you have someone to turn to."

"I'm pretty much boots-on-the-ground all the time. It's the way my life is most comfortable. Dave's cool with that. I'm sure that my dad would have been too. He probably would have made a Ranger out of me, if he'd been given the time. That would have been okay, I guess? I'm good with the drills, but not really much for the rigid command structure, if you know what I mean."

The wily old soldier laughed out loud. The booming sound echoed through the complete stillness of the ammunition bunker.

"Young lady, I know exactly what you mean. I have a bunch of troops that seem to think a lot like you. It's the curse of youth, and easy living."

"I think you're right."

The two smiled warmly and truly at each other for the first time since they had been locked in the bunker together. The soldier was happy to see that the unorthodox scientist he had been sent was not actually crazy. The young lady helping out was happy to see that the old soldier could recognize common ground.

"Well, colonel, what do you say we finish this little science project before Lou calls and starts chewing me a new one."

"Lou?"

"Lou Stenson, NEST operations chief. The dude who thinks he actually is my dad."

The colonel's eyes widened at the mentioning of the SEAL's name, so that Kristin could see the colonel's pupils dilate. The instant respect given to individuals based upon their merit had always been one of the things Kristin had respected about all the branches of service.

"Well, we wouldn't want to make your de-facto dad mad now, would we?"

Kristin chuckled, "No, that's generally a bad idea."

The colonel took a drink of the now warm and dusty soft drink, and then sat the can behind the tools on the workbench. Looking down at the young scientist, cross-legged on the floor in front of the semi-dismantled nuclear bomb, he nodded a firm 'Let's Go' nod to the girl.

"Okay, see that square box, about two-inches square, that I exposed?"

The colonel nodded.

"That is the actual timer. The analog readout is just a readout display. That is the actual timing device. It inserts itself into the trigger actuator behind it by means of a splined-gear drive. The trigger actuator is that 4-inch square grey box behind it."

Once again, the colonel nodded in understanding.

"Now, the off-blue bracket above the timing trigger actuator assembly definitely should not be bent like that. This explains why the timing device isn't sitting square and tight against the trigger actuator. The reason the display jumps when you tap it is because the gear drive inserted in the trigger actuator is slipping."

Kristin stopped her tutorial and looked at the colonel. The base commander nodded his understanding of the mechanics.

"Good news first - we can easily shut the old boy down. Bad news second - I seriously don't think it's fixable. Parts for something like this probably no longer exist. You're gonna want to send it out of stock when we're finished."

The base commander nodded his actual understanding of the implications of her statement. Basically, heads were going to roll.

"I need you to gently grasp the timing device. I'm going to stick my hands inside the casing and find the junction plug, where the timing device plugs into the main firing harness. Once I have it, I will count down from three. Upon zero, we will both pull our individual pieces out. Simple, right?"

"Seems easy enough."

"We need to do it at the same time. If you pull early, a capacitor will discharge inside the trigger assembly and it will go off. If I pull early, lack of electric loading will let the gear-drive spin freely and the auxiliary feed circuit will set the bomb off."

"What keeps it from doing that anyway?"

"See that small hole, what looks like the override eject of a CD-ROM drive?"

The colonel nodded.

"That is a hole for a safety wire. The safety wire keeps it from doing that very thing. Behind you there are a couple pieces of round steel, about the size of a 7 mm pencil lead. Grab one."

The colonel grabbed one of the wires and handed it to Kristin. She inserted the wire into the hole until it stopped and it felt secure. She checked it a second time to make sure it was snug.

"Okay, ready? Go ahead and grab ahold of the timing device."

The colonel bent over top of the young scientist and very gently grasped the small square metal box. He found it surprisingly cool to the touch. Kristin wriggled her hand inside the casing until she was in to the elbow. Exhaling gently, she fished around for several moments before finding what she wanted.

"What do you think, sir? Are you ready?"

The base commander nodded hesitantly. Kristin smiled up at him in reassurance.

"Okay. Three, two, one – zero."

An audible thump echoed off the walls as the base commander extracted the timing device out of the trigger actuator. Pulling up on the housing, the unhooked plug end of the assembly also slid free of the connector boot. Kristin exhaled audibly into the open bomb casing. Neither person moved for a good 30 seconds, waiting. Finally, Kristin relaxed and the colonel followed suit.

"Well, that went better than planned."

The colonel blanched. "What do you mean by that?"

"Old nukes are touchy creatures. They could easily go off as many times as not. I usually just plan on them going off. It keeps me calmer than if I think they just *might* go off."

The colonel was about to come unhinged when he stumbled upon an age-old grain of truth in her words. Plan for the worst. It made sense to him, all things considered. So, he calmed.

Kristin stood and collected her tools. She laid all the tools back in the order that they had been when she started and wiped the dust from the back side of her shorts.

"Now, I did you a favor, can you do me one? The bomb dogs outside are going to be justifiably pissed. I don't want to have to deal with that on vacation. Can you get me out of here without being tossed to the wolves?"

"Absolutely."

"Second. It's my professional opinion that this particular nuclear weapon should have been decommissioned two decades ago. It's also my professional opinion that at some point over the past 60 years, this bomb was dropped. That is the only thing that explains the bracket being bent the way it is. This was strictly a matter of time in the making."

The colonel nodded again, this time with a seething anger that would lead to inquiries.

"Thing three. You remember me saying I was on vacation?"

The colonel nodded.

"I really don't want to spend the next three days doing paperwork on this. What say you give all your bomb dogs an impacted AAM or some such thing, and forget I was ever here?"

The soldier looked down at what easily could have been his own daughter and smiled a very knowing smile.

"Stealthy exit?"

"Exactly."

"Just like an operator. The Rangers would be proud of you."

Kristin smiled back a wry and solemn kind of smile. "Thank you, sir."

The base commander walked to the door of the ammunition bunker and wrapped on the heavy metal door three times. The door slid open, and the senior man stopped everyone outside in their tracks. He could tell they had been prowling around outside the door like a bunch of feral cats. Kristin hopped up on the workbench and rubbed her temples with the palms of her hands. This was her life. She really did love it, but the adrenaline dump at the end left her kind of spent.

The colonel came back into the bunker and waved at Kristin. She jumped off the bench and walked to the heavy blast door.

"I'll escort you out of here, so you don't get any bother. It's getting a little late to be flying you back to Croatia, so my assistant has made you a reservation at a nice beach hotel in Livorno. It's on me. I will send a team to retrieve your gear. You should have your things by lunchtime, if that meets with your liking."

"I appreciate your hospitality colonel. You are entirely too kind. I can make my way back to Croatia to get my stuff tomorrow or the next day."

"Negative. You relax and enjoy the Tuscan Coast. Besides, I'm not having Lou Stenson call me because I didn't treat his little girl right."

They both laughed, and made their way out of the bunker. The colonel deposited Kristin at her hotel in his personal vehicle. He assured her that the reservation was for anonymous military personnel. She was stealthy and gone. As far as anyone could glean, she had never been there at all.

"Doctor Hughes."

"Yes, sir."

"I can't thank you enough for everything. I can't tell you how grateful I am that you appeared, independent of how it all started."

"I'm just happy to have helped, sir."

"If you ever find the need to *just blow stuff up,* you are welcome at any installation where I am stationed. And if you have any screw-ups with your outbound travel, let me know. I'll personally get you a hop stateside."

Kristin thanked the commander for his hospitality with a soft kiss on the cheek and turned for the hotel door. It had been a really long day and she wanted to soak in a bath.

CHAPTER 2

Four antiquated Russian cargo trucks pounded up the worn asphalt roadway outside the small town of Bereza, Belarus, at a uniform speed, dust flying up from semi-worn tires and twisting into spindles on the roadside. They came to a star-shaped five-sided intersection and turned off, twenty degrees to the left, onto a maintained concrete roadway. Each truck maintained its interval with the next and continued on with little regard for the local traffic.

Midway down the kilometer-long roadway, all four trucks came to a uniform stop at an obviously worn, but serviceable, guard shack. The guard, a sharply dressed Belarus Air Force soldier, came out of the all-window building and stared at the one meter gap between the rumbling lead truck's bumper and the road crossing rail, which blocked off the entrance. *They were either well trained or lucky*, the guard thought. The last person who had broken the crossing rail had been sent to Russia. To date, he had not returned.

The guard looked up at the inhabitants of the first vehicle. The driver looked like the average mercenary sort that worked in the area. Once a highly trained soldier, but now, with poor economic times, a gun for hire. It wasn't an odd sight. Commercial contractors helped the lagging Belarus army out from time to time. They were cheaper than maintaining standing troops in out of the way places. Yup, he looked like one of them.

The second man, casually lounging in the passenger seat, was NOT one of them. Tall and physically fit, with a moderate complexion that spoke more of Mediterranean roots than of the Belarus highlands, he was definitely not a gun for hire. He was also NOT Belarus military. That could present a problem. The guard instantly saw visions of the Russian Urals and laid a steady hand against the trigger guard of his well-oiled type 2 Kalashnikov automatic.

The unimpressed driver of the lead vehicle thrust out eight pieces of paper that appeared to be identification cards. The shadowy passenger leaned over to hand out a single piece of paper and leaned back to his original position. The red star and gold wreath of the Belarus military at its top were instantly recognizable to the suspicious guard.

"We have a meeting with Polkovnik Gregor Petrovych. There is our letter of admission and copies of our papers. Open the gate, please." The passenger spoke with a surety that was unsettling.

The guard looked at the pile of paperwork in his hand. It all seemed legit to him. Colonel Petrovych was also present on the airbase. Hell, he'd been there all week. Maybe they were all legitimate? The guard pushed the vision of the Ural Mountains to the back of his mind and handed the driver back the stack of papers.

"You will find Colonel Petrovych with the bunker detail. They are located off the north side of the runway. Proceed straight to the dirt track route and go right. You will cross the concrete bunker road after a kilometer or so."

The guard didn't wait for an acknowledgement, but returned to his glass shack to raise the gate. The shadowy passenger smiled and nodded to the driver, who promptly pulled his foot up off the metal clutch pedal. All four vehicles lurched forward and began pounding down the concrete roadway. The gate guard dropped the gate bar behind the bumper of the last truck and started to feverishly document the whole affair in the gate log. Even if it was all kosher, he wasn't taking any chances on losing his hard-won rank.

The heavy cargo trucks maneuvered down the concrete entrance road to where the well-groomed tank trail crossed it at a crisp ninety-degrees. The convoy hung a hard right onto the tank trail and a funneling plum of dust rose up behind them. The area around Bereza had been without rain for several weeks and that fact was making itself known to the last truck driver in line. They continued pounding the dirt trail, dust plum steadily rising into the air and being funneled to a square vent by the thick tree line on either side of the track, until they came to the smooth concrete roadway that cut perpendicularly across it. All four trucks skidded to a stop.

The dust plum slid past the man leading the small convoy as he deciphered Cyrillic signs at the intersection. Pointing to the right, the group turned onto the well-serviced roadway and promptly left the dust cloud behind. Equally well-serviced driveways extended from the main roadway at unequal intervals and disappeared into the thick woods. At the end of each drive, a massive steel blast door could momentarily be glimpsed jutting out of the earth. The entrance to each of the air base's ammunition bunkers was of good quality, and had obviously been maintained.

As one of two air bases to survive the transition out of Communism, the Bereza Air Base had become the home to both the Belarus Air Force and the Air Defense. The VVS was, as most ex-soviet countries were, a modest and wholly underfunded affair. The airbase housed numerous Mig-29 and SU Series aircraft, mostly the twenty seven series interceptors and twenty five series fighters. They were old and parts were always in short supply, as was pilot training. And, most importantly, jet fuel. Glasnost had forced the Belarus Air Force to stay on good terms with their mighty Russian neighbors, mostly out of sheer necessity.

Viewing the obvious differences between the bunkers and the guard shack, it seemed clear that the Belarus military was spending its tiny budget on maintaining their attack posture. Cold War thinking at its finest. It was prudent since the Cold War wasn't really that cold in the ex-soviet countries of Eastern Europe.

The convoy doglegged left with the roadway and continued down the ammo trail. Circular black tire marks could be seen tattooing the middle of the road in front of some driveway extensions. They had been laid down recently by the heavy Soviet era multi-tire haulers that transported ammunition and missiles from the bunkers to the flight line. A wave of the hand and the whole group came to a halt in front of a well-groomed and obviously maintained bunker driveway. The trucks turned and covered the short distance into the thick woods that obscured the bunkers from overhead view, before coming to a complete stop. A group of soldiers working around the outside of the bunker also came to a halt and began staring down the group of men in the trucks. A slightly soiled soldier loitering near the open blast doors dropped his shovel and disappeared inside the cave-like entrance.

The first truck's passenger looked past the gaggle of men scattered about the entrance to the writing scrolled into the concrete top of the bunker's face. He spoke Russian well enough, but sadly didn't read it all that well. Cyrillic was not an easy language to pick up. Besides, he was here to do business not write a dissertation. The letters over the blast door, ХраНеНИЯ боеПрИасоВ 11, he knew translated to Ammunition Bunker 11. It was the location he had been given the day before during his flight over to Belarus. And, as was his trademark, he was right on time.

Colonel Gregor Petrovych strode out of the open bunker door, hands wide at his side in the very-Eastern European style of greeting. At 5 foot 7 inches tall, with entirely too many good meals around his waist and red cheeks that spoke of a liquor pre-occupation, he was the stereotype of the ex-soviet glory days. The over-stretched seams of his uniform stated as much.

"З ДраьстьуйТе АДрИан. Добро ПоЖаЛоваТЬ В БеЛарусь."

Adrian Beqiri leapt from the passenger side of the lead vehicle and landed soundly on well-worn combat boots. Leaning back, he stretched his 6 foot 1 inch frame out completely, flexing his 225 pound fighter's physique to get the kinks out. He casually ran a hand through his closely cropped dark hair and then straightened to let his likewise dark eyes bore into the pudgy colonel for a moment. Tilting his head from side to side, two audible cracks could be heard in the silence. The colonel began to get noticeably uncomfortable under the mercenary's steely gaze. Adrian relented.

"Good morning Gregor. Let's use English. Less ears to understand." The two men shook hands and Gregor waved off the troops loitering around the outside of the bunker to go do something else.

"So, Gregor, the roads around Bereza aren't what one would call Autobahn quality. You really should do something about that."

"Alas, my friend, it's the cost of independence. We barely have enough currency to keep the planes in the air. How am I supposed to fix roads?"

"Hmm, I see your point. Are we ready?"

"Yes. Yes. All set up."

Adrian gave a quick hand signal to his crew. All four trucks instantly began to move. They slashed up and back and were uniformly reoriented with their cargo tailgates facing the open door of the ammunition bunker. The lead truck backed in fully and stopped just short of hitting the loading dock. Men from the colonel's group quickly and wordlessly loaded a heavy wooden crate into the cargo bed of the truck and secured it in-place with thick straps. The last soldier out of the cargo bed raised the truck's tailgate and secured its latch. He slapped the side and the truck rolled out of the bunker doorway and assumed its previous position.

The second truck executed the same maneuver, and received and identical looking crate. The third truck was backing into place when Adrian Beqiri jumped up on the loading dock with the colonel's men. The mercenary visually inspected the wooden shipping crate sitting on the dock, a heavy and dust- covered, 3-meter by 1.5-meter by 1.5-meter old wooden crate. The stenciled lettering, Последний фондовой, was still visible through the dust layer.

"Last Stock" was a code name for the old Soviet Union's Cold War secret nuclear weapons stockpile. An off-the-books nuclear backup to the official inventory. It was a little something to fall back on if the main stockpile was somehow rendered unusable. The C.I.A. had long ago taken to calling it *Fallback,* in deference to its own secret stash.

Adrian smiled and pulled a small box from his jacket pocket. Laying the device face-up on top of the crate, the needle on its analog meter did not so much as twitch.

"No, Adrian. They are perfectly safe. The warheads here are stored the same as the conventional stock. They will need to be assembled to be viable."

Adrian Beqiri, arms dealer to anyone with money, knew this all too well. Tactical warheads not on-missiles, or bomb drop ready, were stored in a semi-disassembled state to prevent accidents. Warhead live-assembly happened just prior to use or missile attachment. No one wanted live nuclear warheads just lying about. It was the one thing that all nuclear capable countries had in common.

"Just checking the core shielding, Gregor. These things have been

15

sitting in their crates without inspection for a very long time. I don't want any incidental leakage."

"I understand, my friend. I don't need you popping up on the satellites either."

Both men smiled at each other as a group of soldiers collected the crate and began loading it on the truck.

"That's actually how we found them, you know? One of the core shields started to leak. We tracked the tritium fallout down to a completely hidden back bunker. We discovered the fallout by accident. You really never know what's left lying about, do you?"

"How many did you come across?"

"In the stockpile? Five. You have three, and the other two are either unstable or leaking tritium."

"What exactly do you plan on doing with the other two?" The look on his face said that Adrian didn't want the colonel making up stories to the Old Russian High Command.

"Well, I'm certainly not turning them back in, if that's what's going through your head. I'll probably sell them to Al-Qaida or the Taliban. I don't really know yet. Dirty bombs are all the rage in that part of the world. Besides, if they lose a few dozen people handling them, they don't seem to care as much."

"I see your point. Just choose your conversations carefully."

"Fear not, Adrian. I'm not exposing you, or me for that matter. Frankly, I'd rather do business with you. I like doing business with business people. Arms dealers are cautious, and thorough. Fanatics are, well, fanatical."

Adrian stuck out his hand as the third truck exited the ammunition bunker. Colonel Petrovych took it and shook firmly.

"Not to sound too business-like, but when will I be receiving the second half of my payment?"

"You already have it, Gregor. It was deposited in your Cyprus account ten to fifteen minutes ago."

The Colonel smiled broadly, showing a line of smoke stained teeth. "See what I mean – business like. One last question?"

"Go ahead."

"Why four trucks?"

This time Adrian smiled. It was the first time anything resembling warmth had appeared in the man's expression.

"I wanted a spare. Dependable transportation can be hard to come by in this part of the world. I don't have time for any broken down trucks."

The portly colonel laughed loudly as the mercenary jumped down off the loading platform and headed for the lead truck. He climbed back into his semi-reclined position and the trucks departed. The trip out of the airbase was as uneventful as the drive in had been. Transport papers labeled *Machine Parts* were handed off to the gate guard, so he could save face.

The lead truck made a right turn at the five-sided intersection and headed back toward the small town of Bereza. Adrian Beqiri retrieved a satellite phone from his jacket pocket and entered a number from memory. It rang two times.

"Good day, sir."

"No. It went fine. We're leaving now. Yes, sir."

Adrian returned the phone to his jacket pocket and his body to the casual semi-reclined position. A good bit of business done. Now, all that he had to do was get them home and get to work on the plan.

CHAPTER 3

The luxury Mercedes saloon moved smoothly over the macadam in historic Silesia with little of the discomfort that the Belarus cargo trucks had provided. The E40 expressway was a hundred years removed from the cobbled together roads of the old soviet state and the ride reflected as much.

Adrian sat leisurely in the back seat and discussed the movement of AEK-919K machine guns he had procured for a group moving about in Turkmenistan. The *Kashtan* was well known to the men working in the area and ammunition was available in reliable quantities.

The conversation with the tribal leader he had been having over his encrypted cell phone was concluded as planned and the weapons would be heading east the next day. *Good bit of side business done*, Adrian thought. The collapse of the Cold War and its replacement with a state of unchecked terrorism was good for his business. The business these days was constant. No longer did arms dealers need to go looking for clients. Currently, there were so many buyers that middle men had standing lists of individuals waiting to do business. The work was rewarding, but at times also exhausting.

Adrian Bequiri, age forty, 6 foot 1 inches tall at a lean 225 pounds, with closely cropped dark hair and dark penetrating eyes, had been running the daily affairs of the Vakar Arms Network for the last five years. He had been born and raised in the hills of Albania, and found his general education inside the illusive Albanian war college.

Up until he rose to status in the arms trade, killing had been much more useful to him than grade school math. Fortunately in the arms business, the math was easy and straightforward. It was really more a business of dealing with people, which was something he understood.

The man that secretly led the Vakar Arms Network, he had never met. It was well rumored that Adrian had made an impression on the man at some point. So, when the last operations manager fell out of favor, Adrian was first on the list of replacements. Adrian had enjoyed the transition out of the trenches, and did everything in him to make sure he wasn't replaced any time soon.

Though he now resided in Paris, the ex-mercenary was very much at home in the east. The old soviet bloc states and the vast Muslim desert were his primary business area. He moved weapons around Africa, and South or Central America as well, but the east was where the real action was. And as long as the US military stayed active there, it would continue to be.

Adrian turned his head and looked back at the three shiny Mercedes trucks following uniformly behind. The nuclear weapons they were carting down the autobahn were definitely not his normal stock and trade. When they had surfaced in the murky back channels of weapons gossip, it had been his employer who leapt at the opportunity. Adrian would just as soon have let them pass. Heavy weapons were always more problematic. Nuclear heavy weapons were ten times more of a problem than that. But, his employer had been direct, so Adrian had gone shopping.

The E40 made its way up to the Polish-German border with little fanfare. The group of shiny black vehicles navigated the signs and moved from one lane to the next until they drove through the no longer used booth area that had been a Soviet era border check point before the E.U. had rendered them all defunct. Adrian inspected the degradation of the place that he was sure was lost on his other comrades. That was understandable. Most of the men in his employ were still much more fighter than philosopher.

On the opposing side of the empty shells, the E40 turned into the Autobahn 4, and headed north to avoid the border town of Görlitz, and move on toward Bautzen. The fleet pulled up at a service station on the far side of Dresden, and refueled. Continuing on Autobahn 4 East, the group moved across the restored lands of Germany without notice. The convoy swung south on 45 and headed for the city of Frankfurt. Normally, Adrian would avoid large city traffic. It produced too many unknown situations. But for his final destination, the route through the city was his best path.

The route went from 45 to 60 and then to 61, finally turning into route 50 outside Rheinböllen. On route 50 they then transitioned from the AutoRoute to rural roads about halfway between Rheinböllen and Marbach. Adrian calmed significantly as the group made their way south out of Marbach. They were back in known territory again.

The vehicles quietly pulled into the mountain town of Idar-Oberstein and made their way from the Hauptstrasse to the Schlosstrasse and up the hill to the long dead-end street with a pair of nondescript warehouses at its end. Adrian pressed an icon on his smart phone and the large roll-door front of the far warehouse began to lift. All of the vehicles in the convoy made their way inside the building, as numerous guards watched from concealed positions about the grounds. The Idar-Oberstein warehouses had been a favorite of Adrian's for some time. With the cargo they had procured on this trip, they were almost purpose built.

The nukes were in good shape, but they had been packed up for a long time. Leakage of the shielding was a very real possibility. The warehouses were located in a small town, just north of one of Germany's remaining active US Military bases. The small town even had off-base military housing. But more important than its housing, there was a remote nuke site not far away. As one of the large bases to continuously survive base cuts and closures, it was almost guaranteed to still possess nuclear warheads in its ammunition bunkers. The great military powers wouldn't completely dismantle their powerbases. It was just the way of things. Besides, even if the Nuke Site had been closed down, there would be a low level satellite signature for years to come. If the group did end up having a shielding problem, they couldn't have found a better place to mask it from detection. Any spike on the satellite detector hovering over Europe would almost certainly be dismissed due to location. Even if a detection was investigated, the nuclear search teams would be scouring the base, not the surrounding countryside. Hiding in the shadows of a giant was always the safest place to be out of view. That statement was as true with arms deals as it was fairy tales.

Adrian climbed out of the Mercedes with his finely crafted French attaché and watched the group quietly go about monitoring and unloading the cargo. The nukes were being placed in a custom shielded holding locker to minimize problems and all equipment was being checked for residual leakage. All was going according to plan at this point. The next steps would need to be implemented in the morning. At the moment however, there was time for a good meal and a bed. A bed, preferably with a woman in it.

Adrian rose with the sun the next morning as he had done for many years. He graciously dismissed the whore he had acquired the previous evening with a pleasant sentiment and cab fare and then headed for the kitchen to brew his customary pot of black coffee.

His business of the day was all logistical. He needed to move the Kashtans out. There was a request from a Moroccan about a shipment of ground-to-air missiles that he thought would be easy enough to handle. Three or four phone calls later and both situations had been easily resolved. He looked out across the sunny terrace of the rental house he used as his office and smiled. It was going to be one of those good days in the German highlands. He sat down in one of the terrace's comfortable chairs and pondered his last real piece of business. He need to deal with the nukes.

Adrian had approximately two-and-a-half weeks of time for things to happen, if everything was going to go to task. His employer had told him that transport out of Europe had already been arranged. The ship left port in eighteen days. That should be more than enough time to do what needed doing.

The first order of business was people. More to the point, knowledgeable and expendable people. In many ways, he liked using expendables. They usually always took their secrets with them. His core group of mercenaries were all well-seasoned and trusted men. He could count on them, as far as any mercenary can be counted on. They wouldn't betray him, unless it was necessary. That little bit of loyalty deserved honoring. That could not be said for outside contractors. Especially the kind of educated radicals needed for handling the nukes. Besides, none of the people in his crew were competent at assembling Russian warheads. No, expendables were definitely the way to proceed.

Adrian bit his lower lip and thought back on the conversation with Gregor. What was it he had said? *If they lose a few people handling them, they don't care.* And, *Fanatics were, fanatical.* That was all true. They were also good camouflage. Everyone knew that fanatics were untrustworthy and hateful people. Adrian liked the idea of using some poor bastard for his knowledge and hate, and then killing him before the poor bastard could gain any glory from it. Adrian didn't like people that were in it all for hate's sake. He was a businessman. He worked in the arena of supply and demand. He possessed no broken moral compass. But, there were many out there that did, and he would be happy to use them. The best place to acquire those expendable martyrs was Farooqi. Yes, she could always find the right people quickly.

Adrian set down his coffee and picked up his encrypted smart phone. He dialed a number from memory and waited for the electronic ringer. The phone rang three times.

"Noor Farooqi."

It was a nice, matter of fact, greeting. Basically, all business. Noor Farooqi was a well-healed Pakistani woman, of an undetermined age and social status. She had no specific education that anyone knew of, and no known family history. She had made her way out of her native Pakistan to London, where she rose through the social scene by a well-placed set of marriages. At 5-foot 3-inches tall, with long dark hair and large dark eyes, all wrapped in a Mediterranean complexion, she looked much more Israeli than Pakistani. She was thin and fit and basically modest. An expensive set of C-Cups was her only real concession to western civilization, aside from fashion.

Besides being beautiful and manipulative, Ms. Farooqi was also a first class facilitator of personnel for people like Adrian. She was a free-lance intermediary who facilitated people and situations for other people. She was very good at what she did, and that made her both rich and sought out. Just as she was being sought out now.

"Good morning Noor, Adrian Beqiri."

"Adrian. How lovely to hear from you."

"Thank you Noor. I hope you're well."

"Tip top, Adrian. Tip top. Now, how may I be of service to you today?"

"I was hoping you could source me a couple of scientists."

"One time or return service."

"One time use."

"Any particular specialty?"

"Nuclear warhead assembly."

"Country of origin for the nukes?"

"Russian."

"No worries lover, Russian tech is easy these days. Any specific flavor?"

"Hmm, Middle Eastern of some type might be nice. That is, if it won't cause you any heartburn."

"Oh Adrian. Like you, I have no regional affiliations. It's bad for my business model. The educated but otherwise downtrodden minds of the deserts and highlands of the Middle East are easily obtainable. And, blamable later on."

"Outstanding."

"Timeframe?"

"Soon. Say, five days to a week."

"Hmm, sooner means more money. I like you Adrian."

"Price isn't a bargaining point, Noor. Send me a bill and I'll pay it."

"That is why I keep taking your calls love. Now, give me twenty four hours and I'll get back to you. Till then, Cheers."

Adrian sat down the cell phone and retrieved his coffee. The majority of the day's business was done and his coffee wasn't even finished. He had two and a half weeks of quiet German countryside and then it was back to Paris. Well, that was if no other major acquisitions came along. He didn't see any coming. All his usual clients were taken care of. All the miscellaneous orders were well in hand. And soon, the nukes would be out of his hair too. No, it was a good day all around.

CHAPTER 4

Noor padded around the terrace of her high-end SOHO apartment and pondered Adrian's request. She really didn't want to send him anyone from England. That would have been rather simple but, alas, the British pound wasn't what it once was.

She needed to buy some deniability. The scientists Adrian requested were to be of the sacrificial variety, which most-likely meant a large scale terrorist attack was coming. And these days, large scale attacks were usually pointed at the United States.

The American intelligence machine was cumbersome and slow, but it was not foolish. The scientists would be identified as British citizens, accusations would then be made, and as inevitable as sunrise the global stock prices of anything British would plummet. Her portfolio would not enjoy the prolonged dip in the market that would surely come.

Noor stopped her pacing and took up station on the chaise lounge to light a cigarette. She turned her slim silver lighter over in her hand a few times as she pondered. Why was it that America having a tiff with most countries bothered no one, but when they had one with Britain everyone started to panic? It really didn't make much sense in today's economic setting. America having a tiff with China, now that should get people panicking.

She rubbed out the butt of her cigarette and lit a second. Oh well, if she couldn't do it easy then she would do it semi-easy. The Arab would have people tied to the Middle East. He always did. Those people wouldn't cost her too much. The Arab was a reasonable fellow. At least she thought he was a fellow. She had never actually met him in person. In her business, that was better with most people.

She picked up her phone and dialed a number from memory. It rang six times. He was like that.

"Good morning, it's Noor. Do you have time to do some business?"

"Yes, Noor. What do you want?"

"Two scientists. Capable of handling Soviet nuclear items. Of an Eastern – no, Middle Eastern flavor. Expendable."

"How soon?"

"In Europe in three days."

"That's fast."

"Yes, life's difficult. Can you handle it?"

"Of course. How would you like to handle the exchange?"

"Same as last time. You send me the details and put them on a train. My men will collect them when they get off the train."

"That's fine with me. I'll send you details in a few hours."

"And, I will send you money shortly thereafter. Same account in the Cayman Islands?"

"Yes. That account will be fine."

"Lovely. I will be waiting for your next message."

"Goodbye."

Well, at least he was consistent. The Arab was good and reliable, but he really was a douche. Noor wondered if it was a female thing. Business should be done between men, not women? It probably was one of those antiquated Eastern ideas. Oh well, he would acquire what she wanted, and that was what really mattered. He would service her needs. She would, in turn, service Adrian's needs. Everyone would get paid. That was what it was all about, supply and demand.

Noor lit a third cigarette and settled back in the chaise lounge. She would just need to have her man collect the scientists and hand them off to Adrian's men. She would figure out those details once she heard back from the Arab. For now, it was a waiting game.

The odds seemed good that Adrian was operating whatever he was operating from somewhere in continental Europe. That would make the transfer of the men an easy matter to effect. The new E.U. was a friendly place to travelers.

While she had some free time, maybe a bit of shopping was in order? Yes, shopping and some lunch would be a nice distraction to the passing of time. She rubbed out the cigarette in her crystal ashtray and stood.

Noor returned to her apartment from the shopping around mid-afternoon to find two emails waiting for her. Both emails had been sent to her secure server at her apartment. Security was key. One could never be too careful in her business.

She sat her shopping down in the entry hallway and took up station at her computer. She could have sat out on the terrace and checked her messages on the laptop. It would have decrypted the emails, and the day was lovely, but there was something reassuring and business-like about the bulk of a desktop terminal. Remnants of a bygone age. Maybe?

The first of the emails was another business request. It was from a person in Angola, requesting contacts for a reputable transport/security team. That was easy. She knew of a couple of different people in Angola that could handle transport and security details. That one could wait for a bit.

The second email was the one that she wanted. The Arab, true to his word, was on-time with a response. The response he had sent her was fairly long, so she settled completely into her office chair and started from the top.

"Hafid al-Sajjadi, male, thirty five years old. About six feet tall and approximately 180 pounds. Thin, wiry frame, with short dark hair and dark eyes. He worked for the Pakistani nuclear program until he was let go for "a lack of funding" approximately a year past. He holds a doctorate in Collapsed Field Explosion Geometry from Virginia Tech University. His parents both died when their village was shelled.

"Hamal ibn Syed, male, forty eight years old, 5 feet 7 inches tall, approximately 165 pounds. Again, thin, fit, with dark hair greying at the temples, and dark eyes. He had worked for the German Ministry of Science for five years, before moving to the Pakistani nuclear program. He was let go over security concerns. He holds a doctorate in Nuclei Detonation from Columbia University. His father died fighting with the Taliban.

"Both men are currently residing in Pakistan. They will be boarding a plane in the morning for Europe. After a short ride, you may collect them at the Baunhauf, Graz, Austria. They will be arriving on the noon train from Zagreb.

The payment for this service is 200,000 euros. It should be handled according to our previous conversation. Good day."

Noor lit a cigarette and reread the email two more times. Arrangements as agreed upon. The Arab was rude, but definitely thorough. After appeasing herself that everything had been handled appropriately, she erased the last two paragraphs and retooled the ending.

"Both men will be delivered to the Baunhauf in Graz, Austria, in two days. They will be arriving on the noon train from Zagreb. Please remit payment of 500,000 euros for the services. You may collect them in Graz or, for a small fee, I can have them forwarded on to wherever. Just let me know what you would like to do.

Best regards, Noor."

Satisfied, she washed off all the tracking tags from the header of the email and changed her name to Adrian's. She read it twice to make sure it was correct and hit send. She reclined in the chair and smiled. She had managed to make 300,000 euros and go shopping at the same time. The last bit of her email was just a polite prompt. She knew that Adrian would collect them in Graz. It was just the way of things. It was how everyone did business.

The next morning, during her breakfast tea, she received an encrypted email from Adrian. It thanked her for the prompt service, and said that he would handle collecting the men at the train station. More importantly, it said that he had placed 500,000 euros in her drop account in Cyprus. She hadn't even finished breakfast and business was complete. Business was good, and she was done for the day.

A day and a half farther removed, two men from Adrian's security team sat quietly in the main terminal café of the Graz train station, looking directly at Platform twelve's pedestrian walkway. The train from Zagreb was due in, on track twelve, in eighteen minutes. That was more than acceptable to the lead man, Pavel. The wooden benches in the train station's café were definitely not meant for long-duration sitting. He had already reached his emotional limit and would be quite happy when the train arrived.

Pavel didn't mind the waiting. He had handled this type of detail several times. He just enjoyed a bit more comfort than the Austrian people apparently did. His partner for the day, a French chap, was a good decade younger. He seemed quite happy to sit and make small talk. The Frenchman was also a seasoned mercenary, so Pavel indulged him with the small talk. It helped to pass the time.

With standard European efficiency, the noon train from Zagreb pulled to a stop on Platform twelve at noon. The doors sprang open on all cars and the platform was instantly awash in disembarking bodies. The two mercenaries stood and moved to a position where they could see the entire platform. About halfway through the unloading process, two obviously Middle Eastern men exited the third, second class car, and began walking slowly up the platform together. Pavel inspected the men as they walked and matched them to the descriptions he had been given. The two men wore new suits that more hung on their bodies than wrapped them. And each man carried a small shoulder bag and an attaché. Yes, they were the two he was looking for.

Pavel and his man approached the two travelers and introduced themselves in English. It had been assumed from their schooling that both men were bilingual. The hunch was correct and both of the scientists responded in kind.

Package now in-hand, Pavel escorted the men down to track five, where the 12:30 train was departing for Zurich. He handed them their tickets and followed them onto the train. Pavel and his assistant took up station two rows ahead and facing the two scientists. He sat and smiled at them in a reassuring way. As expected, the train pulled out on time. Approximately halfway across Austria, Pavel talked with the men in the connector between the train cars. Explaining the travel plans, he handed each man a full set of documents to use. They would need to go to the lavatory fairly soon and familiarize themselves with the details of the documentation. They were informed to ONLY speak in English from this point on. It would both put-off and accelerate the train and customs people they needed to interact with. Also, Pavel would be able to understand and help out, if necessary.

The group returned to their seats and enjoyed the remainder of the trip to Zurich. The group waited out a 40-minute layover and then boarded a train bound for Stuttgart, Germany. In Stuttgart, they caught a quick connection and followed the German border west to the town of Saarbrucken. That train too, was prompt, and the group was collected at the station by another man. They all climbed into the comfortable Volkswagen van and made their way northeast, to the warehouse in Idar-Oberstein.

The nondescript van pulled into the nondescript warehouses on the hill overlooking the little town, and all five men disembarked. Adrian introduced himself to the scientists and escorted them to a small apartment area within the warehouse, where they might wash, eat and pray. The scientists appeared tired, but otherwise unaffected by the secretive nature of their travel.

Adrian left the scientists to their affairs and made his way back to Pavel. The two men talked out the details of the trip to satisfy Adrian's curiosity. Appearing that everything was going according to task, Adrian relaxed. He knew that normally recruitment was the weak point in any operational plan. One was never really sure what one was going to do or how one was going to act. But much more importantly, one was never sure who was watching. It appeared from all aspects of the post-op briefing that this had gone to task. They could commence with their plan sooner than expected.

CHAPTER 5

Ed Crowley paced about his standard sized, standard color, standard decorations, government office in Alexandria, Virginia. He wore the same perplexed expression he always wore when trying to decide if some random fragment of information spit out of the ether was the tip of a controversial iceberg or just another ghost in the machine.

At 5 feet 10 inches tall and a gamely 270 pounds, with brown hair, blue eyes, and the reddened cheeks and nose of a professional drinker, he wasn't really built for pacing. But, the fifty one year old spy was a twenty nine year veteran of the National Security Agency, so he paced more often than he liked. Wearing his standard grey suit with white shirt, the senior intelligence officer looked much more akin to an aging college professor than he did one of America's top spies. Having been born and raised in Denver, Colorado, his ability with math and his natural aptitude for lateral thinking had brought him to be noticed by the intelligence community when he was still in high school. Pepper, as he was known to the Cold War set, had risen steadily through the ranks at the NSA until he landed in the director's seat for the office that dealt with *Captured Data*.

The *Machine* known as ECHELON was an information producing juggernaut. It produced $1.0 \times 10(16)$ more bits of data in a second than was possible to interpret. Wading in the middle of this never-ending data stream was Ed. His hand-picked team used heavy data algorithms to flash-sift the data stream for nuggets. Once the nuggets were identified, the whole piece of data was extracted from the stream and analyzed by dumping it into another set of heavy algorithms that filtered for key words and phrases and decided if something was data or white noise. Even with eighth generation filtering terminology software and the latest bit-selection algorithms, a staggering amount of white noise was still extracted. So, in the end it was the job of an intelligence officer to look at what was left and decide if it had merit.

The piece of paper that Ed had been carrying around his office for the last forty five minutes had every hallmark of being another ghost in the machine. A ghost, in NSA speak, was a piece of information that seemed credible, but was actually just a bit of someone's otherwise mundane and unimportant conversation. Because everyone on the planet happened to be discussing the news of the day, unimportant bits happened often. Ghosts were a very common theme after any newsworthy terrorist attack. You blow up a building with a plane and everyone is suddenly discussing blowing up buildings with planes. It was just people trying to makes sense of their lives. It was all usually harmless, except for the much less than one percent of the time when people were actually talking about blowing up buildings with planes. Ed blamed the white noise on the advent of the 24-hour news channels – when technology made it possible to report news at any time of day. Ed hated news people.

The phone stationed in the proper government orientation on his standard wooden office desk rang. The ringer intruded into his noise-free thinking space and made him jump. Snatching up the handset, he listened as the voice coming from the super-computing interface station two floors below informed him about the absolute absence of any credible data set regarding any terrorist activity in the usual suspect countries. He grunted something thankful and replaced the handset in its cradle. Being one of the only *Cold War Kids* left at the agency, he had acquired access and clearance for many things that he probably shouldn't have. This was the case with the voice on the other end of the phone. It allowed him to better process data. Extra info that would normally get compartmentalized made his life easier. It would definitely be more difficult for whoever replaced him. He looked down at the crumpled piece of paper in his hand. Maybe, independent of what his gut was telling him, it really was a ghost?

Ed sat down in his chair with a thud and picked up the phone. He pressed the red button on the unit to get an encrypted outgoing line and dialed a number from memory. It rang three times. The director of the Central Intelligence Agency (D/CIA) picked up his direct line and mumbled something that passed for hello into the phone.

Eugene R. Taggart was an imposing man who was starting to show the signs of age. He had made his way out of Eastern European Field Operations at the end of the Cold War and trudged straight to the top of the most well-known clandestine organization on the planet by being an action first, questions second kind of leader. Equally loved and feared by all, he was a spy's spy.

"Hey Gene, it's Ed."

"What's got you calling on an encrypted line? You sound kinda twisted up."

"ECHELON kicked out a nugget from the stream. The data has no external referencing, but my gut is telling me it has all the hallmarks of non-aggregated feed."

"Pepper, save me the techno-babble."

"Oh, sorry. It just happens when I am here. We got an intercept that someone has been talking to The Arab. It would appear that they want to procure a couple of Russian capable nuclear scientists."

"You sure it's The Arab?"

"I wouldn't have called you if it wasn't. It was his cellphone all right. The techs had to chew through some non-Radio Shack redirection and randomizing gear that he was running, but it was definitely him."

"Okay Ed, you've officially got my full attention. So, who was The Arab making a deal with?"

"Noor Farooqi."

"Are you sure?"

"He called her by name, more than once."

"Well, that was dumb."

"That's what I thought. The redirects path out Farooqi as currently being in London."

"Hmmm, the prime minister always says no to us running ops in his grand city."

"I know. He's kinda stuffy."

"How sure are you that it's not a ghost?"

"It took me a long time to make the call. I have nothing paper-worthy, but it feels real."

"Your gut has always been good enough for me, Pepper. Apparently, it's poker night. How is 7 p.m. for you?"

"Can we make it 8 p.m.? My day isn't really going so well."

"Neither is mine. 8 p.m. it is then. I'll make the calls."

"Sounds good."

Ed Crowley hung up the phone and leaned back in his chair. The game was afoot, or so it seemed.

As promptly onto 8 p.m. as his schedule would allow, Ed Crowley pulled into a driveway half full of black armored sedans and SUVs, situated in the quiet section of Forrest Heights and parked his car. He discretely nodded to the two security guards that blended into the tree line by the barn/garage that was also discretely located behind a large two-story house. Pausing at the garage's front door, he waited until the doorway's retina scanner passed over his right eye and identified him. An audible *ping* was followed by the click of a bolt unlocking. It announced that he may enter, and he did.

Ed said good evening to the security guards inside the entranceway as he shook off his overcoat. He placed the coat on a hook next to the other coats hanging on the wall and headed up the stairs leading to the garage's loft. He paused at the top of the stairs and punched an eight digit code into the keypad. The heavy metal blast door released its lock and Ed made his way inside to *The Game Room*.

The Game Room, as it was known, was actually an old FBI safe house that had been de-listed and transformed into an ultra-secure meeting room for the men who unofficially looked after the freedom of their country. The collection of men allowed access into the black-book club was a hand-picked group of patriots. Known simply as *The Group* to the president of the United States, they were the lynchpin of homeland security. In a post-9/11 world, where homeland security in America had transformed itself from something useful into a massively slow monetary drain, an alternative had been sought out before external threats reappeared. From the midst of this intelligence free-for-all had been born *The Group*. The *REAL* functional chief from each operational sector and one hand-picked field operative were covertly tasked by POTUS with the seemingly impossible goal of forming a group that utilized independent and completely open backdoor communications, interaction, and operations to handle all threats at hand.

The president had secretly formed the group after having had enough of the limitless in-fighting and territorial behavior. Understanding that the problems posed by the post-9/11 creation of the DNI and Homeland Security were not making things any better, he pulled a play out of the old Cold War Soviet rulebook and simply went around them all. The key players for his new endeavor were selected out of the NSA, NRO, CIA, DOE, FBI and Justice Department to form an unrecognized collective backchannel intelligence agency. It was something that had never happened before in U.S. intelligence and, as such, it took some time for the professionally suspicious men and women of National Security to buy into the idea of direct and unfiltered communication. But, once it was moving, there was no going back.

Now, even POTUS understood that letting the FBI and CIA play together both internationally and domestically could be legally problematic. For this reason, the members of the group had been allowed to recruit a Supreme Court justice to do their interpreting for them. It had been considered a bold move at the time, but having a full-time justice to interpret impending operational legalities had actually saved them a time or two. It was extremely practical.

Ed nodded to the other men in the room and walked directly to a side table. He removed his Glock Model 20 and his cellphone and placed them in the holder space marked NSA. He picked the cellphone back up and checked to make sure it was off, and then returned it to the felt-lined space. He retrieved an ice-cold Miller Lite from the silver bucket on the next table and loosened his tie.

The NSA chief took a seat at the poker table and listened to a baseball conversation between the DCI and Pat Sommers, the operations director from the Secret Service. Not being a sporting fan, he didn't join in, but sat quietly and waited for the last of the group to appear.

Ten or fifteen minutes passed before the last of the group had finally arrived. A large and imposing figure of a man made his way to the side table and dropped an iPhone 4 and a government issue Colt .45 into the space marked DOE, retrieved two beers from the bucket and made his way to the last empty space at the table. He plopped down in the padded poker chair with a jet lagged look on his face and cracked open the first of the beers. Each of the men nodded hello, as if to say *All-Hail* to some Roman gladiator.

At 6 feet 1inches tall and 210 pounds, Lou Stenson now carried the extra ten pounds that every ex-operator seemed to acquire. With brown hair greying at the temples and brown eyes, he possessed a gaze that could cut through normal men. Even with the greying temples, he still possessed the frame and acumen of a person very accustomed to running with pack and weapon at the ready.

Being only thirty eight, Lou Stenson was considerably younger than all of his peers at the table, but the amount of mileage and scar tissue his frame possessed made him blend in well enough. He had a bachelor's degree in international affairs from Bucknell and had done a brief stint at the State Department before being recruited to the position of NEST operations chief with the Department of Energy.

Where these things were impressive on their own, the gladiatorial praise he was awarded by his elders stemmed from twelve years of active operation as a member of SEAL Team 5, and his still A+ reputation as an active operator. The rumors of his exploits with the team and the different clandestine operations were so fantastical that no one even asked if they were true or not. Truth be known, most all were factual. It was the reason that he was the only non-active Navy person allowed to interface directly with real-world Special Operations. The Special Operations, Navy SEALs and Army Delta Force, were the people sent out to recover wayward nukes. This was the reason he had been casually redirected into his job, and away from State. Operators always wanted to interface with operators, and everyone in the know knew who he was.

Lou had taken the station chief post without any qualms, and enjoyed the Nevada weather quite well. His station in Nevada, and not Washington, D.C., also explained why he was the last one to show. He popped the twist cap off his beer bottle with one thumb and consumed the contents in one long pull. He opened the second bottle the same way, looked at the other men and smiled.

"So gents, what's the big doings in the Capital tonight?"

Paul Spencer, senior systems director at the NRO laughed and started shuffling cards.

"Yeah, Gene, what say we get to the story time part before I'm forced to start giving away my money to you vagrants?" Bob Sloan said, as he munched on a BLT sandwich he had retrieved from the beer table.

"Okay boys, but it's probably better if we let Pepper do that," the CIA director said stoically.

All heads rotated to look at Ed Crowley, who was quietly counting his poker money. He flashed an unconvincing smile and sat down the wad of bills.

"Well, short version, ECHELON stumbled upon a phone conversation between The Arab and Noor Farooqi. She was buying a couple of Soviet nuclear science capable guys."

All men reflected on the information, but said nothing.

"We teched out the cell signal and the source confirmation is definitely The Arab. Reverse trace on the signal led to Farooqi being in London. The Arab has fairly new signal bounce and IPO redirect gear, but it appears that he's currently hanging his hat in southern Pakistan. Probably Karachi."

Again, everyone absorbed, but no one interjected anything, so he continued.

"She was chasing two scientists, delivered to Europe, and would pay by account transfer. Time frame on the delivery was three days."

Bob Sloan rubbed his chin and squinted at Ed through his bifocals. "I don't know, this whole thing reads to me like a bad '80s spy novel. Are you sure it's not a ghost?"

Ed rolled his eyes over to Paul, who was attempting and failing to pop the top off a beer with his thumb.

"The signal geometry from ECHELON was clean. The data pack was transferred to NSA intact." Paul quit with the thumb wrestling and retrieved the bottle opener from the middle of the table. Having a way into his beer, he looked back at Ed.

"The hackers and signal intelligence kids did full system de-integration on the data set. The signal de-masking was complete, and all routing points were accounted for from ringer to hang up."

Bob Sloan squinted at Ed. "So, no ghost?"

"Nope. No ghost Bob. Everything here seems legit."

Lou Stenson stood up and carried the empty beer bottles to the trash can. He poured himself a tall Jameson on the rocks as he considered all points.

"Ed, you said Russian nuclear scientists. Russian Russian, or Russian equipment capable?"

"The second. Noor specifically asked for expendables of Middle Eastern upbringing."

"So, smart and expendable fanatics? They are actually pretty easy to come by in the Middle East. The Russian nuke is the base platform for almost eighty percent of the nuclear community. Finding capable people should be pretty immediate. That probably explains the three-day timeline."

Gene Taggart began to rub his temples, which everyone took as a sign that things were probably about to get worse.

"Okay, let's talk about options," the CIA director said, without looking up.

"Track and bag the scientists," Lou said directly.

"Do that by squeezing Farooqi?" responded the CIA director.

"Shouldn't we see if we can officially locate The Arab? The prime minister of Great Britain is not going to take kindly to undisclosed ops in London. We certainly can't tell them, and you know how they get when they find out." The Secret Service chief had had the unfortunate pleasure of dealing with the prime minister on previous occasions.

"Gentlemen, when was the last time we actually gave a shit what the British thought about our operations? We do what we do. That's what we do." Nathanial Baker, justice for the U. S. District Court, District of Columbia, rolled his eyes while speaking, but kept his tone level.

"The judge has a point, Pat, plus we know where Noor is right now. The Arab would be much more of a drone hunt." The CIA director threw the remainder of his beer down his throat and the Secret Service man nodded in agreement.

The judge looked across the table at Stenson, who was inspecting one of the scars on the back of his left hand. He possessed a lost in deep thought look, as though he was reliving killing whoever had placed it there.

"Lou, what do you make of the nuke issue?"

Hearing his name spoken out loud brought the NEST operations chief back to the present. "Well, if the nukes are a real entity, and for some strange reason I think they are, then the actual target doesn't really matter. If they nuke a U.S. target, we're fucked hard. If they nuke a North American target, we're still fucked pretty hard from the fallout. If they have some humor and nuke a European target, geopolitically, we're still fucked pretty hard. It's sad, but true. Realistically, whoever is playing nuclear football could whack somebody in Africa without bothering us much, but there's nothing in Africa worth a nuke. Nope, I'd say that if somebody is willing to go to all of the trouble to procure a warhead, ready the package and transport said live device, then it's definitely a high-value target. I'd say it's the U.S. or Europe. The borders of both are pretty damned porous these days."

Lou settled his chin on his left hand and looked across at Gene Taggart as all the other men nodded in agreement. The CIA director nodded, too, and then cleared his throat.

"Everyone got the memo about the group having a new CIA field agent, right. His name is Robert Dunn, and he is well capable. I think he will probably want to talk to your girl. Can you track her down for me? They can go pay a visit to Noor, after they get acquainted."

Lou nodded his head as the CIA director looked over at Bob Sloan.

"Most likely they will also want to be talking to Ben Donewoody. Is he currently available to operate?"

Bob nodded in acknowledgement of the FBI field agent's availability.

"He should be free of anything major. If not, I'll make sure that he is."

Good. I say that for now we let the ops people talk a little and get back to us with some actionable intel, so we can move forward with whatever this is."

Everyone at the table responded with approval of the loose plan.

"Okay, then I'd say it's time to start taking Bob's money." Everyone laughed. Paul Spencer started dealing the cards.

CHAPTER 6

Hafid counted the leads on the wired capping assembly. Thirteen plug leads were connected to the firing box installed in the upper half of the warhead casing. He had counted the leads four times, each time coming up with thirteen.

The correct number of leads were connected, and each lead was in good condition. The firing circuit showed no signs of damage from being in long-term storage. What had not managed to survive, or more accurately, had not been installed, was the tag differentiating the twelve firing leads from the one auxiliary timing and detonation lead. Hafid held the bundle in his hands and looked down on them with that disapproving look that only a scientist can conjure. It wasn't disappointment or despair, but more a bland wondering of 'why?'

The firing circuit had an extra lead going into the firing box that looked exactly like the twelve firing leads coming out of the box. The lead was used by Russian ground troops to attach a hand-held detonator, so the device could be remotely triggered. Almost universally unknown to everyone but the Russian high command, it was a design feature of almost every early nuclear weapon produced in the former Soviet Union. The old men in the Kremlin liked weapons that were multipurpose, but even they were smart enough not to hotwire nukes. So, they installed an extra trigger plug. The plug allowed troops to self-detonate weapons when last resorts called for last resorts. The plug normally had a green end cap that differentiated it from the twelve black capped firing leads. Sadly, that was not the case today.

"Hafid, what is the matter? You have been looking at that box for a long time." Hamal ibn Syed looked over his glasses at his younger colleague in a fatherly way.

"Apparently, this bomb's firing box was made on a Friday or a Monday. The assembly technicians forgot to color-code the auxiliary detonating lead."

"Is that a major problem for the firing circuit?"

"Definitely, yes. If you manage to plug the auxiliary lead into one of the twelve firing lead positions the explosion geometry will not provide complete radial compression. The nuke will misfire."

"Misfire how, Hafid?"

"Hmm, this big a nuke. It would probably have enough punch to blow up a good-sized building and you'd get high-quality dirty bomb effects, but definitely no full-compression fusion release. No Hiroshima."

"You said, 'if you manage?'"

"Yes. The auxiliary lead should have one more pin connector in its socket than the firing lead's receiving connector socket. I will need to count the pin sets on the individual leads to figure out which one is which."

"Then you probably should get started with your task." Hamal smiled in a reassuring way and pushed his glasses back up his nose.

"How are you coming on the final assembly inspection, Hamal?"

"I am almost finished with it. All of the inspection tags have been checked and removed. The casing just needs to be sealed up after the firing circuitry is installed."

"Oh, that is good work."

"Thank you, Hafid."

Adrian and Pavel sat off to one side of the operation and quietly observed the two men working. They had been reassured by the scientists several times that the nukes were completely safe and harmless until the firing circuit were installed. So, they watched. The two Pakistani scientists went about their work the same way that two old men would assemble a puzzle in Central Park. Adrian found the whole scene equally comforting and confounding. Pavel looked on, unmoved by it all.

The mercenaries watched as Hafid figured out the differences in the leads and began to very slowly attach the twelve firing leads to the primary charge caps spatially positioned equally around the main explosive sphere. All twelve firing leads needed to fire simultaneously to produce the uniform compression necessary to achieve implosion.

Once the octopus-like conglomeration was attached, the firing box itself was secured inside the warhead casing and the internal positive lead was pushed into place. The leads connector made a sharp click that made Adrian's spine tingle when it snapped into place. A red light on the front of the firing box came on. Adrian assumed that the Cyrillic under the red light said *Power*.

Hafid al-Sajjadi mumbled something in his native tongue that sounded a lot like a prayer and then pressed a black rubber-coated button directly under the small red light. One at a time, in sequence, 12 equivalent-sized green lights came to life across the face of the firing box, showing that the firing circuit was complete and active. Hafid nodded at Hamal and both men smiled. Adrian exhaled audibly in relief. Pavel sat unfazed.

The two scientists went about closing up the casing of the now live nuclear bomb. Hafid pulled the auxiliary timing/detonation lead through a hole that they had drilled in the outer casing cover. Apparently, the Russians had assumed that the casing cover would not get reinstalled, as there was not a grommet-lined hole for the wire to get pulled through. They were really thinking last resort at this point.

Once the weapon was completely assembled, Hafid attached an American made D52A cellular firing trigger to the external lead and waited for a green L.E.D. light to illuminate. The little L.E.D. came to life as it had when the circuit had been bench tested at five different times in the day. The American trigger had been fitted with an adaptor to receive the Russian lead. Feeling confident that the weapon was ready to go, Hafid looked up at Adrian and nodded his approval. He then powered down the trigger and rocked back on his knees to stretch.

The two scientists took a break to rest and have some mint tea while Adrian's men opened the crate for the second nuclear weapon and started removing the extra wood bracing and packing materials. The scientists observed the internal call to prayer and then refocused their efforts on the second device.

The assembly of the second bomb went along mostly as the first. The two men worked as if they were reading from an ABC how-to manual. Each man went about his own task and the two exchanged some general conversation, as they had done during the first episode.

To Hafid's pleasure, the auxiliary lead on the second firing box was properly marked with a green end plug. This removed several steps from the process, and soon enough the second bomb was finished and being sealed up. The American trigger was installed and tested and Adrian was again informed that the device was ready for use. Adrian thanked both men for their hard work and sent them off to relax for the remainder of the day.

Once the scientists were out of earshot, Adrian turned to Pavel and asked if the shipping containers were ready to go. Pavel said that the large sea-land containers were ready and waiting in the other building, along with their manifested cargo. The double-ply containers made to house the nukes were also ready to go. All that was required at this point was to load the bombs, attach the external triggers and load the containers. Adrian asked if the extra metal leads had been installed in the inside of the sea-land boxes so that the firing circuit could pick up cellular signals. Pavel nodded and explained that a large cellular antenna had been fashioned into the roof of each shipping container. They should have no problem with cellular reception.

The arms merchant got up off the couch and walked over to the two nuclear bombs sitting so quiet and still on the floor. Knowing that the serial numbers on the two shipping containers ended with Alpha and Bravo, he had put a big A on the first device with a large black marker, and entered the detonation number into his phone as *Cousin A*. Adrian extracted his phone and checked that the numbers for Cousin A and Cousin B were both still programmed in, then he placed his phone back in his pocket and returned to his position on the threadbare couch.

"What do you think, Pavel?"

"It would seem we are as ready to load them as we are ever going to be."

"You seem matter-of-fact about the whole affair. They aren't crates of mortars, you know?"

"No. They are really big bombs. We sell bombs. Somebody made them with the intention of them being used. We are handing them off to someone who will use them."

"That is a very good point, Pavel. A very good point. Everything else that has been made for war has been used, from mustard gas to smallpox mixed with ricin. Somebody was going nuclear at some point."

"Exactly. At least we're making some money off of the madness."

Adrian smiled at Pavel and padded him on the shoulder. "Exactly."

Pavel smiled back, but said nothing.

Adrian retrieved his phone from his pocket and dialed a number from memory. It rang two times.

"Adrian. If you're calling me, it must be good news."

"Yes, sir. Good news indeed. Those two old items you wanted me to refurbish – they are all shined up and ready to go."

"Very good job, my young son. When will they be ready for shipment?"

"They will be heading to the docks tomorrow. They should arrive at the port in two days."

"Right on time. You continue to run the organization with efficiency, Adrian. Good job."

"Thank you, sir."

"Keep up the good work, Adrian."

Ivan Vakar sat the handset of the phone back in its cradle and pressed a black button on its side to disengage the scrambler. He leaned back in his chair and smiled as he looked out the large windows of his corner office.

At fifty seven, Ivan was no longer the young and hard-charging man he once was. His 6-foot frame now carried some 260 pounds on it, a good piece of which came from good bier and fine food. A head of brown hair which had now turned a salty grey capped a round face with a round nose. His fiery grey eyes, though, had lost none of their flare.

A businessman from Belarus, Ivan Vakar was the owner of a couple of medium-sized paper goods manufacturing companies that were of little threat to anyone. He kept them as they were, to give his public life an air of legitimacy. They produced enough to cover the money questions, but were not his primary means of income. For the last twenty five years, his primary income had come from the illegal arms sales of the Vakar Arms Group. War was where the money was, and war had made him rich.

He realized early on that being an iron monger was not going to produce the public image that he wanted to possess, so he kept himself a silent partner in the whole affair. Opaque Management was what he liked to call it. Arms buyers wanted a face they could resonate with, and a public figure was not that face, so he gave them an arms dealer's face. Little looking was required, as he had known about Adrian for some time. So, Adrian ran the operations and Ivan funded the business. It worked well for everybody.

In his late thirties, Ivan had earned an economics degree from some no-name French college. With that, his little paper goods fiefdom, and his arms dealing money, he waded out into the deep water of European politics. Now, with both the paper business surviving the economic recession of the new millennium and the arms business running at full capacity, Ivan Vakar sat in a fancy multi-room office in Brussels. He had managed to make his way all the way up to the Office of High Representative for the Foreign Affairs Council of the European Union. He was outwardly a shining example of the new Europe.

Internally, he was a seething ball of anger that had been long focused across the Atlantic Ocean, at the high and mighty American Mount Olympus. He hated America. He hated the way it economically held everyone down. He hated the way it lorded over every other country politically. He hated the way its military came and went as it pleased, without anyone's approval. Being from Belarus, he hated what the Russians had taught him in school about the evils of America. He hated it because it seemed that they were right.

America had exported its easy-living, easy-money lifestyle into Europe and turned it into a swirling mire of unemployment and greed. But mostly, he hated how Europe continued to be seen as the needy second cousin in all global affairs. Europe had the businesses. Europe had the armies. Now, Europe had the collected government. It was well past time that the western world went back to being run from the right part of the western world.

Ivan turned from the window and looked up at a painting of the crucifixion of Christ that hung on the far wall of his office. Yes, that was it. He was the new Roman. He was going to stick a stout spear in the side of America's rib cage and put an end to the whole charade. Then, he would leave them for the crows. Europe and the European Union would fill the power vacuum and stabilize world affairs. Yes, it would be a better world without America in it. It would be a better world very soon.

CHAPTER 7

The sun rose high and fast over the white stretch of Mediterranean sand where Kristin was lying. She had waited until the shops opened so she could acquire a new bikini for the day. It was white like the sand, and somewhat smaller than she normally would have liked. But, she didn't plan on doing any running or beach sports, so it would work nicely for making tan lines.

The beach, which was just across the street from the shop, had comfortable lounge chairs with umbrellas. It also had gregarious Italian boys who would fetch drinks from the nearby café for a smile and a few euros. Kristin picked a lounge chair out in the middle of the sea of sand, where she didn't have to look at anything but the surf, and dropped her bag. She tossed the attendant several extra euros and he retreated with a smile, obviously enamored by her scant clothing. She looked down at her form and thought that she probably should have picked up something more conservative. Oh well, it was too late now.

As expected, the young Italian reappeared with his large smile and a shiny plastic card from the nearby café. Kristin inspected the offering and made her decision. She pointed at the mineral water and raised one finger. She then pointed at the Peroni and raised two fingers. The boy nodded his head enthusiastically and headed out across the hot sand at a trot.

Kristin retrieved a bottle of Coppertone SPF 8, Bronze Enhancer, from her bag and began slathering on the oily concoction. She was all but finished rubbing herself smooth when the concierge returned with her three bottles of refreshment. She asked how much in broken Italian.

He responded in broken English that the bill was nine euros. She tossed him twenty euros, the bottle of oil, and then pointed at her back as she laid down in the extended beach chair. The boy couldn't pocket the bill fast enough to start with the massage, but was quite professional with its application. When finished, she rolled over and smiled appreciatively. The concierge smiled from ear-to-ear, the way young men do, said thanks and was off across the sand to the next vacationer.

Kristin adjusted the umbrella so that it didn't block too much of the sun and settled into the chair thoroughly. She pulled a healthy amount of Peroni from the first bottle and sat it on the small plastic table attached to the red beach umbrella's stand. She removed her trademark tiger-striped wayfarer sunglasses and placed them next to the half-empty beer bottle, closed her eyes and calmed her soul. A Mediterranean beach vacation was why she had come to Europe. Croatia, Italy, wherever, a beach was beach, albeit some prettier than others. And this was a beautiful beach. She decided that she would need to send Col. Pickard a Christmas card and thank him for the nice hotel.

The sun was high, the air was hot, and the fine Italian lager was cool. That was all that really mattered about a day at the beach. She knew it wouldn't last. It never did. She just absorbed as much of it as she could as it came along. She was a live-in-the-moment person. Her life experience had taught her that it was pointless to plan too far ahead. You could be fine one day, and hit by a truck the next. She viewed her future in short segments of time which just seemed to happen.

She had a 401K plan and a pension allotment, but they were both Lou's doing. She had never bothered to consider it, so he had filled out the paperwork on her behalf. He had also handled the life insurance and all the beneficiary stuff, too. She had once wondered whose name he had filled in on the form, but assumed it was Dave's. The old SEAL had always been a proponent for future planning. She could never understand why it mattered, especially in her unique line of work. It wasn't like she would ever get to retire anyway.

No. now was now. Now was what mattered. The sun, the sand, and the pleasantness of the beach. Take life as it presented itself – that was her guiding logic. It had been working quite well for over a decade.

47

Kristin closed her eyes and focused her thoughts on her breathing. She had learned the importance of breath control while studying martial arts back in Henderson. She had known the basics of breath control from her range time at Fort Benning. Take a breath holding the weapon, hold the breath while you center your target and depress the trigger. That was in her DNA now. The martial arts breathing was more of a Zen thing. Breathe and reflect. Know your body and react to your surroundings. It had come in handy many times and in many different activities. She had three ex-boyfriends who could attest to its usefulness.

Calm your mind, calm your breath, and engage your target. That was and continued to be the mantra. It helped her to focus and center herself in her own universe. It was good. It allowed her to function when everyone else around her was losing it. And the boyfriends? They never got kept around very long. She wasn't into having or being a possession. Men came and went like the desert winds. She made sure that they enjoyed themselves while they were there, and then she sent them packing. It was just so much easier being single.

Kristin had calmed almost to her baseline. She had expelled all her negative thoughts. She was serene. All was good in her world.

"Doctor Kristin Hughes?"

Kristin's eyes slid open like a cat's. Slow but, all about target recognition. She saw a well-dressed man standing in the line of her sun. Something about him definitely seemed government. Yup, nothing ever lasted long.

"Ich verstehe Sie nicht, sir. Was willst du?"

"Funny, your German has an accent. I wouldn't have guessed that from your file. And I would like to converse with you regarding a matter important to your government."

Kristin wrinkled up her face. The imposing man was standing in her sun. That was just rude. She retrieved her Ray Bans and slid them onto her face to counter the returning glare.

"Hmm, let's see. Armani dress pants and shirt. Very stylish Bexley dress shoes, and is that a Gucci tie? I have to say, I applaud your fashion sense. You are the very definition of European style. You also just ooze spy out of all your pores. Let me guess, a company man? A – Mr. Robert Dunn, isn't it?"

The CIA man blanched white. Apparently, he had never been called out before. Wasn't that what happened to James Bond in like, every movie? Wasn't the damsel supposed to know his name already?

"Doctor Hughes, how did you know my name?"

"Relax Bob, it's not a conspiracy. I got a text from my office when you came onboard. They figured you'd be showing up, eventually. Now, I haven't talked with the shop in a couple days, so why don't you chill, and we can talk. Give the old dude a couple euros for a lounge chair and the young chap a couple euros for some beers, then we can discuss whatever it is that's of national importance enough to ruin my vacation for the second time in two days."

The spy looked at her quizzically regarding the "second time" statement, but said nothing. He turned and complied with the other requests. Soon he was sitting on the other side of the big red umbrella. Kristin watched the man warily as he retrieved a lounge chair and flagged down the café boy. She waved her empty bottle at the CIA man as he negotiated with the concierge.

"It seems the lady could also use a refill, please."

Robert Dunn was the best-dressed person on the beach as he settled into his lounge chair. He loosened his tie and unbuttoned the collar of his light charcoal-colored dress shirt. At 6 feet tall, with closely cropped black hair and grey eyes, he possessed the classic good looks that played very well with European women. Looking about forty, his Mediterranean complexion had already started to brown up nicely in the summer weather. His complexion worked as well as it could to hide numerous small scars, but it failed. The 225 pounds carried on a sturdy frame also played well with the ladies, she imagined. He looked more British than American. She imagined that that helped him move about Europe unbothered.

With a bachelor's degree in chemistry from Boston College, he had been recruited by the boys at CIA headquarters while still in school. He had been involved in several think tank operations before finally requesting a transfer to field operations. That was eight years ago. He had been promptly dumped in Europe to do various things, until Gene Taggart had come calling. That had been six months ago. He leapt at the chance to work on the DCI's direct operations team.

Robert handed Kristin a perspiring beer bottle, and fully eyed her body. The Greek nose set to anchor her blue eyes and long, highlighted blond hair made her quite striking. The athletic body, which was only minimally wrapped by the white bikini, was obviously not for show. She was an outdoorsy woman, toned and sun-kissed.

"Is that an Aida Yespica bikini?"

"It is, thank you."

"I approve. It's striking on you. You have good taste in fashion, Doctor Hughes."

"It's Kristin from here on out. Thanks."

"Okay, Kristin. Robert. Robert Dunn."

Kristin straightened the back of her lounge chair up to the forty five degree position to better converse and observe. Robert settled in closer to the shade produced by the umbrella and attempted not to look out of place.

"Like I said, Bob, I haven't talked to the shop in a while. I'm attempting to be on vacation. So, why don't you just start in wherever you like."

Robert looked at her with a look that said *you're already annoying me,* and tipped up his beer bottle. Feeling it the best way to level the playing field, he began. He started by explaining what the NSA had sifted out of ECHELON, and that it seemed to be authentic. He explained that the traffic led back to the Farooqi woman. She had apparently procured some nuclear scientists for an unknown client, and they had come from someone called The Arab.

He watched the scientist absorb the information, processing each piece and adding it to information that she already knew. When she was finished making squishy faces, he continued with the rest of the information that was in his packet.

Robert finished the dissertation, then removed his shoes and socks. He rolled up his pant legs and also his shirt sleeves. Loosening a couple more buttons on his shirt, Kristin took in the obvious outline of his chest, along with several more small scars. He was clearly the hands-on type.

"So Kristin, what do you think?"

"Well, the scientist angle does definitely scream 'let's build a bomb.' It's a little like a movie cliché, but sadly true."

"That was everyone else's assumption, too."

"The expendable part is interesting."

"How so?"

"It either says something about the materials, or the employer. They are either not going to outlive their work, or they are going to be killed right after their part is complete."

"That's an interesting point."

"I would guess it's the second one. Handling a nuclear weapon for the purposes of terrorism is an incredibly secretive affair. Besides, radioactivity high enough to kill the handlers is super easy to track."

The CIA man nodded his understanding.

"I'll be willing to bet that this Farooqi woman doesn't know which one it is either. It's not the type of thing that would generally be covered. Do you know anything about her?"

"Apart from the official brief, no. I would imagine we will need to make some field-level judgments."

Kristin smiled at him in a way that said he was new to the team.

"Bob, that's exactly what those of us in our little group do. We make field-level decisions."

Robert looked at her quizzically, but didn't jump at a response. Instead, he waited several seconds for it to pass.

"Well doctor, now that you know what I know, what do you suggest we do next?"

Kristin looked at him incredulously. "What do you mean?"

"I was told – I need you to track down a young lady named Kristin Hughes. Dr. Kristin Hughes. She's 5 foot 6 inches tall, I believe currently possessing brownish colored hair, and brown eyes. She's your counterpart for field operations, over at NEST. She is vacationing on one of the Greek Islands. I'd like to give you a better location, but she's kind of a free spirit. You listen to what she has to say, and do whatever she wants. Doctor Hughes is the absolute best and most qualified nuclear weapons specialist in the U.S. command structure. As such, NEST gets to be point on potential operations regarding areas of her specialty. She is the field operations leader for matters pertaining to the group. Just do whatever she asks you to do. And Then – seriously Robert, she's completely capable. I'm sending you her bio so you can get up to speed. Just don't cross her. Because she's a very nice person, but if you offend her it tends to end badly. By badly, I mean that I know a dozen people that would be quite happy to kill you for her, if she was possessed to make a simple phone call. To be clear, Robert, I am one of those dozen people. Or – something to that affect."

Kristin began to laugh in a sympathetic manner.

"OKay, that explains quite a bit, Bob. That speech has Gene Taggart written all over it. The DCI probably told you that just because we had never worked together before. Or maybe just to screw with you? He does have a strange sense of humor. Just so you know, that's not the way it works. The field operations members of The Group are both completely autonomous and completely interactive. We work together as equals, always. If someone's skillset is needed most, then that person gets to have the say, otherwise its level pegging. Nukes and such is probably why he said listen to me. Understand?"

Robert Dunn smiled the smile of relief. He had been unhappy about being dispatched to be someone's overqualified assistant. Being equals was much more palatable to him.

"So, you do the tech stuff, I do the spy stuff, and everyone else does whatever?"

"Exactly. It's easy."

"Well, that's definitely cooler. Now, same question still stands, what's next?"

"First things first, we get you off the beach. Then, while I find my bag, you find us some transport to London. After a nice dinner in Soho, we have a little chat with this Farooqi woman. Sound good?"

"I can give you a lift to your bag, and I have a gulf stream sitting over at one of Galileo's private hangars. We can be off whenever you choose."

"A waiting private jet? I like you more and more all the time." This time, Kristin's smile was genuine. It made Robert Dunn slightly amorous.

"Well, I had to do a little scouting to find you. You are renowned for being a free spirit. Oh, nice listing as a non-permanent military officer, by the way."

"Thanks. Shall we go?"

They stood and each collected their stuff – Robert's gaze fixed upon a quarter-sized, star-shaped scar in the meat of Kristin's back, just below her right shoulder blade. He had been told stories of the scar and its mysterious origins by several old-time company men when he had first made quiet inquiries about things in Kristin's bio. Seeing the scar in the flesh, he had no doubt how it had come to be there.

"Do you mind if I ask you a personal question?"

"Go ahead, Bob, fire away."

"That scar on your back? Is it really true that you did some freelance work for the Israeli government and got shot by an informant? And that the Mossad were so offended you had gotten hurt that they sent a half-dozen men to make sure the informant died badly. I mean, they talk about it in whispers down on the farm."

Kristin attempted to look incredulous. "The scar actually came from a rock climbing accident. I don't know where those other rumors come from. And, I have never worked with the Mossad in any fashion."

Robert Dunn knew a bullet hole when he saw one. But, he also understood that the young doctor was a keeper of secrets.

"Rock climbing? Well, that probably makes more sense."

Kristin could hear the underlying tone of knowing in his voice, but liked the answer he gave. He knew not to pry into things that were better left for dead.

"Mr. Dunn, may I ask you a question?"

"Only seems fair. Go ahead."

"Not to question your credentials, but are you *good* at what you do?"

The spy looked at the scientist in a way that said, *you aren't getting shot on my watch.*

"Yes, ma'am. I am."

"That's good to hear."

CHAPTER 8

The Mercedes truck rumbled north on Autobahn Route 7 past the turn off for Garlstorf and belched out a puff of black diesel smoke as the transmission was set into a higher gear. Now several years old, the red Axor was a little too dirty and sported many more dings than when Phillip had acquired it. The cosmetics were of no never mind to its owner. The sturdy drivetrain in the Mercedes-Benz truck was excellent for hauling the heavy sea-land boxes to and from the port.

Phillip had been hauling containers in and out of the port for some ten years. It was easy enough work, and it kept him deep in the mix of intrigue that the port offered. That very intrigue had led him to a meeting with a shadowy man named Adrian five or six years back. Since that meeting, Phillip had hauled many of Adrian's containers out of different places and up to the container docks in the Port of Hamburg. It was good business. He had to do very little. He just showed up and the containers were loaded on the haul trailer and secured by the men at the pickup point. All the documents to ship the containers were always handed over in a large envelope. And the documents were always right. Once at the port, getting unloaded was always easier when you had one of the shadowy man's containers. He always greased all of the right wheels, so all that Phillip ever had to do was show up in the right spot. He would drive straight into the stacks and one of the mobile pickers would promptly unload him. Once the truck was unloaded and the documents were handed off, he would park his truck in the big lot for the kanteen and have a break. Everyone at the port was always pleasant and Phillip enjoyed the unusual status that Adrian's containers brought. As he made his way speedily up the autobahn, he knew that today would be no different.

There had been some gossip in the streams of conversations in Europe's largest port that his employer was actually a gunrunner, and all of those containers of *Machine Parts* were actually weapons. Phillip never checked into any of the gossip and frankly never cared. He was paid lavishly for work that would have otherwise gotten done anyway. To Phillip, moving containers was moving containers. What was in them was none of his affair.

The Axor and the freshly painted green cargo containers made their way past the Autobahn Number 1 interchange and the signs for the turn off to Hittfeld. Rumbling north, Phillip watched the traffic slowly start to thicken as the outskirts of the massive port and the city began to condense the cars and trucks. He moved the big red Axor into the left lane and passed by a string of slower moving vehicles. He waved casually to another truck with a petroleum tank on the back. He had talked with the other truck driver several times while they both waited to be sent in one direction or another by the port security details. That was another thing he liked about the port, there was always someone interesting to talk to while you waited.

The Port of Hamburg was called Germany's "Gateway to the World" for a reason. That reason was that it was massive. It was the largest of the German ports and it was only outdone in Europe by the ports in Rotterdam and Antwerp. It handled every manner of freight and there was always heavy commotion. The sprawling port consumed all of the branching sections of the Elbe in and around Hamburg. It had so many drop points and different entry gates and railway transfer facilities that a new driver could get lost and not come out for days. As big as the modern city of Hamburg was, the full lower half of it was some type of port facility.

Ten years on, Phillip was a seasoned navigator of all the port color and number code systems for picking up and dropping off cargo. He had been lost several times back in his early days, but that was a long time ago.

The signs for the E45 had appeared and the traffic was now all but consuming the Axor. Phillip made his way back into the right lane and lined up for the Finkenwerder Strasse exit. The traffic around the port would be extra heavy at midday. Phillip berated himself slightly for his leisurely start to the day.

The big transport truck navigated the ramp and the convoluted turn-about on Finkenwerder Strasse that brought the traffic back underneath the autobahn and into the forest of signs that started separating traffic out into the different port routes.

Fortunately for the bumpers on the Axor, the designated turn off onto Dradenaustrasse was only a couple of turns on from the main off-ramps on the opposite side of the autobahn. Phillip always liked making this set of turns. Once on the port road there was no more crazy traffic. The road was definitely congested, but it was all big trucks hauling containers. Everyone in that traffic had the same goal, and they were all headed through one of the same group of gates.

Phillip took his place in the long line of trucks waiting to enter Waltershof and let the Axor idle and rumble. He reached down and picked up the two thick packages of shipping documents held together by a collection of rubber bands. He re-checked the cargo container numbers in his mirror against the numbers on the document packages, and then sat the document bundle back down on the passenger seat. He inspected the containers with both mirrors. They were both unmoved from where they had been positioned on the trailer. All the binder chains looked tight and the containers looked shiny green. Everything about his load was as it should be.

The Axor nudged forward a truck length at a time for some forty five minutes before it made its way to the delivery gate at the far west end of the complex. The gate guard, a portly fellow named Klaus, looked up at the Mercedes-Benz and smiled.

"Phillip – long time. You haven't been to the docks this week. How have you been?"

"Klaus, my old friend. It's been slow the last couple days. Probably the new economy."

The gate guard shook his head in understanding. The European economy and its currency had been taking a beating in the world markets.

"Ah, I understand. So, what's on the truck today?"

Phillip grabbed the big collection of documents and handed the large bundle over to the guard. Klaus removed the bands, checked the cargo numbers against the ones on the containers and looked at the contents sheet. He made several notes on the documents regarding ship name and departure date, and then replaced the paperwork back in the proper manila envelopes. Collected up once more, the portly guard handed the stack back to Phillip and walked back to inspect the containers themselves. Both containers were in new condition. They had no leaks or obvious issues with their cargo. Both the shipping seals and required locks were in-place. All seemed fine, so the guard walked back to the truck's cab.

"Cat litter, Phillip? I thought this company you haul for made machinery parts."

"Not sure, really. I think they bought out another company, or are diversifying, or something. You know how companies are."

"Yes, things change here all the time."

"That they do. Frankly, I'd rather have the machinery parts. This cat litter is heavier than you would think. I burn more fuel hauling this stuff."

Klaus shrugged his shoulders in empathy that times were tuff all over. "The Diaspora is picking up her cargo this afternoon. Drop the containers at the D7 stack. The pickers should already be there getting ready to load."

"A Greek ship?"

"A Greek name anyway. Pretty sure that she's flagged out of Cyprus. She makes runs from here to the ports on the American Great Lakes, or so says the computer."

Phillip shrugged his shoulders. "Whatever works, I guess. Thanks, Klaus."

The port guard waved and reached inside the door of his gatehouse for the button that raised the gate. The Axor rolled into Waltershofer Hafen proper, and headed back east along Zellmannstrasse toward the large stacks of containers waiting to be loaded onto outgoing vessels.

Phillip made his way out into the massive sorting area that contained the large piles of shipping containers awaiting transport. The stacks ranged from two or three containers together to more than 100 in a group. The area was a forest of containers stacked from two to eight high. It was easy to end up turned around in such a place. Phillip rolled the Axor along slowly and cautiously, watching for any cross traffic until he pulled up to the appropriate pile. There was a large D7 spray painted on the tarmac in front of the first container.

Being far enough away from the end container stack, Phillip shut down the Mercedes-Benz and pawed around behind the driver's seat to find his faded blue plastic hard hat. Laying his hands on the old beat-up helmet, he placed it on his head and jumped out of the rig. Phillip set straight to work unbinding the shipping containers from the trailer's carrying frame. He had them all but un-hooked when the large mobile crane appeared from around the corner of the container mountain to unload him.

The mobile crane driver rolled straight up over-top of the truck's trailer and centered himself over the first container. A cradle lowered from the mobile platform and grabbed the container squarely by its top. Steel pins snapped into place and the crane lifted the container off of the truck's trailer. The crane operator placed the first container on top of the second container and pinned them together. Holding part of the total weight with the crane, when the two containers were secured together, both containers were lifted into the air. The crane took possession of the cargo containers and rolled back away from the truck the way it had approached.

Phillip stood by the truck for a couple of minutes watching the mobile crane place his containers in the D7 stack before a man in utility dress appeared in a dry mud-covered golf cart. Phillip handed the man the big stack of documents and pointed toward the two shiny green cargo containers from which the crane was detaching. The man in the golf cart looked up at them and nodded. He said thanks and drove off. Once again, Phillip's job was done. Time to head to the kanteen.

Elsewhere in the port — Adrian watched the container crane unload his cargo and place it in the outgoing cargo stacks, the same as it had done for every other container delivered that morning. Things moved along out in the sorting area as if it were just another day. For Adrian, It was not just another day. There was still a myriad of things that could go wrong. The containers were packed as well as containers holding such things could be packed. The radiation shielding qualities of the cat litter would foul the detectors in the American ports, if they had the bad fortune of actually getting inspected. But still, things happen. Containers get damaged in shipping. They get randomly inspected. Or worse, they get lost at sea.

Losing these two containers at sea would be an incalculable problem. The odds of any one thing happening to the shipment were definitely low, but all the small odds added together made Adrian worry.

"Mr. Adrian, you are finding everything to your liking?"

Adrian smiled, and thanked the port manager for his patience.

"No problem, Mr. Adrian. We get many people that want to see their cargo sent off safely. It's OK, yes."

Adrian asked about the time the ship was scheduled to arrive, realizing he had some hours before it got loaded and its documents got transferred. He explained to the port manager that he was going to go into Hamburg and get a meal. He would be back when the ship was getting loaded. The port manager nodded his approval and offered up the name of one of Hamburg's finer restaurants. Adrian thanked him and headed for his car.

Having enjoyed a fine meal and a good single malt scotch, Adrian decided that he had better head back to the port. Dusk would be slowly descending on the Elbe, and night time sailings would be starting soon. He made his way south and found his parking spot in the visitors section of the main port building, just as he had earlier in the day. He waved to the receptionist and she buzzed him into the entryway of the observation deck. Upon reaching the top of the stairs, he was met by the port manager.

"Your cargo has already been loaded, Mr. Adrian. You can see the tops of your cargo containers in the middle of the central cargo stack there."

The manager pointed down at the loaded container ship and moved his finger around in a small circle. Adrian nodded with pleasure.

"The Diaspora will be casting off shortly. Why don't you enjoy a drink while they undo her lines?"

The manager pointed over to a well-stocked liquor station in the corner of the room and smiled. Adrian slid several well-folded 100 euro notes from his pocket and palmed the man's hand as he shook it. The port manager pocketed the tip like a pro, nodded in appreciation, and then departed. Adrian walked to the cart and eyed a thirty-year-old Macallan. Smiling with satisfaction, he poured two shots into a rocks glass and found a seat in front of the observation deck's large picture windows.

Adrian sat and observed an old Asian gentleman studying a large container ship father down the port's dock wall through high magnification binoculars. He scribbled some notes on a small pad and sipped on something resembling club soda. Considering the man of little consequence, he swirled the glass so the whiskey could breathe and retrieved his cellphone. Punching a couple of buttons, the phone rang two times.

"Good evening, Adrian. How are things in Hamburg this evening?"

"Everything here is proceeding without issue. The vessel is loaded and is casting off her lines now."

"Excellent. You should be ready to meet her in the Port of Chicago when she arrives."

"Plans are already in motion for that. We will be there when she arrives."

"Very good, Adrian, very good. The Roman spear is about to get its chance to pierce some flesh."

Adrian made a quizzical face and wondered if his boss had been drinking or something. He was not known for vague references.

"Yes, sir."

"Good, Adrian. Call me when you get to America."

"Will do, sir."

Adrian put the cellphone back into his suit pocket and took a drink of the scotch.

CHAPTER 9

Ivan Vakar stood in the middle of the large wall of windows that separated his office from the rest of the city and casually swirled a cup of espresso to dissipate some heat. He had never appreciated why every coffee server on the planet felt compelled to produce coffee so hot that no one in their right mind could drink it. Waiting ten minutes for your coffee to cool was just ludicrous. *It was just one more absurdity imported from the West,* he thought as he looked out over the cityscape. Feeling basically content with the small cup's thermal output, he popped a small pink blood pressure pill into his mouth and shot the espresso in behind it. The double shot of coffee was still a little hot and Ivan winced slightly as it slid down his esophagus.

Looking out his office windows, he could feel the plans he had made coming together. Like the Oracles of ancient times, he could feel the spirits in the ether coalescing around him. They all whispered to him of a new Rome, a new republic of men collected together out of self-interest and run by themselves, not by the meddling all-powerful Western world.

This new Rome in his vision would not be Rome. It would be more of a democracy than the dictatorship of the Caesars. Its seat would be in Belgium, not Italy, the place where it had been established. A new European Union that would govern and defend Europe against the evils of the world.

Ivan knew that even after the West was removed from the playing field, there would still be infighting. Historical animosity and resentment covered all areas of the E.U., but that would fade. Collective governing would appear once the West was removed from the equation. America's capitalistic, free economy was just as destructive as Stalin's socialist state had been. It just killed in a more subtle way.

Removing America and all of its politics from the world, and more importantly the European government, would allow Europe to deal with all of the other threats at its door. The Muslim hoard migrating from the East was just as cancerous to Europe as America. Threats were at Europe's door from all sides. Change needed to come, and it would come very soon.

Ivan turned from the window and looked across the room to a painting of Christ on the cross. Rome was coming to take control of things again. Yes, very soon.

Rome. The image of the great Roman Legion marching onward toward the Rubicon came to mind. Collectively, Europe had a formidable war machine at its command. They would not be needed for America. America was a house of cards. With a sufficiently big wound to its side, America would fold on its own. The government-buoyed economy would easily enough be its undoing once the downfall was under way. The Muslims, however, were another matter. The Muslims might need a little bayonet prodding to pack up and leave. The Moors of Morocco and Northern Africa had swept north into Iberia in 711 AD and stayed for some 700 years. It had taken the Reconquista, and the fall of Granada in 1492 AD, to finally drive them back across the strait.

Europe certainly couldn't withstand another 700 years of open conflict. Spain's economy would never survive ten years of it. But then again, this wasn't 711, and these new Muslims weren't the Moors. Yes, the Moors were Muslim, but they were more scholars, architects, doctors, and tolerant of different ways. Vakar scratched his chin and focused on a car going by on the street below. No, the Moors lasted because they had something to offer. In the long run, Europe was made better by them crossing the channel. Better off, but not willing to be philosophically restrained. At its very core Europe was a Christian territory. All the way from the peasant farmers to the red robes at the Vatican it was Christian. That was the Moor's downfall in the long run.

Unlike the Moors, this new Muslim invasion in the twentieth century was much more insidious. They weren't scholars or doctors. They were vermin. They were of no use to anyone. All they offered to Europe was discontentment. They sowed the seeds of anarchy and rebellion. They were nothing more than a cancer on the European Union. This new Muslim plague would be best handled with the military solution. Well, maybe not military – that would make them martyrs. A police action had a nicer ring to it. Yes, kill enough of them and the rest would leave on their own. It was a historical truism. Vakar smiled at the thought.

Once the edges were pushed back where they belonged, Europe would be allowed to fully come of age and take center stage again as the world leader it had always been. After all, every empire that had been built had come from European soil, with one glaring exception. Genghis Khan had managed to sweep down off of the steppe on a pony and conquer pretty much every square mile of ground he encountered. He was the only one to do so. China didn't count. They were a shortsighted, inward looking, sadly self-repressed people. They had a lot of ground, but that wasn't an empire. No, with the exception of the Great Khan, empire was a European invention.

Even in the current state of the globe, France and England had more sway over the governance of far-off lands than the great American machine. If one really looked at the globe, what could America claim? They held a vast section of North America, but that was just bordered ground, like Russia. For all of its military might it possessed nothing more than a handful of tiny islands. Those islands weren't even of any consequence to anyone. Even the vast oil fields of Alaska weren't a sign of empire. They had bought Alaska from the Russians, mostly because Russia didn't want it anymore.

No, America was a child with a shotgun. They knew they had power, but they had no idea how to use it properly. So, they just swung it around like a bully. Oh, look at my shotgun, look at my shotgun.

The thought of the child with the weapon made Ivan frown. His father had taught him the power and responsibility of a hunting rifle at a young age. If he had been given that metaphorical shotgun, he would know exactly what to do with it. Instead, America used it to bully the rest of the world into viewing things its way.

A low-pitched chirp came from the intercom on the desk, and Ivan's secretary quietly reminded him that he had a meeting starting in ten minutes. The soft female voice pulled Ivan fully from his meditations and back to the present. The Foreign Affairs Council did indeed have a meeting starting in ten minutes. Ivan would need to be on time.

He placed the now rock-cold espresso cup down on its saucer, which rested on the corner of his desk, and his eyes settled on a small stack of manila file folders. One of the paper companies back in Belarus had been having union issues. That needed to get sorted out. He would need to set aside some time in the afternoon to address it.

"Unions. America. Hmmph!"

Ivan Vakar turned and headed for the door of his office. As he made his way down the hallway and through the building to the meeting room where the Foreign Affairs Council generally gathered, he passed by numerous functionaries expressing greetings of one kind or another. He was still somewhat lost in thought over his current side project. He knew that mere days onward, the globe would be a much different place. It would be a globe more to his liking. Coming through the rich mahogany double doors and sinking his shoes into the plush, yet sturdy, carpet of the terraced meeting hall, he made a mental note to pull it together.

Ivan glad-handed several members of the council as he made his way down the aisle to the table in the middle of the hall reserved for the High Representative. Even with the day's agenda being a pressing one, all of the council members seemed to be in an upbeat mood. The animated exchanges taking place were a sign of high spirits among the European leaders. When things were gloomy, they tended to be more stoic.

Everyone in the meeting hall noticed Ivan as he quietly made his way toward his seat. By the time he was situated and ready, the last of the council members were taking their seats. Once all twenty seven ministers were in positon, he nodded to the valet and the doors were closed. The affairs of national interest could now begin.

There were only two real points of interest on the docket of the day's business. The E.U. Council had to ratify a proposal from Ireland, letting Ireland offset export dues in the needs of its own internal interests. It was a straightforward matter. The council had done the same for Greece at the start of its economic downturn.

Ireland had a very low export volume per capita and most all of the council members figured that the meager resource would do all but nothing for its economic situation. Nevertheless, it was the first step in buoying up Ireland's economy, so it needed to be done. This council was required to ratify it first, simply because exports were labeled a foreign affairs matter.

As Ivan expected, there was almost no discussion on the matter. The minister from Italy asked if they could go straight to voting, and the motion was seconded by the French. A short time later the proposal was ratified and moving on toward the full council of the E.U. for a final vote.

The secretary speaker slid the docket onto the pile by his side and motioned toward the second folder on the table. Ivan looked down at its label and nodded. The E.U. had been wrestling with how to handle the disproportionate import and export taxes that America applied to goods and services for some time. Some in the E.U. had been working toward a free-trade situation, much like the NAFTA legislation had produced between the three North American countries. Most members saw this as folly. America had always held a stand-off philosophy when it came to fair and level trade. NAFTA had been brokered as more of a peace making event than anything to do with level trade. America out-traded Mexico and Canada a thousand fold. They had very little to lose.

On an Atlantic front, things were different. America had been losing export power since the fall of the wall. Import/export taxation was its way of stabilizing a weaker dollar. Weak dollar or not, European countries could ill afford to just be bullish toward the situation. American economic sectors had a powerful sway on European economic sectors. They needed to be handled, not stonewalled.

Ivan leaned back in his chair and watched as the Portuguese and Polish ministers lobbied against the Croatian minister's view to be more liberal in the council's approach. As he watched, he made mental notes separating the weak from the functionary members. In his new European Union, the weak ministers would need to be replaced, along with some of the functionaries. Men of more substance were required.

The debate went on for a good thirty minutes unchecked. Several more ministers weighed in on both sides. All of the proffered ideas seemed to be perfectly reasonable responses. Of course, that was if you assumed that things in the world would go on as they were. Ivan wanted none of that. The status quo was nowhere in the plan. A fully out-in-front Europe was what he was building.

Ivan removed his wire-rimmed glasses and rubbed the bridge of his nose.

"Ministers. Good sirs, a moment please. While all points are equally valid here, we should be looking down a road where America does not have the economic power that it once had. Its economy has been slipping ever since it became global. All economic models show that it will never reach its 1950s market high again."

The minister from Poland stood, a frumpy man with too many years, and pushed the button on his positioned microphone.

"Mr. High Representative, that may or may not be true. Either way, the American markets are a large section of the markets of every country in this room. They cannot just be dismissed. Not while they still hold power."

Ivan bit his tongue. He wanted to tell them all that in a week or so there would be no great American economy. But, he knew how such news would be received and interpreted. Though all of them would accept it well enough once it was over, none of them would have the backbone to stand with him as it unfolded.

"That may be true as well, minister. But, they still need to be sent a message that they are not as great as they once were. Remember, they are weaker now because of China and Russia. Whatever message is sent to America is also sent to the other two. Sitting between the three, we are far better to look strong than to look weak is all I'm saying."

The frumpy man from Poland sat down and looked put-out by the rebuke of his position. Other ministers picked up the mantle and the conversation continued in debate format for another forty five minutes.

As the noise in the room started to exhaust itself, it seemed that the voices of strength were slowly winning the day over the voices of liberal compromise. That made Ivan happy. The majority of the European players were for Europe. That would make things easier when true strength was needed.

"Ministers, as you know I have a meeting with the U.S. president next week. With your permission, I will express both sets of concerns and let him know that we are spending ample time looking toward our own futures."

All of the ministers accepted the solid tone in Ivan's voice as a signal of the end of the debate period, and nodded in approval. The gavel was struck and the meeting was ended. Ivan sat and watched the group file from the meeting hall. He wondered what next week's meeting with the president was going to bring. Whatever it brought, he planned on still being well over the Atlantic before his little economic care package rained fallout all over the great American Midwest.

The hall was all but empty when Ivan Vakar collected his things and pushed his chair in under the desk. The day had gone about as expected. It was time to go find a nice meal, and then continue on with the plans.

CHAPTER 10

The Hawker 800xp's tires made a screeching noise as they slid across the tarmac at London City Airport in the borough of Newham and made its way to the private jet center. As the jet came up to the yellow paint outline on the tarmac and starting spooling down its Honeywell TFE engines, a crisp black Mercedes sedan pulled up to the associated vehicle outline and parked. The exterior door to the jet separated from the fuselage and dropped into the descending position. Dr. Kristin Hughes stuck her head out of the door and looked around like a little girl on one of those Make-A-Wish shows.

"All right, Bob, you got me beat. Your life is way cooler than mine."

Robert Dunn smiled and nodded toward the door from behind her. "It does have its moments."

As he watched the doctor descend the plane steps in her blue and white striped sundress they had picked up at a small Italian shop on the way into Pisa, he considered that this might be one of them. His new partner in crime certainly could turn heads in a crowd.

The Mercedes made its way straight west across London, hugging the Thames as it went. The city was a mountain of stacked block buildings all jumbled together that whizzed by the car's windows in a blur. Kristin sat comfortably in the rear of the big saloon as it bombed through the traffic and considered that of all the times she had done London, she had never done it like this. It made her wonder if her new associate from the CIA had some sort of side gig going on. Most of the other CIA agents she had interacted with had much less flash than Mr. Dunn. But then again, she had no idea of his background or cover story. That bit would need to be passed by Gene the next time they talked privately.

Robert Dunn watched the outer edge of Green Park glide by the window with one eye and Dr. Hughes with the other. She was an enigma, if there ever was one. Fashionable, and let's face it, smoking hot, with a solid brain, having a doctorate in some scientific discipline that he couldn't pronounce. She ran around the globe defusing nuclear bombs and lounging on the beach. And, she knew people in the international spy circuit that most people in the International spy circuit didn't know existed. She was definitely an enigma. Who knew – maybe if this new friendship paid off well, he could proxy her into a better situation with the company? Yes, under the Dior, she smelled like a promotion in the making. He would need to keep her alive and happy.

The Mercedes rolled to a stop in the parking lot of Café Nero, on the corner of Victoria Street and Buckingham Gate, and idled its way into a parking space. The driver killed the engine and began to exit the vehicle. Kristin sat quietly as the driver opened her door and extended a hand for her assistance. Robert exited the opposite door and adjusted his suit jacket. Kristin smoothed her dress and thanked the driver for his assistance. The driver nodded that completely professional nod, and turned to Robert.

"Jimmy, we're gonna grab a cappuccino and take a walk around Soho. Go ahead and just standby here. We'll be back in, say, an hour and a half or so."

"Very good, Mr. Dunn. I'll be here upon your return."

Kristin and Robert walked to the door of Café Nero, and Kristin waited while Robert opened the door for her. The weather in Westminster was quite pleasant and the shop had not yet turned its fans on for the afternoon. Robert retrieved two portable cappuccinos from the counter girl and handed one to the doctor. Adjusting the lid so that it could cool as they walked, Kristin turned and headed for the door.

The two made their way west along Victoria Street, passing the exteriors of public houses and restaurants. The colorful exteriors of the many shops gave the place a feeling that went back to the '80s, when Soho was known for sex shops and the adult film industry. The odd sex shop could still be found in Soho, even though it had been all but transformed into a fashionable part of the city. It still held political and religious groups, a remnant of the once-thriving sex trade, and a goodly chunk of London's gay population. It seemed from walking its streets that the area had transitioned into a multicultural space inside London, with both rich and poor living well. It was the perfect place for someone like Noor Farooqi to live. She wouldn't even be noticed here.

Kristin pondered this as she walked along looking in the shop windows and making chit-chat with Robert. She had been in the Soho neighborhoods several times and had always liked the area. It somehow felt like Seattle back in the day. Or maybe San Fran? It was hard to say for sure. She just knew that she liked it here. It was comfortable.

Robert pulled up his gait and came to a stop in front of a multi-story building on Victoria Street and pointed to a trash receptacle in front of it. Kristin looked up at the cute stone building and assumed that they had arrived at their destination.

"We're here?" she said, playfully.

"Yes ma'am," Robert returned with a smile.

Robert opened the outside door and held it while Kristin entered into the plush landing on the ground floor. He followed in behind her as if it were any other day in the world. The two walked quietly up the stairs that circled the inner lift and admired the paintings hung along the walls. The landing for the top floor of the building was likewise appointed and appeared quite well-to-do. Robert took in the three doors that circled the large open space and casually pointed at the one toward the rear of the building. "Number two it is", Kristin said smiling, as she strolled over in front of the door.

The door to the apartment was a sturdy wooden affair. The ornate inlaid panels went well with the deep cherry stain. Robert was sure that it was reinforced. Kristin was sure that there was a camera.

"Well, can't break it. Picking it in this setting is problematic. What say we try this the old-fashioned way?"

Kristin looked at Robert, waiting for some cool bit of CIA tech to appear out of his pocket. He simply reached out and pressed the doorbell. The bell rang two times before the door was opened. Robert Dunn looked down on the petite, fit woman at the door and smiled.

"Miss Farooqi, my name is Dunn. This is Dr. Hughes. We received your name from The Arab."

Noor Farooqi, surprisingly, didn't as much as flinch. She nodded and inspected both of her visitors with a studious look.

"Americans?"

"Yes, ma'am," Kristin said quietly.

"Company?"

"I am," Robert said in a matter-of-fact way. "She's with the Department of Energy."

"I see. Well, you've come all this way. Please, come in."

Kristin looked at Noor, and then at Robert. Robert simply nodded and opened his palm to usher her through. The three walked through the lush apartment and out onto the terrace at the rear of the building. The view of Westminster was amazing and surely justified whatever the lease price happened to be. Noor showed them to seats at a wrought-iron table and took up a seat on the opposing side. Noor retrieved a smoke from the pack on the table and fired it with a golden butane lighter. She pulled a long drag off the stick and slowly exhaled in a practiced and graceful manner. If it was meant to convey calm, it was working on Kristin.

"Before we get too far along with other matters; Dr. Kristin Hughes? Of the DOE NEST Team?"

Kristin blushed slightly, unsure of the acknowledgement. "Yes, ma'am."

"I have heard a great deal about you over the years. I must say that your exploits are the stuff of folklore in our business. Is the story of your time in Morocco, five years ago, actually true?" Both Robert and Noor looked at her expectantly.

Kristin smiled a conciliatory smile. "I'm sure I don't know what you're referring to, even if I know what you're referring to."

Noor smiled broadly. Robert looked perplexed.

"A lady should be allowed to keep some of her secrets." The two women nodded to each other as Robert looked perplexed.

Noor stood from her chair. "May I offer you something while we talk? A Pellegrino, or a whiskey, perhaps?"

Robert Dunn removed a silenced Glock Model 20 from under his jacket and placed it on the glass table top.

"Fine. Straight to business is fine." Noor retook her seat and situated herself.

"Absolutely no offense to you Mr. Dunn, but I get the impression that Dr. Hughes is the brains of this operation, and you are the muscle. In this particular instance, the muscle will not be necessary. I work in an untrustworthy business. Go ahead and ask your questions. If I know the answer, I'll be happy to give it to you."

Kristin smiled wryly, somewhat knowing that that was coming. And also, that it stung Robert's ego a little.

"You talked to The Arab looking for a pair of nuclear capable scientists. What type of scientists, specifically?"

"One of them had a doctorate in explosion geometry, and the other's was in nuclei deterioration."

"So, they were warhead scientists?"

"That was my impression, yes. They both had held jobs in Pakistani's bomb works at one point or another."

"Who made the purchase request?"

"Adrian."

"Adrian who?" Robert said matter-of-factly.

"Adrian Beqiri. He is the main figure, or should I say public face, behind the Vakar Arms Network. He is Albanian, I believe. Now living somewhere in Europe."

Robert scribbled down notes into his smart phone as she talked. He was hoping someone would know something about all this later on.

"Noor, what were the timing and transfer requirements for the scientists?"

"It was short duration. Under a week. That was why I used The Arab. He delivered them to a random point in Europe and Adrian's men collected them there."

"What random point?"

"I believe The Arab sent them to the train station in Graz, Austria."

"And when was this?"

"They arrived three days ago."

"Where were they headed to next?"

"I don't know."

"What was the specific package they were working on?"

"I don't know. I simply facilitated the personnel. The rest is strictly an 'I don't need to know item.'"

"Was it a one-way package deal?" Robert asked.

"Yes. They specified expendable, Middle Eastern, men."

"So, it's a fallback plan of let's blame it on Pakistan."

"That would seem the case."

"What can you tell us about Adrian," Kristin asked.

"Other than what I said earlier? He has good encryption and pays promptly. As far as his business goes, I am not sure of its extent or from where he runs it. We do all of our business over encrypted email and cellphones. But, I would think –"

"Go ahead," Kristin said in a reassuring way.

"Vakar Arms is a local conflict type of arms merchant. As a general rule, it deals in small arms and munitions, and the occasional guided missile. Or, they always have with me. This strikes me like something that is well outside of its normal operations."

"So, they don't tend toward heavy weapons as a rule?" Kristin seemed to take the information less well than Robert.

"Heavy weapons are expensive. Nuclear weapons are very expensive. There are several arms dealers in the world that handle those types of arms sales. Vakar Arms has not typically been one of those dealers. I wouldn't think they would have the backing to handle such a speculation type sale."

"Speculation?" Robert's eyes narrowed slightly.

"They were either speculation buying to sell them later, but that's doubtful since it's a lot of money to tie up if you're in the small arms business. Or, they were shopping for someone else who had the money to buy them, in which case they were shopping outside their normal sales market."

"I see your point."

"I'm a facilitator. I get people and things that other people need. I don't ask about their business agendas, though I do wonder at times."

"Okay," Kristin said, trying to get back on track. "If Adrian was going to handle a package that required nuclear scientists, where do you think he would be doing it?"

"It is most likely somewhere in Europe. Otherwise, he would have had the scientists delivered to a spot outside the E.U. There wouldn't be any reason to bring them here, unless what he was doing was also here."

Kristin and Robert exchanged a look and Robert retrieved the Glock from the table.

"Now that I have been forthright with you, I have a question."

Robert nodded and looked at Noor intently.

"How did you end up at my door?"

"The Arab," Robert said matter-of-factly. "ECHELON pulled up his end of the phone conversation the two of you had. He used your name while talking to you. Also, his encryption isn't nearly as good as yours."

"Thank you. That's good information to have."

"I have one last question," Kristin said.

"Please, go ahead, Miss Hughes."

"Why did you open the door?"

Noor Farooqi looked at Robert Dunn and smiled. She patted him on his shoulder and turned to face Kristin.

"The options here are, end up pumped full of drugs and strapped to something uncomfortable; or just open the door and be reasonable about things. As I said before, this is an untrustworthy business. Someone out there had already betrayed my trust, or you wouldn't be here. I am simply passing that betrayal along. Don't get me wrong Dr. Hughes, I'm fully aware that one day I will open the door and there will be a pistol in my face. I don't live waiting for those issues to raise their head. When that day comes, that day comes."

Kristin considered her own lifestyle for a moment and nodded in agreement.

"You have a lovely home, Miss Farooqi. Thank you for your time."

Noor smiled and all three stood.

"May I ask a professional courtesy, Mr. Dunn?"

"Certainly."

"Could you blacken up one of my eyes? It's a professional image thing, you understand."

Without a response, Robert's right hand snapped out at Noor like an attacking cobra. The impact of his knuckles in the petite woman's eye socket was chillingly audible. His fist had no more than retracted when the whole side of her face began to expand from the infusion of blood. To her credit, her knees buckled and she swayed in her stance, but she didn't fall down.

Kristin looked at Robert in shock. Robert looked at Noor with respect. Noor nodded slightly and waved her hand toward the door. The NEST agent and CIA spook quietly exited the informant's apartment, and then the building. Night was coming to the great city, and the hustle was starting to pick up. Back at Café Nero, they climbed into the waiting Mercedes and their driver started the engine.

"Jimmy, let's try the Green House over on Hay's Mews, please."

"Very good, Mr. Dunn."

The Mercedes pulled out into the busy night traffic and headed west. Kristin and Robert sat quietly looking out opposite windows.

CHAPTER 11

Kristin Hughes stood in the kitchen of the London flat that the CIA utilized as a safe house and listened to her CIA counterpart explain the previous evening's encounter with the Pakistani woman. She calmly stirred the coffee cup that she had just removed from the Keurig machine on the counter and watched rivulets of steam rise up through the air in front of her. Outside the kitchen window, couples walked along paths in the small park and some young men played pickup soccer.

She had traveled well, and ate well, and slept well since she had met Mr. Dunn. The shock of last evening's ending had faded to memory. She understood why it was necessary, and why he didn't prolong the event with hesitation. The rapidness of it had shocked her at the time, but now that was all in the past.

Though she had been enjoying her time, she just wasn't sure what she should make of Mr. Dunn. He seemed like a good enough guy. But still, there was something about him that was — off. Her last CIA partner, Jim Bosworth, he was a great guy. They had gotten along very well, and worked together flawlessly. He was sweet and protective. Sadly, he was now also deceased. He had been gunned down while in Africa some six months back. It was all mysterious, cloak and dagger operations. Kristin had known better than to ask anyone in the group too many questions about his death. There were some things that were not discussed. The CIA was a clandestine operation.

The NEST operative/part-time spy pulled herself from her memories and stirred her coffee. Her jitters were probably just new team member cohesion issues. They would pass. She retrieved a second cup of coffee from the fancy coffee machine and padded out of the kitchen.

Entering the safe house's small study, she found Robert Dunn sitting at a desk in front of a computer with Gene Taggart's image staring down at him from a fifty inch flat screen monitor mounted on the wall. With the time change, it was evident to both that the CIA director had already had a long and trying day. Kristin handed Robert the steaming cup and smiled broadly at the camera on the laptop sitting on the desk.

"Uncle Gene! You look tired. Is Washington not treating you well today?"

"Kristin, my girl, you look as lovely as ever. And, Washington never really treats me well." They both laughed. Robert Dunn looked perplexed again. "How are you and Mr. Dunn getting along?"

Robert turned his head to see Kristin as she considered her response. She paused only long enough to give the impression that she was being thoughtful.

"He does seem to live quite well, which is nice. Otherwise, time will tell I guess."

"Roger that. Glad to hear you two are getting along. Now, even though life has made me a little surly, let's get back to business."

Kristin sat on the arm of Robert's chair and took a sip of her coffee. Robert gave up two more sentences that summed up the previous twenty four hours. The CIA director on the monitor rocked back in his chair thoughtfully.

"That about covers what we got from the Farooqi woman," Robert said in an automaton voice.

"I've heard the name Vakar Arms before. They surface on the international radar from time to time. I don't really have any useful intelligence regarding them or their activities. It's my impression that they are, or maybe were, a small arms dealer. They mostly sell to cave dissidents over in the sand box, or the rebels in Africa and South America. I'll check with the others and see if anybody has an active dossier."

"Do we really want to involve outside agencies, sir?" Robert looked unsure about trusting other government organizations. He was a child of the modern game. He was still territorial. The CIA boss adjusted his gaze at Kristin and smiled.

"Seems he's still a little new. Don't worry dear, he'll come around."

Kristin looked down at Robert over the rim of her coffee cup.

"We have lots of ways around 'official inquires.' The members of the group talk to each other all the time. And about lots of things." Kristin shifted her gaze back to the laptop camera. "Gene, tell Uncle Ed I say hi and hope he's well." In a showy, under her breath kind of way, for Robert's benefit she added, "Uncle Ed runs the NSA. He's pretty cool, for a spy master."

"Will do, Kristin."

"Now," Robert chimed back in, not really feeling part of the club, "Is there any information available on this Adrian Beqiri?"

Eugene Taggart's surly expression returned and fixed itself on Robert Dunn. He stopped short of verbally lashing the field agent, and just glared at him a moment.

"The company computers have nothing on Beqiri. I would suggest that that would be your next logical step."

Kristin nodded in agreement. She smiled into her coffee. It seemed she was running around Europe with the CIA for the summer. The CIA director caught her look.

"Not you, young lady. Lou said to tell you that your vacation is over. He wants you back home, ASAP."

"Uncle Gene?" Kristin pouted her best school girl pout.

"Kristin, let the company do — what it does. As soon as we have any actionable intelligence, I promise you'll be the first to know. I suspect everyone will end up involved in this before it's over."

"So, no more vacation?" Kristin turned her mock pout up as far as it would go. Gene Taggart gave her his fatherly look.

"You have a first class ticket waiting for you at the American Airways counter at Heathrow. And the luggage you left in Croatia should be at your apartment in Vegas by the time you get there. Have a good flight, Kristin."

"Thanks, Uncle Gene."

"Robert, go to ground. Find the trail that leads to Adrian Beqiri. Find him. Then, find out what he knows."

"Yes, sir."

"Good." And with that, the connection to Langley was severed. The CIA director's face was replaced with a small spinning logo for International Logistics, which was Robert Dunn's false front employer.

"So — Uncle Gene?" Robert looked at Kristin expectantly.

"What?"

"Spill."

"Oh, come on. The guys that run the group, well, except for Lou, are all old enough to be my dad. It makes them happy."

"And who's Lou?"

"He's my boss. DOE station chief for NEST operations."

"And he is?"

"An enigma."

"So, he's badass or something?"

"Yeah, he's badass. Badass like Batman."

Robert Dunn rolled up his face in a confused expression. He really couldn't get his head around her mind at times. Sometimes she was academically serious and quite well spoken. Other times she was aloof and almost like a teenager. She possessed all of the features of a stunning beauty, which made the juvenile outburst kind of sexy. But, in the end, she was just a very strange woman.

Kristin finished her coffee and put her hand out to take Robert's cup. Robert looked up not completely realizing what she wanted. Getting the whole picture, he shook his head no. He wasn't finished yet.

"I guess I'm off to Heathrow. Give me a shout if you find anything cool."

"Will do," Robert said, obviously already somewhere else. "I have to contact some people."

Kristin raised a single eyebrow, like Star Trek's Dr. Spock would, and then turned and padded back toward the kitchen. Robert sat quietly with his fingers tented in front of his nose. The small International Logistics logo quietly spun around on the display screen on the wall.

Kristin Hughes hailed a black cab down on the corner and headed west toward Heathrow. The trip across London and out to the international travel hub was quiet and pleasant. The city traffic wasn't heavy and the old cabby jabbered on in that way that always make tourists happy. Londoners were all very good about utilizing their number one attribute, which was simply being British. The cabby was in full effect, and his rolling oral history about recent politics made the ride go by quite fast.

Her boss had put her back on the clock, which meant that all of this now was reimbursable. She covered the relatively steep cab fare with an extra heavy tip for all the banter. The cabby smiled broadly and tipped his hat to say thanks, as gentlemen in Britain do. Kristin thanked him and headed inside to find the ticket counter.

It took her a few minutes and several forms of official U.S. government ID to explain to the customs agent why she had no entry stamp in her passport. Fortunately, she had done a few favors for Downing Street. As such, her name was on one of those lists that made these types of things go away quickly. She had pretty much pushed the 12:45 boarding time to its limit, and the plane was all but full when she jogged up to the boarding desk carrying nothing but her ticket. The gate agent inspected her lack of luggage or purse and efficiently processed her boarding pass.

It was somewhat of a female anomaly that Kristin Hughes, a smart, educated doctor of explosive things and sometimes fashionista, didn't carry a purse. She had points that came and went when she was obsessed with fashion. Fashion, but not purses. Her natural avoidance of the purse came from two very specific life circumstances. First, she had always been and was currently mobile. Starting in the military brat system, then college, and now as an unplanned globetrotter, she had always made it a point to be ready to go at a moment's notice. Her father had distilled in her the virtue of traveling fast and light. Second, and more to the moment, was her chosen line of work. As a NEST operative, she usually carried a small backpack. The pack carried everything for defusing, inspection and imaging that she might need on bomb duty. A purse would be excess baggage in those circumstances. And as a sometimes secret agent lady, she didn't need all of the negative potentials that one offered up.

As was the case with most all female military personnel, she carried her ID and cash and such in a standard issue, Velcro closure, OD–green nylon wallet. She just jammed her passport into her back pocket and she was on her way. The only real inconvenience of this lifestyle was cellphones. Her iPhone 7Gz (G being for government. And the series z, with special extra-heavy encryption, and a hyper-accurate GPS locator) didn't really fit in her skinny jeans pockets. If she was wearing a jacket, that was fine, otherwise it was just one of those things that she dealt with.

She downed two whiskey-rocks and tried to sleep, but her mind was having none of it. Her gearbox was in full go, so she looked out her window seat window and pondered the situation at hand. She understood Lou's pull-out well enough. Even as the de facto first field operative of the group, she dealt with the immediate threats to America. It was the CIA's specialty to chase leads around the globe and deal with the nastiness that it brought. It was the FBI's job to chase them around America. It was her job to jump in once the threat was real. The problem was that she could just feel in her bones that this was real. She was sure of it. The feeling had everything to do with the visit to Noor's apartment. The middleman in the game had been too forthcoming. That was out of character for a middleman. It was obvious to Kristin that she was passing on as much information as justifiably possible, so she could wash her hands of her involvement. She obviously didn't want anyone burning her after the fact. She wanted to be done with nukes. If it had been rifles or stinger missiles, she would have been much more elusive.

No, her forthrightness meant the nuclear option was legitimate. This left questions that needed to be answered. All the questions seemed to boil down to where, what, and how long? Where had the nukes come from? What was the intended target? And, how long did she have until they detonated? Her whole life usually ended up boiling down to these three questions. It was all stress or no stress.

It seemed a safe guess, judging by the scientists that had been chosen, that the weapons were of Soviet design. The old Soviet arsenal was full of Swiss cheese like holes when it came to nuclear safeguards. The Soviet bloc would be the easiest place to procure such weapons, if that's what was going on here. And Pakistani scientists would be the most comfortable with the Soviet weapons. The whole Pakistani nuclear bomb works was based upon the old Soviet design. The scientists that were chosen would surely be able to comfortably handle the Soviet weapons.

As for the where, it seemed a safe bet that the where in this game was American soil. Somewhere in the continental United States. Sure, there were numerous places around the globe where setting off a nuke would cause global chaos, but any terrorist worth his salt would jump at a chance to stick it to the good old U.S.A. Everyone knew, especially the terrorists, that despite all of its boasting, America was a pretty soft target. Getting a bomb to a location where it could inflict massive mayhem was considerably easier than the average person might think. Besides, nuclear weapons were not precision strike weapons. They were good was good enough weapons. Get it to the secondary blast range and you were on target. More importantly, the EMP had a larger radius of punch than the kinetic blast wave did. No, close enough was all you really needed with a good-sized nuke.

As for how long till boom time, well that was always a problem. Not how long till they implemented their plans – that time had come. But how long after they livened up the weapon did you really have before it detonated. That was the real problem. That was also the knife edge that she lived on. If they found it, how long did she have to work on it?

The plane pushed through the clouds and leveled out for its cross-Atlantic trek into Chicago O'Hare Airport for her connection on to Las Vegas. She knew that as soon as her boots hit the ground, she was going to be having a frank conversation with her boss. She was ready to get fully in the game. Time was definitely not on her side, she could just tell.

The flight attendant came through the cabin and she asked for a couple more bottles of whiskey. Maybe if she got drunk, she would be able to get some sleep.

CHAPTER 12

The Diaspora plowed through the North Atlantic swells with the ease of a much larger vessel. The slimmer line of the middle-aged container ship let her cut the swells coming down from the Arctic nicely. Even in the midst of summer, the North Atlantic shipping lanes could be problematic. The captain didn't have the issue of constantly having to be on the lookout for icebergs, but the summer storm swells could wreak havoc with his ship just as well.

The Diaspora herself was no fishing vessel. With a thirty eight meter beam, the Guangzhou class freighter was a full-fledged ocean going lady. Too big to traverse the Panama locks before its modification, she plied her trade running between Europe and the Americas. As an 8500 TEU vessel, the Diaspora had spent a decade running the randomly unsettled waters of the North Atlantic. She was one of a hundred similar sized ships cruising around that part of the globe.

The ship and her captain had been making a pretty standard run from Hamburg, across the Atlantic, and down the St. Lawrence Seaway to the numerous Great Lakes ports for about five years. She was a well-known sight in the ports of Canada and the United States. That was one of the reasons Vakar had picked her to put his cargo on. She was an everyday carrier. Nothing out of the ordinary came on an everyday carrier. She was simply full of containers that supplied the vast North American machine.

The big lady cut through a sturdy whitecapped ocean wave and her bow rode smoothly down the other side into the trough behind it. The route the Diaspora had chosen on this voyage had been the standard route along the southern edge of the northern land masses. She came out of the North Sea and into the Atlantic, where she skirted the bottom of Iceland and Greenland on her way to the Labrador Coast. Once she was up against the Canadian Shelf, she would turn south and head for the mouth of the mighty St. Lawrence River for her entry into the seaway.

A trip which could be somewhat torturous in the winter was now relatively calm during the High Arctic summer. That didn't mean that the summer was without its problems. One such summer storm had swept down out of the Davis Strait and slammed into the big ship halfway to St. Johns. The sea's lashing had buckled in a group of containers along the upper mid twenty-foot equivalent unit, or TEU containers. Five containers on the top row of containers toward the bow, in the forward most TEU, had been dislodged and swept overboard.

Some container damage on the high seas was to be expected. The containers themselves had a defined life cycle, and the beating of the sea was one of the things that was expected to end their lives. Completely losing containers was another matter entirely. Lost shipping containers meant insurance company inquiries and reams of paperwork for the captain. Although, in the end there wasn't much actual explaining needed. The container was there at one end of the journey and not at the other. Therefore, it had to be lost at sea. The captain filled out the necessary paperwork for the insurance companies and their underwriters, and then carried on.

This straightforward approach to handling the situation had two interesting side effects. First, unknown to most everyone outside of the shipping world, there were shipping containers scattered all across the bottom of every shipping route on the globe. Goods that went over the side were simply written off and left for naught. Second, it left an interesting little loophole that could be exploited by shady men such as Adrian Beqiri and the underpaid ship captains with which he did business. Upon occasion, ships would pull up and unload a container or two onto another vessel. Then they would write them off as being lost at sea once they made port. The insurance company would reimburse a percentage of Adrian's lost machine parts, and containers loaded with weapons could now move along unbothered by maritime inspectors. Some greased palms, some good route planning, some creative paperwork, and one could move arms pretty much anywhere.

On this particular voyage, no one had any desire to lose anything. So, when the summer storm had stripped the forward containers from the Diaspora, it had made Adrian's man onboard nervous. The lost containers had been but three rows ahead of the two freshly painted containers of kitty litter he had been safeguarding. He couldn't imagine the fury of the bosses if the two shipping boxes had been swept overboard. And he didn't want to.

Rupert, a seasoned merchant marine crew hand and lifetime employee of the Vakar Arms Network, had inspected both containers closely the day after the storm. Their holding pins were secure on all corners and they showed no signs of either damage or leakage. He had made the inspection while walking the deck with the two Pakistani scientists. Adrian had decided to ship the scientists with the bombs, just in case. It was now Rupert's job to make sure that both packages arrived in America and got offloaded without incident. He was the babysitter of the moment. It was easy enough work, and the storm notwithstanding, it had been uneventful. He had sailed with the captain before on other vessels. The captain knew his outside affiliation and made his life somewhat less miserable than others would have. Mostly because the captain was also on the take. It was just a good arrangement for everyone.

Rupert watched the bow of the big lady cut through the whitecapped North Atlantic from one of the deck walkways on the aft tower, and smiled. The smoke from his German cigarettes was blown free as the breeze coming over the bow pushed everything aft. The day was calm and the sky was blue. The ship was making good time and would be gliding past St. Johns in mere hours.

He looked down on the deck scene below, large stacks of containers cut by well-defined walkways. The two scientists stood about midway down the starboard walkway looking out over the endless blue. Rupert didn't know why they were here and he really didn't care much. His man had called and said that he needed to look after the two men, so he was looking after them. Besides, how much mischief could they really get into in the middle of the ocean? He really didn't have to start earning his money until they made port.

Down on the deck – Hamal held onto the top railing of the walkway with a strong grip and watched the whitecaps come and go. He had never seen the ocean before and would be happy not to be so far out in it. When he had flown to America for college, he had been too scared to look out of the plane. He didn't enjoy the flying, so he had stayed to reading the magazines and just waited it out. He didn't enjoy ocean travel either, so now he held tight to the handrail and waited it out.

Hafid stood next to him, casually leaning against the wall of shipping containers. In contrast to his new compatriot, he was enjoying himself quite well. The smell of the salt air and the rhythmic roll of the ship gave him comfort and made him think back on earlier times. As a young undergraduate student in Miami, and then chasing his doctorate at Virginia Tech, he had spent countless days at the beach. He greatly enjoying the calming power of the sea. He also liked the scene that beach life presented. He had been very happy in America. He was happy to be going back to that country now. He was a realist, so he knew the deal with the nuclear weapons would not end well. These types of things never ended well. But he had decided that he would disappear before that happened. He had plans of heading back to Miami. He would do what needed to be done when they landed, and then drift off and find a Greyhound station so he could vanish.

Hafid fished a package of German cigarettes out of his pocket and removed one. The tobacco was not as strong as the Pakistani brand that he usually smoked, but the flavor was good enough. He lit the cigarette and drew in a large lung full of air as he studied his older friend.

"You probably don't need the death grip on the railing. I don't think you're going to fall over."

"I'm not taking the chance. I don't like ships," Hamal said studying his grip.

Hafid drew another lung full of smoke, expelled it, and then shook his head.

"Relax Hamal. The ship is fine. We're actually making pretty good time. We'll be in America soon enough."

"And you know what happens when we get there? Bad things happen."

"True Hamal, but America is vast. There will still be room enough for us to disappear into."

"You're being naïve, my young friend. Our fate will not be that pleasant."

"Naïve how? We were paid to do a job. That job is done. I no longer owe them any debt. Once we make port and the containers are offloaded, I plan on discreetly drifting off."

"I wish you the best of luck."

Hafid extended the pack of smokes to Hamal, but the older man just shook his head. Hamal had heard stories about other men accepting such opportunities for employment in the past, during the time of the Soviets. None of those men ever came home. No, he had no illusions that he could just walk away from the job he had accepted. He recognized he was about to be at his end. If his younger friend wanted to run, so be it. He didn't plan on stopping him or helping him too much. He should have known what he was getting into.

A whitecap slid by the side of the ship and stirred up the salt air. Hafid smiled at the increased salt smell. Hamal studied him skeptically and continued to hold onto the railing. Hafid pitched the dead butt of his smoke over the side with a flick of his finger and began to go about firing up another. Hamal looked past his counterpart and half nodded his head. Hafid straightened up slightly and slowly turned his head to see Rupert ambling down the walkway. Hafid rolled his eyes at Hamal and went back to his relaxed position. Rupert strolled up to the two scientists and inspected Hamal's death grip on the railing.

"I don't think you need to worry about the pitch of the ship quite that much."

Hafid laughed out a full lung of smoke through his nose, in a kind of snorting fashion. Rupert smiled and bummed a smoke from his pack.

"I don't like ocean travel that much. The train however, is very nice." Hamal slowly let go of the railing, but reattached himself as soon as the ship moved. The others laughed loudly. Rupert looked fore and aft to check for other crew members before speaking again.

"Did you get a chance to inspect the containers this morning, or were the deck crews being a bother?"

Hafid smiled and nodded at their handler. Hamal did the same, minus the smile.

"I checked them both before breakfast, when the watch was slow. Everything is fine."

Rupert smiled at the report. Unknown to him, both the containers had been fitted with external plugs for the weapon's systems. They could be checked for readiness without having to open the containers. The plugs themselves had been disguised behind standard bolt cover plates. Many containers had them, so they looked completely normal to the crew. All Hafid had to do was slide the inspection plate to the side and insert the external firing control into its plug. All the lights had lit up green, meaning that when he had checked it, the weapons were ready to go.

Adrian had sent the scientists along so they could double check the weapons before the ship made port. Knowing that the ship had an unloading schedule for ports in both Canada and America, Rupert wanted to get those checks done, whatever they may be, prior to entering the St. Lawrence River. It seemed that everything was going fine.

"That's good news. Now, we have a nice quiet boat ride the rest of the way in."

"That sounds nice," Hafid said, expelling smoke.

"There's fresh coffee in the mess," Rupert said as he turned and headed back up the walkway.

Hafid nodded in acknowledgement, as did Hamal. Hamal watched as the German walked away, and could feel that his life was only a short time from being done. He thought that he needed to take some time to pray. He needed to be ready, at the end.

Hafid looked out past his older friend, and took in the view of the sea. He smiled contently. He thought of South Florida and its sunny beaches, teeming with bikinis.

CHAPTER 13

Kristin pulled up to the gate guard at the air force base north of Las Vegas and smiled as she handed over her ID card.

"Good morning, Dr. Hughes. You may go ahead and proceed in."

The young and efficient airman handed back her military identification card and smiled as he pointed a white glove toward the base side of the guard shack. Kristin motored onto base in her Mini Cooper and made a left onto one of the main roads. Tyndall Avenue ran down the western edge of the sea of asphalt which made up the aircraft handling area.

Kristin pulled the Mini Cooper into her designated parking space outside of a nondescript building sandwiched between the south end of the runways and the base golf course. She actually loved being at Nellis Air Force Base. In so many ways, it reminded her of her Army brat upbringing. The feeling of being a civilian contractor was not completely removed from the feeling of being a military dependent. The sensation it gave her every time she came to work was reassuring.

Kristin punched her entrance code into the metal door's keypad and waited for the click. Proceeding through the door, she waved to the guard behind the one-way mirror and waited in the secure anti-chamber for the internal door to be released. A quick set of stairs up to the second floor and halfway down the nondescript hallway to the nondescript door, where she found her boss waiting. She bounced through the door and dropped her gear bag onto one of his leather chairs. For his part, her boss just pointed one finger toward the coffee pot on the side table and another toward the empty leather chair in front of his desk. He inspected his troop as she retrieved a cup of hot, black, road tar and slid sideways into the chair.

"Two questions. Did you enjoy your vacation? And, why was your phone off on days three and four?"

Lou Stenson eyed Kristin with his interrogation look. Kristin shrugged it off and sipped on her coffee.

"Let's see – left the phone charger in Samos, battery died on the ferry. Acquired a new charger in Split, and recharged said electronic device. And, the trip did have its moments."

"There was a bit of back channel rumbling that your new base commander friend quickly squashed. But just the same, I'd like a debrief on whatever this Camp Darby affair was. I'd like to be able to defend your actions, if necessary."

"Let's be clear about something. I didn't ask to go. Somebody came and found me. I assumed it was you."

"I didn't know you were in Italy until you got on the plane." The two looked at each other quizzically. Kristin raised an eyebrow as if to say, "what the hell?"

"It would seem that your reputation is starting to precede you. That can't be a good thing, considering your predisposition toward crazy clandestine side projects."

"Oh, come on Lou. I'm not Jane Bond. I just do work that needs doing."

"That's what keeps me up at night." The big Navy SEAL looked over the desk at her with his fatherly gaze, which was finely crafted to be both comforting and intimidating. Kristin wasn't swayed in either direction.

"Lou, you know you don't need to worry about me. I'm a big girl. Besides, from what I've seen of you sleeping on the couch in here, nothing keeps you up at night."

"Very funny."

"Now, to the matter at hand. What has The Group been discussing regarding our terrorist threat?"

"I talked with CIA this morning. Their man is snooping around Europe as we speak. FBI has heard the names before, but has no active files on Beqiri or Vakar Arms. As usual, NSA and NRO are awash in too much data to data mine efficiently."

"So, sitting in the dark?"

"The group is doing its thing. We will know what there is to know, as soon as we can know it. Until then, it's your job to wait it out and be ready to ASSIST."

"I got news for you, Lou. My gut is telling me that this is a real world op. And we're already out of time to be sitting around. Everything about this deal smells real."

"I think the same thing. BUT, you're not going off half-cocked, chasing ghosts. That only leads to assets getting exposed and/or hurt. You get me?"

"I get you, sir." The affirmation came out quietly and Lou could tell that she was revisiting some past event.

"Don't dwell on the past, kid. Let the dead lie. That Middle East business was a long time ago."

"Sometimes, it doesn't feel that way."

"Well, that's also part of what we do and who we are."

"Yup."

Lou Stenson looked at the young lady in front of him and wondered just how many times she had been forced to make the tough decision. As an operator, he had made the decision on numerous occasions. But part of his world-class training was the ability to be mentally prepared to do such things. His young "bomb dog" learned it all by trial and error. She had stepped into a job that turned out to be so much more than the application let on. None of the other NEST operatives had any real idea of Kristin's more clandestine activities, nor would any of them be able to handle her job if they did. She was a singular person. Most in the business couldn't be trained up to her natural situational awareness, much less be able to function critically at her working stress level. Still, making the tough choices took a toll on the best of people. What kind of toll was it taking on her?

"Lou? Earth to Lou. You look like you're spacing out."

"Nope. I'm right here, right now."

"Thanks for the VH1 Van Halen reference. Now, can we get Ed, or Bob, or Gene on the horn and see if there's anything new afoot?"

"You do realize that those three men are possibly the three most powerful men in the country? You should really use proper last names."

"You're my boss, and I don't use yours."

"I see your point, All the same –"

"Phone, please."

"Who actually runs this place anyway?" The imposing figure behind the desk laid his palms across it in a sign of aggression. Kristin yanked the stretchy band out of her hair and shook her mane of bottle-blond hair loose.

"You do, Mr. Stenson. And you do it marvelously well. Phone, please." Kristin summoned her best innocent five-year-old smile and turned it up to a beaming level ten. Lou leaned back in his chair and pressed the red button on his desk phone. Two low clicks came through the speaker, followed by a dial tone. Lou nodded at the door and Kristin jumped up to close it. The dialing was complete by the time she regained her semi-reclined position seated crosswise on the chair.

"Lou, figured you'd be calling soon. You got your number one bomb dog there with you?" Paul Spencer, senior systems director at the NRO had a jovial tone in his voice.

"Yes, Paul, she's here. She finally decided to honor us with her post-vacation presence."

Lou smiled. Kristin mocked him with a sneer.

"Well, Dr. Hughes, you did have a high-impact vacation. Just to let you know, I have been listening to the DOD traffic with great interest ever since it went down. You seem to have stirred up a fairly good-sized hornet's nest inside military command."

"It wasn't my intention. I was on a beach in a different country. Am I going to get in trouble over this?"

"Ha ha ha ha ha! No, ma'am. All of the gunfire is internal. There is some heavy European Theatre traffic bouncing around about the inability to account for and maintain their nuclear arsenal. It's all going up-chain, and none of it has your name on it. Trust me, if anything hit the grid with your name on it, the NSA will expunge it immediately."

"Thanks for assist, Paul. We both appreciate her being looked after."

"Least that I can do. It's pretty much my fault that she's in the middle of it anyway."

"How so?" Lou Stenson was now staring at his speaker phone with clinched teeth.

"President was out-of-pocket when the flash traffic came through?"

"Yes. He was at a private conference for the upcoming G8 Summit thing in Chicago."

"The flash traffic was captured by Pat Sommers at the time. He called me and asked if I knew where Kristin was vacationing. So, I stared into my crystal ball for a moment and then sent a fighter jet over to retrieve her. I had received a couple of other calls from group members during the hunt, so I had assumed that you were in the loop. I am sorry about that."

"No worries, as long as it didn't end up FUBAR, it's ok. Just, call next time."

"Roger that on both fronts."

From the outside, everyone assumed that Paul Spencer was your average everyday tech head. He was some guy that had had an Apple IIc before everyone else as a kid, then went on to Cal Tech or some such place before getting a cool job at a start-up in Silicon Valley. The assumption was he was one of those guys who wanted to give back after 9/11 and went on the government plan. It was all a useful bit of camouflage for someone functioning inside the beltway.

Paul Spencer was, in point of fact, a third generation Army soldier. His grandfather had seen the end of WW II and the bad side of Korea. His father, a Medal of Honor-winning infantry captain, had died in Vietnam. Lt. Spencer had gone through West Point and then did graduate work in systems security at MIT. Then he moved on to earn a doctorate in artificial intelligence from Princeton. Lt. Spencer had done tours in South America and Europe, all times trying to find a place for himself in the Army family. It was not to be. But in one of the Army's many insightful moves, knowing they couldn't keep him they decided to put him somewhere that he could do the most good. So, just days after 9/11, he was quietly introduced to the director of the NRO. In the semi-virtual world of the National Reconnaissance Office, Paul Spencer's military training and crazy intellect came fully online. The strides that he ushered into the electronic reconnaissance field were immediate.

Having been introduced to The Group by the president, he had proven his worth on countless occasions and was considered by all to be a senior member. Being in the "position of knowing," as he called it, he made it his personal mission to always know the location and situational status of all of The Group's field operatives. This was why the Army had been able to locate Kristin so quickly.

"So, Paul, what does the crystal ball have to say about this Vakar Arms business?" Kristin had always referred to the American intelligence machine as a crystal ball. To her, it all seemed like Nostradamus trying to divine the future. Though she conceded that they really did have better luck than the French mystic.

"Frankly, nothing of consequence. Now that they are officially aggregated into the filtering algorithms, data should start to amass. That traffic would all have been an NSA level matter, until now."

"So, we're talking to Ed next?"

"I talked to him this morning. We are both feeding all of our data over to the Hoover Building. It seems that FBI had some sort of almost empty file already started on Vakar Arms. Don't know what it stemmed from."

"Affirmative, Paul. Good talking to you. We'll hit up Sloan and see what the what is."

"Anytime, Lou. He should have whatever is to be had at this point. Glad to hear you're back safe and sound, Dr. Hughes."

"Thank you, Dr. Spencer."

Everybody laughed a little and the line went dead. Lou rebooted the phone and punched in a new set of numbers. The call made connection and rang two times.

"Good morning. You have reached the offices of Shadrach, Meshach and Abednego, LLC. We are currently busy planning for the Apocalypse. Please leave a message."

"Good one, Pepper."

"Lou! How's things out at Nellis?"

"Hot and sunny. How's things inside the beltway?"

"Your standard issue hornet's nest."

"Okay. What do you know about this Vakar Arms business?"

"The whole mysterious nuclear terrorism plot against somebody or something undefined? Next to nothing. You?"

"NOT funny, Bob," Kristin retorted at the phone. She was missing out on all of the underlying humor that the two others were enjoying.

"Kristin, seriously. Until you all stumbled across the connection, it was less than nothing to us. All the conversation over cards beforehand was speculation. Now, it's another one of those things that you chase around in the dark with a flashlight. We are at the start of the chase. As soon as we get some actionable intelligence, YOU will be the first one we call."

Lou looked over the desk at his field operative, who was outwardly fuming, and gave her that *"hush, troop!"* face. She complied.

"Pepper, what have you worked up on Vakar Arms so far?"

"Realistically, next to nothing. They did a couple of arms deals with the Yucatan Cartels about 5 years ago. It was a straight cash-for-guns deal. Vakar supplied light arms, ammo, and some undefinable amount of explosives and the cartel paid in small denomination Euro bills.

It was pretty much everyday drug business in our eyes. We really didn't stay with it long. That seems to be the only time that Vakar Arms has come up on the radar. At least in Mexico. There are rumors that the organization primarily operates in Eastern Europe, the sandbox nations, and Southeast Asia. We are building out the information in the file as we speak."

"Are they primarily small arms?"

"Yes. They're part of that whole shipping container bunch. They don't seem to have the infrastructure or general want for the heavy arms business. At least that's the vibe we're getting. We'll know more soon."

"Okay, say all of that is accurate. How could they handle a large-magnitude deal like nukes?"

Bob "Pepper" Sloan was long in responding to the DOE operations chief's inquiry. The senior FBI man knew that things in the international arena were seldom, if ever, what they appeared to be.

"The biggest problems with the nuke market are availability and money. In reality, availability is the only actual problem. If you can find the nukes, then finding the money is a much easier affair. Truthfully, does a small arms merchant with no real infrastructure have the capital to purchase nukes if he could actually locate them? I doubt it. Those events are usually one time auctions. But, if Vakar had backing from somewhere else, it could be doable."

"What kind of backing are we talking about?" Kristin said.

"Funny you should ask. There's a rumor on the street that Vakar Arms actually got its name because it was secretly owned by Ivan Vakar from Belarus, but, frankly, that's just ludicrous."

"How so?" Kristin prodded a second time.

"Ivan Vakar? Please. He's High Representative for the Foreign Affairs Council of the European Union. People in that level of government don't need to traffic arms. He gets his money from owning a mid-level paper plant in Belarus, not from running around pretending to be Doctor No."

"So, he has a cool job, which by proxy makes him not ruthless. We have had many ruthless people in government before." Lou looked at Kristin incredulously as she spit out the words.

"My dear, we have a lot of ruthless people in government right now, but I highly doubt that the European Union wants to do-in the United States."

"All right, I concede."

"We have several people in our European field offices that are in the arms game. All of our field guys and gals are out on the streets doing what they do. The CIA is also out doing what it does. Just as soon as we have anything useable, you'll definitely know."

"That's all we can ask for, Pepper. We'll be standing by over here, just keep us in the loop."

"Sounds good, Lou. You two take care."

The line went dead for a second time. Kristin reached down and retrieved her coffee cup from the government-issue carpet on the floor. The cold liquid slid down her throat with all but no benefit. She stared into the cup's black liquid and pondered all the information that had come out in the phone calls.

Lou Stenson rolled his head, from one shoulder to the other. Several loud cracks could be heard coming from his neck, which pulled Kristin back to the here and now.

"The rest of your group is doing training. You should rejoin them for the next couple days, until we know more."

"Lou, we need to be about this NOW."

"We need to let shadowy people do shadowy things first."

"But –"

"No buts."

"Fine."

"Good. Now get out of my office so I can do boss stuff."

"You mean play solitaire?"

"Yes."

"Fine."

Kristin stood, grabbed her gear bag out of the chair and headed for the door. Lou Stenson looked at the coffee cup perched on the edge of his desk and shook his head.

"You forgetting your dishes?"

"Gentleman hosts the party, gentleman does the dishes."

And, the door closed behind her before her boss could rebut.

CHAPTER 14

The Diaspora exited Lake Michigan into the outer breakwater of the Illinois International Port District at no more than an idle. Her cross-lake velocity had given her ample momentum to enter and navigate the waterway's wide mouth with ease.

The captain throttled up the engines and engaged the large drive units in reverse thrust to slow the ship to a stall. Looking straight down the throat of the port canal, the large rail bridges had all been raised to allow ships to enter farther into the waterway. He looked past them at the South Ewing Avenue Bridge, which was down to allow the flow of the commuter traffic, and wondered if the train bridges were actually being worked on. Most often, the two sets of crossings went up and down together.

The bridge situation was not of great concern, as the Diaspora was headed for a slip ahead of the crossings. The captain had tied up to the primary container unloading area at the mouth of the port many times. He would watch as the bulk cargo ships would make their way past, heading inland through the maze of bridges to the mountainous unloading facilities that could be seen far off. He had also watched the grand Great Lakes ore ships come and go, delivering their unprocessed cargo to the steel plants along the lake.

The steel plants of the Midwest could be seen to the south, all the way down to the curve in the bottom of the lake. The huge foundries and blast furnaces inhaled the ore and exhaled building products. The materials coming and going along the coast and in the port was almost constant.

The steady traffic of the port was one of the things that the captain of the Diaspora liked about the Port of Chicago. Being at the first of the unloading areas made for good viewing of the many ships that traversed the canal. They ranged from large international haulers, like the Diaspora, to tugboats pushing pan-shaped flat-bottom barges. There was usually always something to see.

The tugs that tended to the docking of the larger vessels came alongside the Diaspora and hailed her over to the local marine channel. Acknowledging the summons, the captain signaled his readiness to dock. The tug operators went to work and in no time the large ocean-going vessel was lined up in her slip, bow facing out to the lake. The tugs held the large vessel fast as stevedores on the dockside produced the throw lines that were used to haul up the large diameter mooring lines. The deckhands pulled up the lines and tied them off before the stevedores on the dock took up the slack and secured the ship to her station on the pier. The engines were spooled down to a standing idle and the gangways were lowered to the dock.

The captain radioed the tugs and thanked the other captains for their assistance before picking up a large stack of customs papers and heading off the bridge. Where the real customs paperwork was now all electronic pdf files, which had been sent along to customs days before, it was still a maritime theme that every piece of cargo required a traveling manifest. The captain presented them to the custom official and they were promptly reviewed and stamped. The offloading could begin.

Rupert watched the captain enter the customs house from the small window in his cabin and checked his watch. They had made port in late morning. Knowing the unloading routine of the Port of Chicago quite well, he knew that his containers would be offloaded today.

Where it would take the better part of twenty four hours to offload all of the containers, Adrian had made sure that his containers were loaded close to last. This would make them some of the first to be offloaded. It was always best to have your cargo handled first. That strategy minimized the time people had to wait around the docks. That minimized the potential for problems. Both Adrian and Rupert hated problems.

The U.S. Port System had been upgraded many times in the wake of the 9/11 terrorist attacks. All of the unloading areas in the port were now rigidly restricted. Identification cards needed to be displayed at all times. Roving patrols from Homeland Security and Border Patrol were now all but a constant presence. Rupert wasn't worried about being bothered, per se, as his TWIC – transportation worker identification credential - card and passport were both in good standing. It was more that people waiting and milling around the docks attracted attention, ships or no ships. He wanted to avoid bothersome questions from the harbor authorities. He definitely wanted to keep his two Pakistani charges from having to answer any pointed questions. Muslim-looking men were of great interest to the authorities these days.

Rupert sat quietly at his window and waited. Not long had passed and the dockside carry cranes began to move toward the ship. The ship's large hauling derricks started to swing out and crews began to get things underway.

The captain came out of the customs house with two men from Homeland Security and another in a Harbor Police uniform. They all laughed at something and then parted ways, with the captain heading back toward the ship. The captain gave a big, circular wave of his hand and the first stack of containers was swung over the side of the Diaspora by the unloading derricks. Rupert smiled at his reflection in the porthole glass.

The next three hours passed with a nap and a quick review of the overall plan. It took approximately four hours for the offloading derrick to hook onto the stack containing his two containers. Rupert watched as the stack was transferred to the dock and then picked up by the large mobile crane and driven off toward the stacking area. The hard work on his end was now half done. Time to do the second bit.

Rupert got up and grabbed the lanyard attached to his TWIC card and his yellow floatation jacket with the Diaspora's logo on its back. Going out the door of his cabin, he found the internal passages of the ship were all quiet, as all but a handful of crew were busy with the offloading. Rupert walked the length of the main hallway to a room by the exterior hatch. He banged on the door twice. It opened and Hamal looked out at his handler.

"Time to disembark, boys."

Both men jumped to and retrieved small bags and bright logoed floatation jackets. Rupert gave them the once over and nodded. They looked just like any other dock worker or crew member. The three men made their way out of the ship's superstructure and across the deck to the gangway that descended to the dock. Hamal led the way, happy to be putting his feet back on solid ground. Hafid took the middle and Rupert followed behind. Everything on the docks looked normal and as calm as could be expected during offloading. This made Rupert calm. One never knew what the situation at the ports was really going to be.

Where U.S. Customs as a whole was still a large, slow moving, quite porous affair, the port security was different. Considering that the US Ports were the most porous part of the border system, they were an ever-changing situation. The different ports were like little fiefdoms, and their individual moods changed by the day and the vessel.

Today, everything around the port seemed calm. Fortune was with them. Rupert picked up the pace a bit to get out in front of the other two men as they crossed the yard. The three men moved naturally, and his two associates carried on about things that they were going to see once in the city. Rupert threw in a couple of bars he wanted to stop at as he opened the door at the Customs house.

The three men walked up to the Customs counter and its ubiquitous yellow do-not-cross line as they continued the conversation of museums and theaters. The Customs agent waved Rupert forward and he stepped up, placing his passport on the desk. The Customs officer inspected the picture page of his document and matched it against a photo on the TWIC card hanging around his neck. The agent slid his passport through the automated reader and surveyed the information that came up on the computer screen.

"You guys aren't staying to offload?" The Customs officer had a nonchalant tone, and a matter-of-fact persona. Rupert smiled a smile that could only come from someone getting away with something.

"We spent a bunch of extra hours working on the ship because of the gale we plowed through. Captain was in a good mood. I didn't question the good fortune."

The Customs officer looked over at the manifest stack and the big red sticker signifying lost cargo and nodded.

"You hit big trouble?"

"Not really. We made way through one good blow that wiped some cans over the side. It jammed the tops on some others. Otherwise, it was pretty nice to be at sea."

The Customs agent nodded, as his story matched the one given by the captain earlier on. The passport was stamped with a flourish and slid back across the counter.

The two Pakistanis produced new German passports, with information that would not raise any suspicions. Both were stamped and handed back. The three men headed for the door, making it almost to the exit before the Customs agent turned his chair in their direction.

"Gentlemen, the Diaspora is set to sail in two days. When do you plan on leaving the country?"

Rupert smiled at the Customs agent. This was a formality in port. It was their way of saying, "don't get drunk and end up in jail."

"We'll be on the ship when she sets sail again. Actually, we all have to come back in the morning to do a container count. Captain's way of leveling out letting us go early. Shouldn't take more than a couple hours, though."

The Customs agent laughed. "That's just mean. I'll make a note that you guys are coming back."

Rupert waved thanks and the three men disappeared through the door. As Rupert saw it, things were proceeding exceedingly smooth. That was nice for a change. Usually, in the smuggling business, if Customs went well, so did the rest of it.

All three men jumped into a cab and headed out of the port. The cab went straight out of the port on the normal route and drove to a hotel halfway between the Port of Chicago and the city. The large but outdated hotel was a way station for a great many merchant sailors coming and going through the port. The desk staff could muster up a couple to four languages between them, as they too were all immigrants. And the hotel accepted every tradable currency.

Rupert spoke English, paid dollars, and received a key to a room on the second floor. All three men smiled and headed for the stairs. They were no different than the last 500 men who had walked through the door, and the desk staff forgot them as soon as they were out of sight. Rupert slid the plastic card into the slot in the door and waited for the click. He pushed the door open and the men entered the large double room. All were dropping their bags when the door that connected their room to the adjacent one opened.

"You are right on time. Did you have any problems with the Customs people?"

Rupert walked over and shook Pavel's hand in a sturdy manner.

"No. Everything went just fine. We are on the schedule to go in first thing tomorrow to do the container count. We'll do the cosmetics then."

"That should work out well. We have a truck scheduled to pick up the first one tomorrow afternoon. As soon as I know that they're ready, I'll send one on its way."

"With the drive back down and what not, I can't imagine it'll take any more than three hours to handle it all. No reason it shouldn't be complete by noon. All you need to do is change the container numbers in the port computers."

"The numbers have already been changed. Now, what do you say you and I have a drink. And your traveling companions can have some time to get cleaned up."

All four men nodded, and Rupert followed Pavel into the adjacent room. Hamal stretched out on the broken-down mattress, and Hafid looked out the window at the city skyline in the distance.

Afternoon passed by quickly enough. The Pakistani men calmly talked and read magazines to pass the time. Pavel talked to different men handling logistics and drank with Rupert. The conversation in both rooms was light, and noncommittal. A man arrived about dinner time with pizza and some dishes from a local Mediterranean restaurant. All the men ate in relative quiet, the room's TV making most of the noise.

The conversations that did take place in the two rooms were mostly in English. Pavel would speak in his native language on the phone, and some German with Rupert. Hafid had learned some Ukrainian from his roommate at Virginia Tech. What Pavel was speaking wasn't that, but it was close enough to be understood. Hamal soaked up the German part with ease, and the Pakistani men kept each other up to speed with their handler's conversations.

There was a palpable sense of finality building in the hotel as the hours passed. Nothing was said, but most everyone here knew that when the nukes were final inspected and all lights were green, the two scientists would no longer be of use to anyone. Rupert still didn't know what was in the containers, just that whatever it was needed a final inspection. That could make it a hundred different things. It could be a nuke, or it could be chemical or biological. It could also be a number of different computer-based options. Rupert was the guy in the chain that just did what he was told and didn't ask questions that didn't need asking. Pavel liked that about him. It would make things easier when the time came.

CHAPTER 15

Lou Stenson paced back and forth across the expanse of his utilitarian military office's wall of windows that looked out over one of the air base's runways. The view of planes coming and going on the runway didn't give him its usual comforting distraction. He knew all of the members of The Group were currently doing the best job that they could do. The spooks on the team were all world class in the intelligence game. They would do what needed doing. He just had to let them do their recon, so his team could start up active operations.

Lou looked out on the tarmac apron and watched a mechanic fiddle under the hood of a desert camo Humvee. From its appearance, the mechanic was going about his tasks with purpose. At least he was doing something.

Lou cracked his neck and went back to pacing. SEALs spent great amounts of time waiting for the Op Order to come down. Normally, they would fill idle time with training. Downtime was training time. Now, being somewhat removed from being a fulltime operator, Lou had no need to constantly reinforce his skill set. Now, he had time for pacing. But, still, idle time was wasted time. Maybe a tumble or two in the gym would help?

The big NEST director of operations scratched his chin. That did sound like a good idea. There were two other members of the NEST Ops Teams that were certified black belts or better in a martial art. They could both give him a proper fight. He considered that for a moment. Most everyone from both of the field teams stationed at Nellis were either out doing training operations or down in the burn rooms working on technique. There must be a bad ass kicking around the shop somewhere.

Lou made his way through his office door and out into the hallway. A quick flight of regulation metal stairs and he was on the first floor. He started down the long central hallway that gave access first to the classrooms, then on to the burn rooms, and finally the rec areas and the TO&E. The TO&E was in the two big hangar areas where all of the NEST field operations gear was kept. TO&E workers maintained all the bomb detection equipment, radiation sensing devices, and numerous scanner units in this area. The civilian-looking helicopters and light aircraft that sometimes carried the teams and gear were also maintained and housed there.

The large cargo aircraft that transported everything in the inventory around the U.S. territories were actually military aircraft borrowed from the inventory at Nellis Air Force Base. The flight crews stationed at Nellis had couriered his crews many times. And the NEST chief had given many thanks for their professionalism.

If there was anyone more uncomfortable with waiting for information than Lou Stenson, it was definitely Kristin Hughes. Lou stopped in front of one of the hallway's classroom windows and watched Kristin casually tinker with an old World War II timing trigger. He could tell by the way that she poked at it with the number 11 screwdriver that her heart was nowhere in it. He was happy that her back was to him, so he didn't have to undergo the same fusillade of questions that he had already been subjected to three times this morning. She definitely was not a patient young lady.

He watched as she poked her head with the eraser end of a pencil and noticed the highlighted pink strand in her otherwise blond hair. It wasn't a ribbon, though she had been known to do that. No, at some point in the recent past, she had been bored/frustrated/agitated to the point of dying her hair funny colors. Lou thought hard about the last couple of days. She had not had the highlights when she returned from Europe. Come to think of it, she hadn't had any funny colors in the just-out-of-bed hair style she was sporting this morning as she was rifling him with unanswerable questions. When the hell this morning had she found time to dye her hair?

Lou started to ponder if Kristin wasn't in fact starting in on one of her rebelling-against-the-man phases when he happened to notice that she was now looking at him. She was actually looking at a four-foot-square mirror in front of her bench that held a reflection of him in the hallway. The SEAL grabbed a bit of his short crew cut and made the universal gesture for WHAT THE FUCK?!? Kristin responded with her patented bored-geek smile. She started to turn around but Lou threw up a big palm as if to say stop. So, she did.

The NEST operations director turned and continued down the hallway, taking in the various activities going on in the training areas. He had spent a good ten minutes watching Jim Bonner and his second work on a mockup of a warhead from the Multiple Re-entry Vehicles on a Trident II. The MRV bus on a Trident II could secure a dozen warheads and each one of the real thing was a handful.

The MRVs were basically dispersed individual warheads. In a sense, it made the Trident a nuclear shotgun, of sorts. The W88 warhead that the two men were wrenching on was a new-use tactical nuke. It was basically a bunch of HMX-based plastic explosive wrapped around a beryllium reflected plutonium core. The plutonium core punched a deuterium-tritium fuel core that was boosted by enriched lithium 6. The whole affair was sandwiched into a cone hat-shaped cover and secured to the bus by a locking ring on its flat end.

None of the radioactive load or the plastic compression explosives were actually in the training unit. All ordnance used in the training simulators in the burn rooms was of the flash-bang variety. It was a relatively safe option for training. It allowed the technicians to get real world feedback on failed techniques, as the flash-bangs would leave your head ringing for a good couple hours.

Lou smiled and quietly watched the two world-class operators efficiently sidestep the booby traps on the device and remove its internal actuators. He was starting to rethink the sparring when Bonner sat down his tools and nodded to his second. His second nodded affirmation and Bonner slapped the big red button on the end of the work bench that stopped the timer on the wall. Lou inspected the large LED readout proclaiming twenty two minutes and forty eight seconds had elapsed. They had set a very good time. Nukes, even new series nukes like the

W88s, were touchy creatures. These two had tamed the beast in a very respectable time.

The boss threw the two men a big thumbs up through the observation window, and then pointed at Bonner and made some quick karate hand moves he would recognize. Bonner nodded three times quickly and then pointed at the nuke. He started picking up his precisely laid-out tools when – "Mr. Stenson, please take a priority call in your office" – came over the building's loudspeaker. Lou looked at Bonner, shrugged, and made a slashing motion across his throat with his thumb. Bonner returned with a head nod and went back to picking up his tools.

When Lou Stenson rounded the corner of his office's door frame, the blond/pink-haired Kristin Hughes was already waiting in one of the chairs that fronted his desk. She hadn't wasted any time getting up the stairs.

"Nice hair," he grumbled as he passed her chair and headed for the phone.

"Pick up the phone."

"Pick up the phone, please. Pick up the phone, boss."

"Fine. Please pick up the phone, boss."

"Thanks, Barbie."

Kristin scowled at the ex-Navy SEAL with a "don't-make-me-kick-our-ass" look. Lou Stenson laughed out loud at the gesture and sat down in his chair.

Pressing the red button on the desk phone resulted in numerous clicks before a voice appeared. That meant there were more than two parties on the line. That meant information dispersal. Apparently, the game was officially afoot.

"Lou, glad to see you could join us. Gene, Pat and Ed are on the call with us. This is just a quick overview of a larger conversation we can have over cards. I assume you have Dr. Hughes with you." Bob Sloan spoke in a matter-of-fact tone of voice. If one didn't know better, they would think he was giving a systems briefing to new recruits.

"Affirmative Bob, Kristin is here with me. Go ahead and get to it, if you choose."

"Okay then, we have had our field ops guys and gals out beating the bushes ever since Gene's man and Kristin spoke with the Farooqi woman. As usual, most everything we came up with was worthless."

"That's not shocking," Lou responded as he looked across the table at the simmering Hughes.

"One of our men stationed in one of the German field offices, however, had some luck."

"Go on."

"Turns out that Vakar Arms does most of its small arms shipping in containers, aboard outgoing cargo vessels. It's pretty much standard procedure for the smuggling sect."

"Sounds right. We occasionally insert into hostile ports that way," Lou pointed out, as it was a black ops go-to move.

"Well, Vakar Arms works almost exclusively out of the Port of Hamburg, Germany. They have a couple of greased manifest and container guys that eliminate most all of their headaches."

"Bob, if this is an overview, can we get to the meat and the bone?" Pat Sommers had that needing to get back to work sound.

"Sure thing. Turns out that our mystery man, Adrian Beqiri, personally oversaw two cargo containers get put to sea approximately seven days ago. Two shipping containers loaded aboard the cargo ship Diaspora. A Greek ship, flagged out of Cyprus, and headed for several stops along the St. Lawrence Seaway before ending and offloading at the Port of Chicago."

Lou looked up from his desk and noticed that Kristin was literally bouncing up and down in her chair at this point. She was obviously at the point of attack. He reached out and hit the mute button on the phone.

"Hey, calm the fuck down, troop. This is a briefing, not an op order."

Kristin re-attached herself to the chair and drew a measured breath. The big SEAL hit the mute button again.

"What's the quick story on the ship, Pepper?" Eugene Taggart's voice was all business.

"She's an ocean going container ship. Moderate in size. She's been making the same run into Chicago and Montreal for a couple years now. Sometimes she makes her way as far as Thunder Bay, but usually only summer season. She's a transport."

"Bob, does your field guy know what was in the containers?" Kristin's tone was measured, as if she was addressing a scientific committee.

"Load manifest for both boxes, confirmed by both conversations with the dockworkers and a peek inside the computer manifest system by Nate Baker's guy, says two loads of cat litter."

Kristin Hughes' eyes dilated fully and she literally turned pale. Eugene Taggart, the CIA director, expelled an audible breath. Pat Sommers was first to speak.

"Bob, sounds like that card game is going to need to be pushed up to this afternoon."

"I appreciate the concern Pat, but let's not jump to conclusions."

"Gentlemen, the only thing better than cat litter at shielding radiation for smuggling is granite. I think it's safe to say that A + B + C = D. A great big booming capital D. What is the real-time status of those containers?" Kristin had become obviously agitated, though her tone was still measured. Lou Stenson could feel that his field team was just about to get greenlighted.

"Both containers were offloaded at receiving, Port of Chicago, as of today. Anything else will need to be face-to-face."

The CIA boss was next to speak, and it only calmed Kristin a small amount.

"My field ops guy, Mr. Dunn, is on a more hands-on hunt for info. Should be tracking down the trucking guy. Hopefully, that conversation will lead us to Mr. Beqiri. Bob's people pulled a useable photo of him off the Hamburg port closed circuit TV. Lou, you should get Dr. Hughes and her team under way. We'll update everyone that needs to know as it unfolds."

"I'll have the NEST Field Team in route to Chicago shortly. Bob, you should notify FTC Chicago, regarding FLYNET activation. Also, you'll need to send me the info over the crypto. I'm not going to make the East Coast by this afternoon."

"Get on a plane anyway. I have a feeling that I know what the target is. And, if so, most-likely when it is." The Secret Service chief spoke with purpose.

"Roger that, Pat. Just as soon as I get things under way here."

Bob Sloan re-inserted himself into the conversation with an unintended authority that seemed to mute everyone else on the call. Everyone in The

Group understood that once an op was initiated, it needed one command voice. If not, it created chaos. Everyone in the group was a Type A personality and was used to taking charge. They would naturally go off on individual priorities if not kept in-check. Since the containers were on U.S. soil, it was officially an FBI problem. Realistically, NEST was now in full control, but FBI was more of a public face, so FBI got the football.

"Individually, you all know what needs to be started. Lou, get on a plane. Dr. Hughes, head out and I will get you the full field op SITREP while you're under way. Pat, we are gonna need some real-time info from your end by this afternoon. Let's everyone get moving and we'll fill in the pieces as they come at us."

"Sounds good. We'll speak again soon." Lou hung up the call and looked up to tell Kristin to get her butt moving. She had already gone, and his office door was slowly coasting to a stop against the wall. Lou Stenson raised one eyebrow and looked at the door for a brief second. Then, he picked up the phone and hit the direct-line button for the Air Force Flight Operations Office. It rang twice.

"Duty Office, Johnson."

"This is Lou Stenson, NEST operations chief. FLYNET is requesting transport. Nellis Group to Chicago. Lift off, ASAP."

"Affirmative NEST. O'Hare, Midway or Gary International?"

"Gary, Indiana."

"Affirmative. FLYNET is at your command. Transport on the hangar apron in thirty minutes."

"Affirmative Flight Ops. Thirty minutes."

The NEST chief hung up the phone and turned to look out the windows of his office, which happened to overlook the hangar's runway apron. Two F-250 pickup trucks with camper backs and a stripped down Sikorsky HH-60G Pave Hawk with exterior pods for x-ray and neutron detectors were already lined up on the apron. Next to them, several cargo boxes of equipment had already been staged. It seemed his young bomb dog was running at full speed.

The big SEAL surveyed all of the action unfolding below him and wondered if they weren't already too late to be of use. He hoped that whatever Pat thought about when it would happen was a long time off.

CHAPTER 16

Rupert, Hamal, and Hafid appeared back at the port entrance man-gate at 9 a.m. sharp. All three men looked bright-eyed, which made the gate guard question their evening's activities. Rupert gave him the old *"we're headed there next"* story as he slid his TWIC card into the automated reader. He punched in his seven digit pin and the light on the card reader turned green. A mechanical beep followed the green indicator light. Hamal and Hafid followed suit, and all three men proceeded through the gate into the port's container complex.

The group grabbed the first golf cart that would start from a small cluster of machines by the entrance and headed off into the maze of containers, known as the stacks. Golf carts were a common way of moving around the interior of the port's secured area. They required little enough maintenance and didn't add to the noise. A tall orange flag on the back of the cart made them visible to the mobile container cranes. That being said, several still managed to get run over each year.

The three men made their way back out to the proper row of containers without bother. No ships were offloading, so there was little movement around the container yard. Rupert stopped at the first of the tall stacks and parked the golf cart. He removed the count sheets from his backpack and gave an equal amount of the papers to each of the other men.

They dispersed with purpose and began to inventory the containers that had been offloaded the day before. They cross-checked the lists with the containers and crossed the numbers off one at a time as they went. Each man worked deliberately, and in just over two hours the last of them returned to the cart with his checklist completed. Hamal and Hafid gave their lists back to Rupert and commented that all the containers were accounted for.

"Our two are five stacks down and two stacks in," Hafid stated in a conversational tone. "They are the top two containers on the stack, which will make them a pain to get at, but otherwise they look fine."

Rupert tossed each of the men a can of Pepsi which he had retrieved from his pack and sat on the corner of the beat-up golf cart's seat. Popping the top on the aluminum can, he took a large gulp and smiled.

"Well, that could have been worse, I guess. Let's have a small break, and then we can go take care of things."

The three relaxed in various positions and discussed a variety of topics. Rupert was really starting to genuinely like his two new comrades. They both seemed nice enough. He knew, however, nice men didn't last long in his business. It was kind of sad, but it wasn't his problem.

The group jumped into the golf cart and headed to the stack that Hafid had identified as containing the right containers. Rupert took a casual walk around the area to look for trouble and could not believe his good fortune. The two green shipping containers were in a location invisible to both of the nearest security cameras. He had expected that he would have to disable at least one camera, but it now looked as if that wouldn't be necessary. He might get in and out of this deal without getting noticed, for a change. That thought made him smile. No arguing with the port agents and Customs guys.

Rupert walked back to the golf cart and removed two rolled up bundles from his bag. He placed one in his pocket, and with the other in-hand, went back and started scaling the container stack. Once all the way to the top he kicked out a leg so he could stand, wedged between the two stacks of containers, and let the rolled up four-inch-wide industrial sticker unravel. He peeled the first couple of inches of the protective paper from the adhesive backing and placed it squarely over the numbers on the outside of the container. Peeling the paper down and rubbing the transfer smooth with his palm as he went, Rupert worked his way gingerly down the side of the container until it displayed a completely different identification number.

Rupert leaned back against the other container stack and inspected his work. The sticker was the same bright green as the container's paint and matched it perfectly. It looked very proper. Looking down to the ground, Hafid gave him a big smile and thumbs up response.

Rupert straightened himself and moved to the other end of the container to repeat the process. Hafid scaled the stack and acquired a similar position between the two stacks of containers in the row. Working confidently, he jacked into the hidden port and checked for the green light that signified everything was still working properly. He had checked both devices and returned to the golf cart by the time Rupert had finished applying the numbers to the other end of the containers.

Hafid sat on the cart and watched as Rupert changed the container numbers on the second container. He moved quickly and calmly, as if he had done this numerous times. Though the sound of equipment could be heard moving around the dock area, none of it seemed to be headed in their general direction. Rupert returned to the ground and retrieved yet a third set of numbers out of his backpack. Hafid and Hamal said nothing, but watched as Rupert scaled an adjacent stack of containers and began switching out the numbers on a random container. The container was a faded red color and it looked as if this might be its final voyage on the seas. Rupert worked with the same pace and calm that he had shown on the first two containers. The background on the third set of numbers was a neutral white color and made an obvious transition against the faded red side of the container. Hamal looked around quickly and noticed four other containers had the same appearance. This was obviously a standard theme with container shippers. Rupert returned to the cart and sat down next to the other two men. He retrieved a second can of Pepsi and inhaled the contents of the can.

"What's in the red container?" Hafid was younger than the other two men, and still somewhat curious. Rupert put the empty can back in his bag and shrugged.

"Hell if I know. The computer said machine parts, but I have no idea."

"But what purpose does it serve?"

"I don't ask questions that I don't need answers to. It just is what it is." Rupert smiled at Hafid in a calming kind of way.

Hafid sat back with a perplexed expression. Rupert put the golf cart in gear. Hamal said nothing, but the purpose seemed obvious enough to him.

The three men made their way back to the head of the lot and parked the golf cart where they had found it. Making their way into the port control office, Rupert handed the stack of inventory papers over to the man at the logistics counter. The two men exchanged some light conversation as the port agent matched Rupert's stack of papers to the stack that the port control people possessed. The port agent nodded and stamped the stack approved, not noticing that the two stacks varied by three small numbers. The port agent gave Rupert a quick hand salute and the three men exited the office. They made their way back through security and grabbed a cab that happened to be waiting outside.

Everything that Rupert had been required to do was done. All he needed to do now was report in with Pavel at the hotel and catch the ship out of the port in the morning. Hamal and Hafid also knew that their part in this affair was at an end. Hafid looked out the window at the distant city skyline. Hamal sat quietly.

Once at the hotel, all three men returned to their respective rooms. Hamal walked in and sat at the small table. Housekeeping had come and removed the food containers from the previous evening. The smell of the cheap Mediterranean food still managed to hang in the air like a ghost. Hamal smiled at the table top, the smell calming his now fraying nerves.

Hafid went to the bathroom and retrieved a toothbrush and hotel-sized bottle of shampoo. Returning to the room, he walked to his small bag on the bed and opened it. He retrieved a clean shirt and pair of pants, along with a thick sweatshirt. He changed his clothes and stuffed the old clothes into the bag. He stuffed the toiletries, his passport, and wallet into the pockets of his pants and turned to look at his older compatriot.

"I think this is where we part ways, old friend. I wish you well in your journey." Hafid smiled warmly at the older Hamal in a gesture of solidarity.

"May Ali always look upon you warmly." Hamal closed the two steps between them and embraced the younger man.

"You can still come with me. We'll get out of here together."

"You go. Live your life. I'll stay here and see how it all plays out. I think I'm in a good place with Ali."

Knowing it was final, Hafid embraced his friend a second time. Hamal returned the embrace genuinely and then released the younger man. Hafid walked to the side table and snatched up an ice bucket sitting next to the television. He twirled it around on his palm as he exited the room.

In the hallway, as expected Pavel had left one of his men stationed to keep an eye on the foreign men. The bulky man looked at Hafid with a questioning look. Hafid held up the plastic ice bucket and twirled it in his palm again. The bulky man nodded and returned his attention to his European language newspaper. Hafid walked casually down the stairs and along the hallway to where the ice machine was located. He placed the bucket on top of the rattletrap machine and exited the side door located next to it.

Once outside, Hafid walked quickly down the side of the building and across the parking lot to the street. Only a moment more and he was around the corner of the block and out of sight. He continued on foot for two blocks to a corner gas station/convenience store, where he made change for a five Euro coin and called the nearest cab company. Again, he made change for a twenty Euro note with the Indian man behind the counter which the hotel people had told him took all currencies, and purchased a map and a can of Red Bull. He had no more than finished the drink when a fairly beat-up Chevrolet cab came wheeling into the pumps. Hafid waved to the cabbie and slid into the rear seat.

"Where to?"

"Could you please take me to the nearest bank that changes money, heading north, please?"

"Sure thing."

Hamal sat by the window at the little table and wondered how long it would be before someone came to see about them. Surely, it wouldn't be too long. They didn't seem the sort to put off ending arrangements. The older man sat quietly with his thoughts for about an hour before the knock he had been expecting came to his door. Hamal opened the door to find Pavel taking up all the space on the opposite side. He backed up so the other man might enter. Pavel seemed calm and unbothered, which bothered Hamal greatly. The Eastern European scanned the room and then looked at Hamal quizzically.

"Where is your friend, Dr. al-Sajjadi?"

"He went downstairs for ice a little while ago. I assume he's talking to the lady at the reservation desk."

Pavel shrugged his shoulders and looked over at the white plastic tray that held the ice bucket and four plastic wrapped plastic cups. The bucket was indeed gone. Pavel walked to the door and barked something to the bulky man in the hallway. Hamal had no ear for East European languages, but from its tone he figure that it implied immediacy.

Pavel walked back to where he had been standing. Hamal waited patiently.

"I wanted to stop and thank you both for all the help you have given us over the last several days. We truly could not have gotten to this point without the two of you."

Pavel had no more than gotten the words out of his mouth when the burly man came crashing through the open doorway. He exhaled a sentence that made Pavel blanch and then turn red-faced. Pavel narrowed his eyes on Hamal like a striking jungle cat.

"Where exactly is Dr. al-Sajjadi?"

"He went downstairs to get ice."

"I will ask this question of you one more time. Where is the other scientist now?"

"He went downstairs to get ice and has not yet returned."

Pavel turned momentarily to look at the burly man. The burly man said something that, to Hamal, sounded like ice machine. Pavel paused, which made Hamal question the situation. Then, Pavel turned back around to face the Pakistani.

"Ice."

"Yes. Ice."

"If you say so." Pavel smoothly slid the suppressed Beretta 9-mm pistol out of his waistline and leveled it, pulling the trigger twice as it came on point. Two bullets thudded into Hamal's forehead with no time for the action to even be recognized. Hamal's head whipped back as he fell, spraying a crimson line out into air. It looked as if someone had flicked a loaded paint brush. Hamal's lifeless corpse landed supine on the soiled carpet of the hotel floor. Pavel pointed the barrel at Hamal's heart and squeezed off another round for good measure.

Feeling finished, he turned and looked at the burly man a second time.

"Lose the body and the carpet. And empty the room. Once you're done, meet me back at the plane. Okay?"

The burly man nodded and started into the room. Pavel looked around the room, but was sure that there wasn't anything to be found which would tell him where the other scientist had gone. In the end, it probably didn't matter. The work he was needed for was complete. The first bomb would be picked up by the trucker in an hour or less. The other bomb was in a secure holding area. He would be unable to stop anything. It would be better if he were dead, but it was fine this way, too.

Pavel exited the hotel and decided to take a couple laps around the immediate area on his way out of the city, just in case. People did do stupid things all the time. Maybe he would find the other man a couple blocks away, walking off somewhere.

CHAPTER 17

Hafid al-Sajjadi sat in the window of the truck stop at a small table and watched the traffic coming out of the Port of Chicago. It seemed to him that some eighty percent of the truckers that pulled out of the port security gates also pulled into the truck stop. They got fuel for their rigs, coffee, or showers before they left for whatever part of America their load was headed toward. It seemed so common place that Hafid wondered why the truck stop wasn't just hooked directly to the port itself. Everyone that came or went seemed to stop here.

In the short amount of time that he had been on his own, Hafid had managed to change his euros into dollars, find clothes that made him look American, and rework some of his long-dead Virginia accent. Now, sitting at the truck stop he looked American. Well, as American as anyone could who was drinking coffee at a truck stop and looking kind of lost.

He was amazed how easily the American sounds and mannerisms had come back to him over the last hours. He remembered his return to Pakistan after his schooling had finished. He had fought so hard to suppress his Americanisms and to be more Pakistani. Now, all of that had resurfaced just as if he had only been gone a short time. It made him wonder if he wasn't really more American than he was Pakistani. It was silly, he knew, but the thought was there.

He sat and wondered what would make these men want to set off nuclear bombs in America. Certainly, they were terrorists. But terrorists for what? He knew enough about global stability to know that what was about to happen would most certainly cause global chaos. There was no way that a major blow to the U.S. would not negatively affect every country on earth to some degree. There would be loss of security, economic meltdowns, and most definitely a global food problem. It seemed a bad idea, no matter what your goals were. The math was just bad.

Hafid took a large pull on his coffee and considered the days that would come after the explosion. What America had that most other countries did not was size. America was vast. The Russians had realized this problem decades ago. There was no way someone or some other country could do in America all at once. You simply couldn't throw enough missiles at it to get it all at one time. There were few countries that had this edge. The U.S., Russia, China, Brazil – that was about it. A case could probably be made for Chile, since it was so stretched out, but Chile wasn't a threat to anyone. Most of the countries that Pavel and his men came from could be wiped clean with just two or three good-sized warheads. Europe and the Middle East were made up of countries that were easily disposable.

Hafid finished his coffee. The burnt taste of the fluid as it went down his throat told him that the pot had sat on the warming plate for far too long. The nasty taste made him wrinkle his nose as he pushed it down his throat. It seemed that the only thing about Pakistan he would miss was the coffee. The coffee from the mountains was rich and robust. It hung in your mouth and you enjoyed it being there. It was hot and welcoming.

He was sure that when he got to Miami he could find some decent coffee. Maybe he would get a job in a coffee house? He had heard that coffee houses were all the rage in the states right now. He liked that idea. He no longer needed to be a scientist. He had done that. He had proven himself and his intelligence. Now, he could go work in a coffee house and just be happy. A waitress from the truck stop came along and pointed at the empty coffee cup. Hafid nodded yes and smiled. The middle-aged woman filled the cup and wandered off without any chit-chat.

Hafid smiled and looked out the window as he thought about his new life. He would get a job in a coffee house and maybe find a cheap apartment out by the beach – somewhere that getting around would be easy. Somewhere he could spend his time relaxing at the beach, or enjoying the many things that Miami had to offer.

When he was in America for college, he had stayed away from forming relationships. Back then he knew he couldn't stay, so it never seemed worth the heartache. Back in Pakistan, there was no one that even came close to his idea of an ideal woman. Now that he didn't need to return anywhere, maybe he would find a woman to share his life with?

He would also need to figure out the green card situation. He knew that there were places in Miami where someone could buy one for a reasonable price. He would need to search out one of those places when he got there.

As Hafid was pondering the green card situation, a moderately worn-out blue Kenworth pulled out of the security gates at the port. Hafid stopped pondering and watched the rig intently. The Kenworth sat and waited on the traffic light stationed at the intersection in front of the truck stop. Hafid couldn't see what the big truck had for a load, but it had to be a container of some type. He checked his watch. According to Pavel, his container should have been picked up approximately an hour ago, which would make this pretty good timing. He was sure that getting the paperwork done was time consuming. Hafid knew that the containers were neither heavy enough nor big enough to require a transport permit, so it should be a straightforward matter for the driver to get his load released.

The traffic light turned green, signaling the truck that it was clear to move. The big blue truck pulled straight through the intersection into the expansive parking area and began to follow the signs to the diesel fueling pumps. Hafid scanned the numbers on the shiny green shipping container and smiled. As he had expected, the trucker picked up his load and headed straight for the truck stop.

Hafid and Hamal had been paying close attention to all of the other men's loose conversation. He knew that one of the containers was to be picked up. And he knew where the truck was headed. He didn't know if the driver was one of the arms dealer's people, but from the talk it seemed unlikely. All he really needed to do now was ingratiate himself to the truck driver and get a ride south, along with the nuke.

He had figured that the driver would get fuel and then come into the shop to pick up food and stuff. It was what all the other truck drivers had done. They got showers, or coffee, or bags of snacks. He hoped that this man would do the same. If he just got fuel and left, then Hafid's plan was in trouble. All Hafid could really do as the big truck pulled up to the pumps in lane six was hope he stopped like everyone else.

The rig pulled level with the pumps and rolled to a stop to idle down. The old truck sputtered a little as the driver shut down the big diesel engine. Hafid studied the scene as he drank his coffee. The pot of coffee had been fresh, and that made him happy. A middle-aged man climbed out of the truck cab and stretched. He looked as American as anyone, with his worn-out baseball hat covering salt-and-pepper hair. Hafid studied the man hard for a moment and smiled even more. The trucker looked as American as someone in a Norman Rockwell painting. That was very good. Americans were basically both trusting and generous. He looked at the truck driver and thought, *this really may be possible after all.*

The truck driver began filling up the tractor-trailer. He stretched again and looked around the yard. He walked back to the container and checked the restraints holding it in place.

Hafid watched the man inspect everything as he filled up the truck. He was happy that the nukes had been packaged for a sea voyage. The truck was by no means new. The box was going to bounce a lot on the way south. Fortunately, he didn't have to worry about the device going off. Even though it was technically armed to detonate, it was also packaged specifically for this trip. It would be fine for the next couple of days, until someone attempted to remotely detonate it.

The truck driver finished fueling up the Kenworth and returned the nozzle to the pump. He removed his baseball hat and scratched at his hair. Seeming satisfied by something, he locked the rig and headed for the storefront doors. Hafid smiled at the table top and got up.

The Pakistani scientist paid his bill for the coffee and made a bit of small talk with the clerk as the truck driver went through the store toward the restrooms. The driver came out of the restrooms and headed for the large coffee station. Hafid slowly made his way toward the door. The driver went to the counter and paid for his drink. Hafid studied a map taped to the wall as the driver made small talk with the clerk. Hafid nodded his head as if he were talking to himself, then reached out to open the door for the approaching truck driver.

"Thank you, son."

"You're welcome, sir. St. Louis fan, aye?" Hafid pointed at the Cardinals baseball hat the man was wearing.

"Yes sir. They're having a good season this year."

"I'm more of a Marlins fan, but I haven't seen much ball this season."

"You should. They're having a pretty good season, too."

Hafid was instantly happy that he had tried to keep up with the baseball over the years. His initial nerves were evaporating quickly.

"Is that where you're headed? St. Louis?"

"Yup. Picked up a load at the port. I'm headed down to the St. Louis Transfer. Where you headed?" The driver took a pull off his coffee and smiled at Hafid.

"South, generally. Down to the coast, and then over to Florida. I've been doing some work in Chicago, but it's dried up. Time to move on. I've got friends and family in Florida. It seems a good a place as any. You wouldn't be in the mood for picking up strays, would you? Since you're headed that way?"

"You hitching?"

"Yes, sir. It's still the cheapest way to get around." Hafid smiled a jovial college smile that he had perfected long ago. The trucker smiled back and laughed a little in response.

"Well, you seem like the decent sort. Sure, why not? I did some hitching back in my younger days, too. You can do a lot a walking at times."

"Thank you, sir. I do appreciate the lift."

"No worries. I can get you as far as St. Louis. From there, you shouldn't have any trouble finding a ride farther south. It'll be nice to have someone to talk to for a couple hours. Come on."

The truck driver pointed at the blue Kenworth parked by the pumps in lane six and turned toward the rig. Hafid nodded at the directions and smiled, then he followed the driver off toward the pumps.

CHAPTER 18

The hulking grey C-17B banked a hard right coming off the runway and began its climb up out of the desert depression that held the city of Las Vegas. Several members of the crew lurched to grab ahold of solid objects as the airframe turned on its axis. Kristin Hughes sat unbothered in her webbed jump seat and rode out the change in rotation. Her mind had given itself over to action mode. Once there, her situational awareness was much improved. Things like the plane pitching one way or another didn't register in her thought process.

In her head, she was calculating the big bird's flight time from Las Vegas to Gary, Indiana. She knew that FLYNET had full sky priority, which would give the plane a direct path between the two. Still, it seemed like at least another four hours to get that far north. Kristin silently cursed herself for not taking the private jet at their disposal. The private jet could get her there in seventy percent of the flight time. She could have had some looking around done before the crew landed.

Kristin refocused her gaze on the cargo plane's metal decking and shook herself out of her head games. The plane had leveled off and was once again stable. They had already passed through the choppy air produced by the heat coming up off the desert floor.

The inside of the big C-17B's cargo hold there was a beehive of activity. The "bomb dogs" were all busy working on equipment, checking monitors, and unpacking items. Up front, the NEST pilots were giving the helicopter the once-over. They would normally give it the once-over at least four times as monitors and detectors were added to its external pods.

Giving the crew a quick visual inspection, Kristin decided that everyone was doing whatever they should be doing. Her bomb dogs were the best of the best. They didn't need anyone looking after them. Kristin unsnapped her seatbelt and pulled herself up out of the jump seat. Stretching, she felt two vertebrae pop back into place. She made a mental note to start taking yoga classes again, whenever this was finished. She retrieved her backpack from under the seat and headed toward the nose end of the cargo bay.

Glen, a strong-bodied ex-warrant officer, was just exiting the helo's cabin when Kristin reached the prep area. He smiled and gave her a big thumbs up gesture. She leaned in and cupped her hands between her mouth and his ears.

"Can I borrow your cockpit? I need to make a phone call."

"Yes, ma'am." Glen smiled and pulled the helo's door open. Kristin had tried numerous times to get Glen to stop calling her ma'am. But it was all for not. Glen Adams was twice her age, and Army through and through.

Kristin climbed into the cockpit of the helicopter and closed the door. Instantly, all of the noise from the cargo plane and all of the havoc of the cargo bay was gone. The extra acoustic suppression required by the bird's detection equipment made it quiet and serene inside. She grabbed Glen's flight helmet and fashioned it onto her head. Rifling through the outer pocket of her backpack, she retrieved a cable adaptor and plugged it into the helmet's headset cord. She plugged the other end into her encrypted iPhone. Pressing the phone icon, a dial tone came up in the helmet's earpiece. She smiled and dialed a number from memory. The secure network that the encrypted phone linked to was not visible to the comms and navigation gear on the airplane, so she had no worries about causing problems to the flight crew. It was the same with commercial carriers, which was incredibly helpful. The phone rang three times.

"Hello."

"Bob. It's Kristin Hughes. What do you know these days?" She could hear him exhale and knew she needed to start calling him Robert.

"Know about what?"

"I want to know about the containers, and about your talk with the truck driver."

"According to the FBI ground team, there are two containers. One numbered 1456463GHB. And one numbered XPK141462. Both are said to be a newly painted shiny green color. They were both loaded onto the ship headed for America. I did a little private snooping and found the same info on the ports computers."

Kristin scribbled furiously on her note pad to keep up with the CIA man as he talked. She read back the numbers and colors to confirm them.

"Okay, Robert, what did you get out of the truck driver?"

"I'm on my way to have that conversation now. I would imagine that he will be forthcoming of any information he has."

"Hopefully, he'll know a little something about Beqiri."

"Agreed. Somebody has to know where he is. He will be the next thing I track down, after the trucker."

"Thank you, Robert. The NEST team and I are on our way to the Port of Chicago to start looking for those two containers. Hopefully, we'll be ahead of whatever plans are afoot. Text me with ANYTHING new. If I don't respond right away, it means I have my hands in a nuclear bomb. Don't worry, I'll get back to you."

"Okay, I'll let you know if any new information comes to light." And with that, he was gone.

Kristin cleared the call and pulled up a number from her contacts list. The connected call rang two times.

"Sexy Kristin Hughes! What can I do for the bomb doctor?"

"Big Ben! I'm headed for the Port of Chicago to find a live nuclear bomb. What are you up to?"

"I'm headed in the same direction, Chicca. Should be there in about three hours."

Special Agent Ben Donewoody was a long standing *Group* member, and the FBI's assigned field asset. Special Agent Donewoody was a twelve year veteran of the FBI, and had spent his career earning a solid reputation for the handling of exterior threats. He was a man who most judiciously handled dealing with outside agencies, which was what had brought him to The Group's attention.

He had been recruited by the FBI out of college. A BA in political science and a master's from UCLA in international affairs made him good FBI material. At 5 feet 9 inches and 185 pounds, he was now trying to maintain his college sports physique. At the age of thirty seven, he was finding it harder every year, though the field operations kept him pretty active.

Raised in Southern California, and now living and working out of Portland, he had an easiness about him that naturally made people comfortable. He and Kristin had been fast friends.

"Looks like I'm about an hour behind you. There are two packages to find. Can you get the gates opened for us at the port? It will make things easier."

"No worries K. I'll see you on the ground, once you hit town."

"Thanks, Ben! Later."

Kristin sat back in the cockpit seat and watched Glen fiddle with an electrical connection. She had been pondering a simple question for an hour or so, with little closure. What the hell would make someone want to blow up Chicago? Other than it was in the middle of the country, it was just another dot on the map. Did they hate deep dish pizza? She couldn't really get the why. People were strange creatures.

Glen caught her eye as if to say, *hey I need my seat back.* Kristin unplugged her gear from his machine and hoped back out into the noise of the cargo bay. She threw Glen a sturdy salute. He smiled and returned the gesture. Kristin turned and headed back toward her seat.

At the same time a little farther to the east, on a different plane – problems were getting explained.

"The whole thing went smoothly enough, sir. Only minor bumps along the way." Pavel looked out the window of the private jet as it flew east above Lake Erie, and he tried to sound reassuring to his boss.

"That's good, Pavel. So, everything on your end is a go?" Ivan Vakar sat in his office in Switzerland and drummed his fingers on his desk. He had officially gone too far to back out at this point.

"Both packages made their intended destination intact and functional. They were properly handled and are in good operational condition. The first package is static. The second package is enroute to it final location. All went well on that front."

"On that front?"

"Yes. Well. We did have one small hiccup. One of the expendables is still breathing."

"Interesting."

"The younger of the two. He did everything he was supposed to do for us, and then slipped out the back door of the hotel."

"How?"

"He grabbed an ice bucket out of his room and said he was going to the machine. When he got to the ice machine, he continued on out the door and disappeared. It was actually quite embarrassing. We made a search of the immediate area on our way to the airport, but he was schooled in America so he most likely just blended in."

"That sounds like something out of a bad movie, Pavel. How can he hurt us?"

"I would think he's of minimal concern. Both packages are live and available for Adrian to deploy. All of the conversations in mixed company were in various languages. Even if he did go to the American authorities, who would take him seriously? He would get grilled at some local FBI field office until it was way too late to mount any kind of response."

"I have a contingency plan to keep the authorities from being too much bother. However, I don't know."

Pavel furrowed his forehead. He didn't know of any contingency plan, but wasn't about to ask.

"We have several private contractors on retainer in the U.S. I could send one of them to continue looking around, if you'd like?"

"Yes. That's seems like a good idea. There's no need for loose ends now."

"Very good, sir."

Pavel smiled out the window. That could have gone worse. Ivan Vakar continued to drum his fingers on his desk. The thumping in the phone's earpiece was somewhat off-putting to Pavel, but he sat patiently.

"Next, Pavel. What is Adrian doing right now?"

"He is still in Germany. I came west to handle the landing and such. He stayed to deal with the Chad arms shipment. The containers were getting ready to be sent out and the people from Chad were getting skittish with their money. Why do you ask?"

The drumming stopped. Pavel took this as a sign that he asked a question he should not have asked. He had been dealing with the European much more directly since the nuke issue had started, and it left him suspect. He enjoyed his new spot in the limelight of the wealthy and powerful, but it was most definitely a double-edged sword. He was now wondering if he hadn't just cut himself.

"It turns out that at least part of our plan is out in the open. The port people we utilized to handle our packages in Hamburg were approached and questioned by some FBI people. They wanted to know about the two containers that Vakar Arms had shipped out recently."

"How do you know this?"

"Because I have a man in Hamburg that watches over my interests. He informed me of the FBI activity at the port."

"So they know about the containers?"

"Well, they know about two containers. If your renumbering was successful, they will be chasing a ghost just as we planned."

"So, all is Okay then? We had planned for this problem early on."

"That's true. The more immediate problem is that they found out the name of our truck driver. That was definitely not planned for. What can he give them?"

"He did all of his dealings through either me or Adrian. He did all of his pickups at the warehouse in Germany. He picked up the last two containers there as well. We probably should lose the warehouse and its crew, and the truck driver, too. Just to be cautious."

"I concur, Pavel. We should do both of those things. But that might not be enough."

"Sir?"

"I think we may need to give them a body to tie the whole thing off."

Pavel swallowed audibly. He was pretty sure that he had just outlived his usefulness to Ivan Vakar.

"Even though I plan to slide a dagger into the heart of the foul American machine, that doesn't mean that we can't get some extra use out of the proverbial fallout. I mean, arms sales will continue long after this is done. Maybe, if we give the Americans a little Vakar Arms blood to lubricate the gears of complacency, then that press would work for us in our sales long after they have ceased to be of concern."

"Sir?"

Ivan Vakar started drumming his fingers on the desk again. This time they sounded to Pavel like the *drums in the distance* found in so many old movies. It made Pavel's spine twitch.

"I'll tell you what – I think it's time that we cleared away some of the loose ends. When you get back, why don't you visit the port and take care of our dock worker. Take care of the truck driver, too."

"Yes, sir. I'll handle it personally."

Pavel made every attempt to sound in command of the situation. He tried, though the drumming of Vakar's fingers was working on his psyche.

"Yes, personally. Let me know when you have that in hand. Then, we'll need to shut down operations in southwest Germany."

"Yes sir, Mr. Vakar."

"Very good, Pavel. Have a safe flight. I look forward to our next conversation."

The line went dead. Pavel snapped his phone closed. Had he just sealed his own fate? Maybe. He needed to be looking for an exit plan, as the Pakistani scientist had done. He was a good judge of sketchy situations. Vakar had just told him he was going to give up a body to the Americans. Everybody but the truck driver and senior port agent had dealt only with him, so the body had to be his, didn't it? It certainly seemed that way.

Pavel took a couple of slow breaths and attempted to steady himself. He would definitely need to consider all of his options before doing anything rash. Still, he needed to act in his own best interest from here on out.

He leaned over and told the burly man across the aisle to contact an asset in Chicago to find the Pakistani. The burly man nodded and started digging in his suit coat for his phone. Pavel straightened back up and looked out the window at the big lake below. Things had definitely changed.

CHAPTER 19

All twelve tires comprising the main landing gear on the C-17B Globemaster III let out a howling screech as they slammed into the tarmac of the Gary International Airport runway. The nose gear was soon to follow, and only a second of roll passed before the four big Pratt & Whitney turbofan engines staled their forward thrust to arrest the plane's positive motion. The rapid deceleration sent all loose items sliding forward across the cargo bay floor, making the loadmaster frown. The jar of the landing woke Kristin from her last minute nap. She opened her eyes in time to see her backpack go sliding off toward the forward bulkhead. Kristin tilted her head to take in the loadmaster's expression and then shrugged, as if to offer an apology for her violation of airlift etiquette. The loadmaster smiled and shook his head, as if to say *civilians.*

The large, grey Air Force heavy lift aircraft turned nimbly in a tight 180 degree turn at the far end of the runway and started back down the ribbon of pavement. The aircraft's pilot passed by the small main terminal building and moved onto the far end of the runway. The pilot throttled back the four large jet engines and brought the aircraft to an idle in front of a private aircraft hangar that was the home of a flight training center. The Globemaster III came to rest next to a civilian Boeing 727, and began its slow and methodical shutdown process. The jet engines were not even halfway to complete idle before the rear cargo ramps were already on the ground.

The C-17B's loadmaster began to bark orders to the NEST crew members about how to properly unsecure their items from the deck of his airplane, as a dozen armed Air Force security specialists flowed out of the plane to establish a perimeter.

Lou Stenson, the NEST operations chief, had called the owners of the hangar facility ahead of the aircraft's arrival and explained that the DOE would be commandeering a section of their apron for its use. The hangar crew had seen the show one other time, when the NEST team had made a surprise visit to the Chicago Air Show, so they did nothing to interfere with the Air Force operations unfolding around them.

Kristin exited the aircraft and pulled out her cellphone. The air around the big machine was an equal mix of spent jet fuel, grease and noise. Kristin found it oddly comforting. Ben Donewoody answered on the second ring and the conversation was a short one. Thirty minutes till onsite, ten minutes to unpack the helicopter. Ten minutes to heat up the engines. Ten minutes of flight time to the port. Maybe just a little faster, if it was possible. Ben responded with, "get after it," and hung up the phone.

Kristin turned around to see the crew unfolding the rotors of the helo. A blacked out F-350 pickup and matching trailer were being backed down the ramp and onto the runway apron. Personnel from both NEST and the Air Force scurried about like ants dragging an intruder from their nest. A man from the aircraft training school was talking to the copilot and pointing toward a tanker truck marked as jet fuel.

The black pickup truck had no more than been freed from the cargo plane and its four person crew was inside and headed for the gate. Kristin took a second look around and smiled as the helicopter's rotors started to spin. Her pilot looked out of the windscreen at her and jerked his thumb toward the backseat. It was time to go.

Kristin jogged over to the pilot of the Air Force transport plane, who was standing stoically on the ramp inspecting the scene.

"Thank you for the flight, sir. We'll call you when we're headed back this way."

"You mean if you're headed back this way? No worries, doctor. We'll be standing by and ready."

Kristin nodded and jogged back down the tail ramp toward her waiting helicopter. She had no more than pushed her torso through the sliding door and the skids of her transport lifted off the apron. Kristin managed to gain her seat and was just pulling on her headset when her pilot notified Midway tower that FLYNET was airborne and would be assuming control of the airspace. The Midway tower flight controller hesitated only slightly before confirming the national security directive and relinquishing control of South Chicago's airspace to the DOE crew. The pilot gave the tower their destination at the Port of Chicago and the requested clear zone of influence. The tower said they would clear all traffic from their airspace until further notice.

Kristin nodded to herself to confirm that the playbook was being followed so well. She pulled a small note pad from her backpack and reviewed the notes she had taken while talking to Mr. Dunn. She had no more than read them once through and she felt the helicopter bank hard right and start to descend. She looked out through the windscreen to see the container area of the port stretched out below. A half-dozen road flairs had been thrown down to mark a landing area for the helicopter, and a man stood nearby wearing a trademark blue windbreaker. The large yellow FBI letters could not be missed. They made Kristin smile, despite the circumstances.

NEST's pilot put the Sikorsky helicopter down on the mark and began to spool down the rotors as Hughes and her two main bomb dogs jumped out of the side door. She turned and looked matter-of-factly at her team.

"Get the detectors up and running. Drop a solid net over this whole area. What we're looking for is here, somewhere. The readings will be faint, so mark anything suspicious."

The team members nodded and ran off. Kristin jogged several steps toward Ben Donewoody and gave him a quick hug.

"Good to see you, surfer boy! Which way to the port office?"

The FBI man smiled and pointed toward the Customs control office. He started to respond, but his recently arrived comrade was already on the move. The NEST and FBI team went crashing through the door of the port office and ran into the already unamused faces of a facility representative and a surly looking Customs agent.

"Who's in charge of the container inventory?"

A middle-aged man sitting behind a weathered counter raised his hand.

"Over here."

"Sir, my name is Dr. Kristin Hughes. I work for the Nuclear Emergency Search Team. This is Special Agent Donewoody of the FBI's Critical Incident Response Group. You unloaded a vessel here recently, named Diaspora. We need to know where her containers are located. Please."

The man behind the counter tapped the keys on the old institutional keyboard and scanned the screen.

"Containers from the Diaspora were all stacked in container rows H, J, and K. Approximately eighty percent of them are still here in the docks."

"Eighty percent? Where are the others?"

"This is a cargo port. Cargo begins getting shipped out as soon as its Custom stamps are verified. The containers that have left could be headed anywhere in the U.S.A., Mexico or Canada. ."

Kristin looked at Donewoody, who just shrugged his shoulders. She rammed her hands into her pockets and retrieved her note pad.

"Okay. We are gonna need to go out and take a look at the containers that are left. Is it possible to locate these two containers for us?"

Kristin handed the note pad over to the man behind the counter, and he scribbled down the two numbers. Ben Donewoody ran a hand through his slightly non-regulation blond hair and sighed.

"If you would like to get started with your work, ma'am, I can bring the container locations out to you when the system is done scanning."

"That would be great. We will be out in the container field. Please hurry."

"Yes, ma'am."

Kristin picked up the note pad and turned for the door. She stepped off at a brisk pace and Ben Donewoody made to follow, when he paused and looked over at the Customs agent.

"All of the Customs paperwork was in order when the ship was unloaded?"

"Yes, sir. All paperwork was correct and all containers were properly accounted for."

"Okay, thanks." Ben turned and exited the room.

Kristin Hughes came back out of the small port building to find her team assembled and ready to go. Two operatives from the pickup truck were sitting on Honda ATVs. Both racks on the ATVs were loaded down with detection equipment. Standing next to the ATVs, two more men stood wearing large backpacks. They held scanner heads that were cabled to the backpacks they were wearing.

The two men from the helicopter were also standing off to one side. They both wore backpacks similar to the one Kristin was carrying and looked ready for action. Kristin came front and center of the group and looked at them expectantly. Finding everything to be squared away, she gave them a universal nod of approval.

"All right, the containers from the ship are in rows H, J and K. A Team, take row H. B Team take row J. FBI and I will take a pass down row K. Jim, you go with A Team. And Brian, go with B Team. I will fill in the gaps once we know what's what."

Everyone in the group gave a uniform, single nod of the head. Brian Smith, an ex-Army EOD Tech that Lou had picked up in an Afghanistan troop draw down was Jim Bonner's second on the big jobs. He was absolutely as capable as either Bonner or Hughes. Smith turned and extended a hand to Bonner. Bonner took it and shook firmly. It was tradition.

"See you on the other side."

"And you."

With that, the teams dispersed and headed out into the metal maze. Kristin put on her backpack and pulled her phone out of her pocket. Checking the display, the phone showed *No Service*. She stuffed the phone back into her pocket and jogged toward the back of the black F-350 pickup truck. The driver of the truck was standing at the tailgate of the truck's rear cap looking at a large suite of electronics. She could hear the onboard mounted generator humming along nicely. Kristin stopped where the driver was standing. Ben came up next to her and stopped to listen.

"Everything OK on the scene, David?"

Maj. David Lessor was an active duty Army special communications officer. Having a doctorate from Princeton, and vast real-world operational experience, he was one of the people that the Army loaned out for the good of all mankind. He was precise, very squared away, and good friends with Kristin's boss.

"Everything is five by five, Dr. Hughes. The cellphone signal shield is up and running. It is good to a radius of 15 miles. The alpha and neutron detectors aren't as much as twitching. If there's a nuke here, it's either well-shielded or it's special."

"Well, let's hope it's the first one. Thank you, David. Donewoody and I are going scouting. Let me know if anything changes."

"Roger that, ma'am."

Special weapons, devices made with exotic materials or having unique geometries, had a way of avoiding conventional detection equipment. She thought that everything, so far, had pointed to a conventional nuclear device. But, what if they had pulled the cores and made something else? She pushed the thought from her mind and decided to worry about that if the time came.

Kristin and Ben made their way to Row H. The crew had managed to inspect about one third of the containers in the large row. The two moved on to Row J and found that the second team was making about the same progress. She reflexively looked at her watch and wondered how much time they really had to work the problem.

The twosome proceeded on to Row K, where a proverbial mountain of containers framed in a narrow little street. A large yellow K was painted on the concrete at the start of the street that seemed to run a good 300 yards off into the distance. The metal shipping containers on both sides were stacked four or five high most of the way along the row. Kristin looked at the vastness of it and sighed.

"Ben, this might be the one that gets us."

The FBI man looked down the long row and rolled his eyes in mock surrender.

"Let's worry about that when it happens."

Kristin pulled a Geiger counter out of her pack and pushed the power button. The red LED light came to life and a green light on the counter bar blinked twice and then faded. Though not even remotely as sensitive as the detection equipment the other teams were using, it would let them know if they were standing directly next to one of the bombs. The two started into the row, inspecting cargo container numbers as they went. Kristin looked at the lower level numbers and Ben Donewoody did the upper rows with a small pair of binoculars. They found nothing as they went. These containers seemed as nondescript as any other containers anywhere.

The two had been at the inspection for a solid hour before Ben finally stopped and stuffed the binoculars into his jacket pocket. He removed a bottle of water from the other pocket and broke the seal. A quick gulp and it was half gone. He handed it over to Kristin and smiled. She had no more than downed the remaining contents of the small plastic bottle when both ATVs came around the far corner of the row and drove to where they were standing. Right as they stopped and shut off their machines, the port official came around the other corner in a beat up golf cart. He puttered down the row to where the team had mustered and pulled to a stop.

Amanda Fields, a sturdy woman with a master's in social politics and a natural ability to find things, sat on ATV number one. Brian Johnson, a 30-something ex-Coast Guarder sat on ATV number two. They both had that no-joy look on their faces.

"Nothing of suspicion in Row H, ma'am."

"Same in Row J, ma'am."

Kristin was about to thank them and tell them for the thousandth time not to call her ma'am, when the port official approached.

"Dr. Hughes, might I have a moment?"

Kristin turned her attention to the port man and nodded.

"We might have a problem," he said. "Are you sure about the container numbers you are searching for?"

"Yes, sir. Those are the container numbers that got loaded in Hamburg."

"Well, then that is a problem."

"How so?"

"All of the container numbers off of the Diaspora, including the ones lost at sea due to storms, have been filtered through. Yours are not among them."

"What do you mean?"

"I mean your numbers are not in our system."

Kristin, Ben, and the port man looked at each other with a perplexed expression.

CHAPTER 20

Walker Jackson stood stoically looking out the windows of his office and taking in the immaculately manicured lawns that surrounded the building. He had always liked this view. He could see the opulence of the place where he worked, but he could also see the traffic of the city whizzing by just beyond his gated drive.

He thought back to a television show he had watched. It showed the building and grounds back in a day before the trademark fencing had appeared. The endless procession of cars and trucks that occupied today's streets were the replacement for a much less-congested flow of carriages and gentlemen on horseback. The thought of that simpler time made him smile. The smile made him think that it might be time for a vacation. Nothing fancy, just a weekend somewhere a little less stressful.

His job had a lot of stress, but Jackson had known that going in. Anyway, there was too much that needed doing right now to be wandering off for the weekend. He was shaking the thoughts of the beach from his brain when the multi-line phone on his desk buzzed. He turned from the window and hit the intercom button.

"Good morning, Margery."

"Good morning, Mr. President. Ivan Vakar from the European Union Foreign Affairs Council is on the line for you."

"Hmm, Ivan. I wonder what the EU wants out of us today."

"I didn't inquire, Mr. President. He's on line two."

"Thank you, Margery."

The president took up a comfortable position in his leather chair and looked down at the blinking button for line number two. He paused to consider his office administrator in the next room. Margery was as efficient and thorough as they came, with just enough dry sarcasm to keep him on his toes. She had been that way ever since she had taken the job, back when Jackson was a newly elected legislator for the great state of Nevada. It had been a long time ago.

Jackson snatched up the handset and whipped his feet up onto the edge of his large desk.

"Ivan, good to hear from you. How are things in Belgium?"

"Good morning, Mr. President. Everything in Brussels is quite lovely this afternoon. How is the weather in Washington?"

"It's a sunny, blue sky morning. Just the way I like them. Now, what can I do for you today?"

The pleasantries were out of the way. It was time for business. The president knew that the call was a quick topic outline for the upcoming G8 summit meeting. He wanted to just get it over.

"I was going over my notes that I had prepared to bring with me to the summit meeting and just thought that I would give you a call. To exchange ideas, as it were."

"That seems to be the theme of the week, Ivan. I spoke with the Japanese prime minister earlier today, and with the Italians and Russians yesterday. Sometimes, I think it would just be easier to get everybody on one of those Go-To-Meeting links."

President Jackson laughed comfortably. Truth be told, The G8 countries had met over secured video link on several occasions. It worked efficiently enough for the day-to-day stuff, but nothing beat yelling at someone in person.

"It can be difficult to get everyone together, at times."

"Very true. But, all nine of us do seem to enjoy Chicago quite well. It should be a good summit. Now, what's really on your mind, Ivan?"

"The trade discrepancies with the EU, Mr. President. The EU has had many talks about how to approach the issues with the U.S. Frankly, the NSA listening post business currently in the news has not helped to desensitize the matter any."

Walker Jackson drummed his fingers on top of his desk blotter. He knew this was the topic that was coming. Still, he didn't like being told things. Pompous people annoyed him. Sadly, on days like today, diplomacy was the thing that needed doing.

"Ivan, I've talked to the German chancellor and the French president at length about this very topic. I had little control over how things were handled before I came into office. I am in the process of settling down that situation now. It shouldn't be an issue that would either block of falter any constructive trade conversations."

"I agree, Mr. President. I just wanted to keep you aware of any feelings that are still lingering in the air on this side of the Atlantic."

"Consider me duly informed. I wouldn't worry, Ivan. I have blocked out some time after the G8 business is concluded to sit and discuss the EU trade issue with you and the other representatives that will be present. We will be able to talk more liberally in Chicago."

"That sounds wonderful Mr. President. I have also saved some extra time for more-relaxing ways to spend the weekend. The theater in Chicago is always very good. I enjoy it."

"Well, in that case I'll block out some time that weekend as well. We can have dinner before your show. Things don't always need to be so business-like. I already have dinner plans with the Russian president while he's in town, but I'm sure we can work something out."

"That sounds excellent."

"We can discuss it in a couple days, when you arrive."

"I agree. I am looking forward to seeing the city again. I appreciate you taking time out of your tight schedule."

"No worries, Ivan. We've all got too much to do, and people to answer to about it. No reason to be antagonistic all the time."

Both men laughed. Jackson's laugh was genuine. Vakar's laugh was less so.

"As a side note, Mr. President, I was also curious about why your emergency teams were running around the Port of Chicago."

The president paused and looked at the phone in his hand. There were emergency teams doing ops in the port? What was that all about? Vakar caught the pause in the conversation and smiled to himself.

"I wouldn't worry. You know how security at these things gets. You get heads of state together and everyone's security teams start freaking out. It's just the Secret Service boys being over cautious."

"Very good, Mr. President. I had assumed as much. I just thought I'd ask."

"Once again, no worries Ivan."

"Yes, Mr. President."

"Well, Ivan, I've got a light blinking on the phone already. I must be getting late for something somebody thinks is important. It was great talking with, Ivan."

"And you, Mr. President."

"Have a wonderful evening. We'll find some time to talk in Chicago."

"Have a nice day, Mr. President."

President Walker Jackson set the phone's handset down in its cradle and drummed his fingers on the desk blotter for a second time. It had better be an exercise. He reached out and snatched the handset back up.

"Margery, is Pat Sommers in the building?"

"I'll check, Mr. President."

The president spun around in his chair so he could stare out the windows of the Oval Office. He was hoping it would calm the bad vibes that were brewing. It was one of those times that, if something really was going badly, he wished someone would have informed him from the jump. If there was badness afoot, and Vakar knew, everyone else would be calling very soon. That annoying man really did like to be a thorn in his side.

A quiet knock came from the door of his private study, followed by Secret Service Special Agent Pat Sommers appearing in the Oval Office.

"Pat, what in the name of all that's holy is going on in the Port of Chicago?"

"Mr. President?"

The president spun back around so he could look at his liaison to *The Group*.

"The special operations people that are said to be doing the special operations over there as we speak."

"Yes. Those people."

"YES. Those people."

"The group received some actionable intelligence. The field ops people in Europe confirmed the plausibility of the information. NEST and FBI field teams are following up on the thread at this time."

"PAT!"

"Fine, Mr. President. We're reasonably sure that someone shipped at least one nuclear device to the Port of Chicago via the Port of Hamburg on a merchant vessel named Diaspora. Intel seemed solid. FLYNET was activated, augmented by FBI CIRG to hopefully handle the situation before things migrated to a critical level."

President Walker Thomas Jackson stared stonefaced at his lead security man. He was attempting to properly add nuclear device, Port of Chicago, G8 Summit, and field operations together in his mind without losing his composure. It wasn't really working.

"I want you to say all of that again, slowly, Pat."

"From your look, Mr. President, you actually heard it all correctly the first time."

"And – when was someone going to read me in on this?"

"As soon as the threat could be positively verified."

"You just said that you have actionable intelligence. How many players are in the loop here, Pat? Give me a quick timeline."

"ECHELON did the pickup of the call via a European listening post in the UK. CIA field ops, accompanied by NEST Field One, conducted a real-world follow up. Intel suggested that a basically translucent group known as Vakar Arms had come into possession of two Russian-designed nuclear weapons. The packages had been green-lighted by two Pakistani kite scientists while the nukes were still in Europe. The live packages were supposedly placed on a westbound merchant vessel in the Port of Hamburg. The vessel's port paperwork was sneak-peeked by European FBI and followed up on by both local group and field CIA. At that time, the intelligence was deemed actionable. A crypto, group conference, activated FLYNET to investigate/handle the issue."

"Suspected time in country?"

"Approximately, 1.0 days."

The president glared at his Secret Service man.

"Suspected time till detonation, as if I don't already know?"

"Unconfirmed, but suspected approximately two days. Most likely detonation scenario will be concurrent with the start of the Summit."

"Okay, now for the big one. Who else knows?"

"FBI Europe knows a little bit of what they were sent to search out. Otherwise, just The Group. Now, you. And, obviously, the Vakar Arms people."

"Do we know anything about these Vakar Arms people?"

"FBI had a super-thin file on them from something several years ago. They appear to be mostly a European-based arms sales business. Small arms sent to whomever. The nuke business seems way too big an endeavor for them, as a rule. FBI is quarterbacking the whole effort."

"Could Vakar Arms possibly be connected to Ivan Vakar form the EU?"

"We are tracking on that right now, but it seems unlikely."

"Find out for definite. He's a shady bastard, if ever there was one. I really don't like him. Although, it does seem a stretch for a sitting EU cabinet chair to be involved in such an operation."

"We agree."

"Next super important question. When did you really plan on telling me?"

"– When we had rock-solid information to pass on. That being said, I had no intention of letting you actually go to Chicago. Right now, even with the prevailing winds, D.C. is outside the fallout zone. It's a continuity of government thing at play, sir."

"Pat, you have the NEST field leader call me when they have a minute."

"Dr. Hughes? Yes, sir."

"Do we know the actual status on the ground in Chicago?"

"Not in real time. Last I knew, NEST and FBI were searching the port container area."

The president stared down at the seal in the carpet that separated the seating area in the Oval Office, and played out global politics in his head. It was a thing he learned from playing the Risk board game as a child. All scenarios he saw in his mind's eye ended badly. Well, most all of them. There were two that showed some promise.

"Pat, notify The Group that I will be leaving for the Summit on time.

It will be the vice president's job to handle continuity of government if things go apocalyptic."

"But, Mr. President –"

"No buts, Pat. It wasn't a request. It's what's going to happen. If there is a potential for dead world leaders, the United States of America is not going to look like the cowardly lion."

"Yes, sir."

"Now, let's get up to speed. Oh, and find this Dr. Hughes for me, please."

CHAPTER 21

One-and-a-half days until the Summit start.

Cold rain and misery had settled in over the greater D.C. suburbs as night fell. Lou Stenson's private Air Force jet touched down on the runway of Bolling Field, just north of the Anacostia Naval Station, as the other members of The Group were assembling in the game room. The jet's low approach over Bolling Air Force Base on its way up the east side of the Potomac river was necessary to stay out of the heavy traffic leaving Ronald Regan International Airport on the opposite side of the river. All of the private jets coming and going from the Washington, D.C., area were a constant problem for the tower operators of the heavily traveled airport. Lou Stenson's plane was just one more set of tail numbers lost in the crowd.

The DOE station chief casually stepped out of the private jet as if he were settling down on a Caribbean island for holiday, and walked purposefully to the waiting SUV. The armored SUV was a Secret Service courier vehicle that Pat Sommers had pulled off duty and sent to fetch the DOE chief. The two man team with the vehicle was fully professional, and other than exchanging pleasantries, left their transport quietly to his thoughts.

The drive down Interstate 295 and across the Potomac River out of the District was a quiet and unbothered affair, thanks to the dismal weather. The armored vehicle pulled into a nondescript property in the south Alexandria suburbs and came to a stop next to several other similar vehicles. Lou Stenson thanked the two men and exited the vehicle. They watched as he walked casually to the door of the building in an angular downpour. They were sure that the man was not one to be crossed.

As was standard practice once inside the fortified room, Lou dropped his credentials, weapon and phone in the slot marked DOE and shook off the rain clinging to his clothes. He skipped his usual beer ice-breaker and went straight for the bottle of Jameson Irish whiskey sitting on the liquor cart.

"Kinda reminds you of those thunderstorms you get out in Vegas, aye Lou?"

Pat Sommers carried a light tone in his voice that masked the serious nature of the gathering. The ex-SEAL slid the liquid down his throat in one smooth pull from the rocks glass and presented a blank, though amicable, expression.

"More like Nicaragua in the late '90s."

Pat Sommers shrugged it off as manly banter. Ed Crowley, NSA representative and the only man in The Group to have access to Lou Stenson's *Ghost Bio*, blanched and looked down at the poker table.

Lou took his place at the table and sat his now refilled glass in the small depression at his space.

"It's been a long day, we're in the middle of a live op, and I'm in a fairly shitty mood. What say we just get to it?"

Eugene accepted Lou's churlish statement and nodded in approval.

"Okay, Lou, you go first."

"FLYNET is active on the ground in Chicago. FBI is assisting with the ground ops. Currently, a search of the port facility has yet to produce the containers."

Bob Sloan, FBI director of operations, nodded his head in agreement. Pat Sommers rubbed the side of his forehead at the presence of a forming headache. The remaining members stayed stoic.

"Are the field teams meeting with any jurisdictional resistance?" added Nathanial Baker, United States District Court chief justice.

"As of right now, no. Everyone is yielding to either jurisdictional authority or FBI badges. The real problem here is that we are chasing a whole pile of unknowns. Why, when, form of geometry. We need to get rid of some of the ghosts."

Ed Crowley, The Group's NSA representative, looked at Bob Sloan and nodded.

"Pepper, what do we know for definite?"

The FBI man turned his head and looked at the Secret Service man.

"I think Pat should probably go first."

"Okay, I can probably do both the when and where/why at this point. The city of Chicago is most likely the primary target area. It's a safe bet that even if there are two packages and they get split up, Chicago is the end game."

Lou Stenson wanted to ask questions, but he took a drink instead.

"The when is presumed to be approximately one and a half days from now, to coincide with the start of the G8 Summit being held this weekend."

Most members of the group stayed silent. Lou Stenson, a relative newcomer to this level of geopolitics, blanched.

"Crap! I forgot there's a G8 Summit in Chicago."

"Yup. Some of the dignitaries are already in the city. The rest are on their way."

"Well, isn't that just messed-up!" Lou threw the remains of his drink down his throat and stared at Sommers.

"You forgot there was a G8 Summit this weekend? It's the only thing being broadcast on pretty much every news channel."

"I don't really watch a lot of news since I left State."

"Seems fair."

Lou drew a breath and calmed visibly. The older spooks in the room calmed as well. The DOE chief stood and walked to the liquor cart.

"All right, Pat, are we semi-confident about the timing coinciding with the start of the summit?" Lou just grabbed the green bottle full of liquor and headed back to the table.

"No matter your actual agenda, for maximum damage, it doesn't make sense to pull the trigger before the start of the summit. So, barring an exterior motivator, we have at least a day and a half. Noon, day after tomorrow."

Lou nodded in agreement and poured two fingers into his glass. Eugene Taggart, CIA DCI, extended his hand and Lou handed over the bottle.

"Seeing how it appears that we have a slate-clearing run in action, what is the status of POTUS?" Nathanial baker asked quietly.

"He is fully in-play at this point. I gave him the brief after a call he had with Ivan Vakar this morning. He's heading for Chicago as planned. VP is headed for the bunker to handle the continuity of government issue."

Lou smiled as Pat laid out the president's agenda. Joint chiefs and Capitol Hill boys were being left out in the dark, as the fallout would not make the D.C. area. It seemed the actual status of the individual dignitaries was unknown, but the president said that he would notify them if he chose. There was a secret defense bunker in Chicago, left over from the Cold War days, but it was unknown if it would take a direct hit of this magnitude. Anyway, they would all be in for the ride at this point.

"He knows the status on the ground and is still heading into the AO. Ballsy. He's got my vote next time." Lou nodded to himself and tossed the two fingers of whiskey into the back of his throat. Eugene handed back the bottle and Lou refilled his glass. Lou stood and looked at the group.

"If it is acceptable to the group, I need to send a text to the field ops team. They should be brought up to speed."

Everyone nodded in unison and Lou headed for his phone. Even though he knew that Kristin was under a dead cell canopy, the text would sit in the ether and wait for her to emerge. It would find her, eventually. The remainder of The Group sat quietly and waited for Lou to return to the table. He sat down and put his palms up for all to see, as if to say, "*no phone, we can continue.*"

"Pat, you said that POTUS was talking to Vakar earlier. Pepper, where do we stand with Vakar?" Ed Crowley had that all-business tone. The FBI director took up the mantle of the conversation.

"As near as we can tell, from everything we can put together, Vakar Arms is fronted by a man named Adrian Beqiri. He's a forty-year-old Albanian currently living in Paris. Vakar Arms works primarily out of Europe. As near as we can tell, right now, any connection to Ivan Vakar of the EU is coincidental. He doesn't seem to be an arms dealer, just an asshole."

"Dunn has got his teeth into the Beqiri trail, but it may take a bit. The man's good at being illusive." The DCI reached out to the DOE chief for the whiskey bottle and it was handed over.

"The timing of it all is highly irregular," Bob Sloan agreed, "but, it does seem to be un-connected."

"By the by," Pat Sommers interjected, "when the old man found out about the nuclear bomb agenda, he was understandably put out. When you re-establish comms with NEST Field One, he would like to talk to her directly."

Lou raised an eyebrow, but didn't respond.

"I think he would like a little personal assurance update from the doctor," Pat said somewhat parentally. Lou nodded in understanding.

"No problem, Pat. I'll make sure she gets on comms with you, so you can redirect her."

Pat Sommers nodded in acknowledgement. Paul Spencer, senior systems director at the NRO, cleared his throat so he could pull attention in his direction. He had started rubbing his temples, the way he always did right before a migraine headache slammed into his world.

"Now that we're done stirring the pot, as it were, what are the unknowns left to be known?" He stood while talking and wandered to the liquor cart, where he removed a bottle of Hornitos tequila and a bottle of Tylenol. He shook four large 1,000 mg pills out of the bottle and dropped them into the bottom of his glass. He filled the glass and swirled it around as he walked back to his seat.

"Nice one, Paul. That's gonna screw with your blood pressure meds." Gene Taggart had a sporting smile on his face, and everyone laughed.

"Actually, you want to avoid the NSAIDs and the ACEs, because mine is an NSAID inhibitor. Tylenol and the opiate-based pain killers are the preferred approach. Now, back on topic." Paul stared into the bottom of his empty glass and hoped that the pills and booze kicked in before the pounding and light sensitivity did.

"How do you stare at a computer screen all day, when the diffused light makes your head pound?" Lou Stenson seemed genuinely interested. Paul looked up and scanned the collection of spooks at the table.

"Looking after your cubs for the last twenty years is what has given me the migraines." He smiled and everyone laughed again. Paul refilled his glass and sat the bottle out toward the middle of the table in case anybody else was interested.

"All right, first we don't know the number of the packages. We know there are two containers, and we are assuming they put a nuke in each one," Lou Stenson started.

"We don't know the actual entity behind the nukes. We know that Vakar Arms purchased them, but why and for who?" Ed Crowley's continued.

"We don't know anything about Beqiri, or the two Paki tech heads that he bought." Gene Taggart's tone was back to gruff and direct.

"It's safe to assume from the price of a good Soviet nuke that there is no redundancy at play here. That means we also don't know the intended destination of the second package," Bob Sloan said, as he stared at the bottle of Evian water in front of him.

"To that point, there are probably fifty important things that we don't know about the actual packages, but we can safely conclude that they are either timer or switch activated." Lou looked up at the ceiling. There appeared to be a bullet hole in the ceiling above the FBI director's chair.

"Why can we assume timer or switch?" Pat looked curious.

"Any other trigger setup or group of setups wouldn't have survived the ocean crossing in the freight container. Almost a sure bet that it's a cellphone trigger, like the sandbox IEDs. Even a timer trigger has a certain amount of instability. This package is designed for maximum impact. Somebody is going to set if off intentionally."

Everyone around the table nodded at varying rates. The line of logic made perfect sense, when spoken out loud.

"Okay, so what needs to happen to forestall this situation?" Nathanial Baker audibled his voice to take in the roll of moderator.

"First and foremost, we need to find and disable the nukes," Lou said matter-of-factly.

"We then need to find Beqiri and squeeze the truth out of him," Gene Taggart said coldly.

"We also need to find the Pakistani scientists and see what they have to say," Ed Crowley threw in.

"While all of that is going on, we need to avoid an international political disaster," Pat Sommers added in an unamused tone.

Everyone nodded in agreement to the last.

"It seems that everyone is on the same page here. I'm not going to stay. I'm going to head over to Fort Belvoir and sit in with Paul's boys at Area 58. I'd like to have as much info about what's going on as possible. The Aerospace Data Facility seems the best place, short of being there." Lou Stenson stood, as if to signal that things were done here. Everyone else followed suit. He turned to go, but paused.

"Pepper, your field ops guy is out in Chicago with the Kristin. Did he happen to take a fast plane, in case they need to cover some ground? Or, can he get one?"

"That he did, Lou. And, I'm a little ahead of you on transport. I've got a couple of fighter jets from the Illinois National Guard standing by, just in case. All she needs to do is ask."

"Thanks, Pepper." And he headed for the door.

CHAPTER 22

"You're absolutely sure they don't exist in your inventory?" Kristin Hughes stared down the long row of shipping containers as a sinking feeling started to form in her stomach.

"Yes, ma'am. We ran the inventory list from the Diaspora three times," the dock agent said.

Kristin twisted a chunk of hair around her index finger and stared at the shipping containers. A James Bond villain image started to run through her mind. They always complicated the plot with something extra that the audience wasn't expecting. It always pushed the secret agent right to the end to solve the situation.

"It's a rope-a-dope." The words came out quietly, almost questioning.

"It's a what?" Ben Donewoody wasn't even sure he had heard her say anything.

"It's a rope-a-dope. A feint."

"So, they're not really here?"

"No, they're here all right. They just aren't in the original boxes anymore, or the numbers have been changed, or something."

Everyone looked at the lead NEST operative with the incredulous look that college professors possess after listening to wayward students. The search team had detected absolutely no presence of anything emitting radioactivity, and the port agent had no history of any such containers showing up. It all seemed too much.

Kristin turned to the port agent, who was still standing next to his battered golf cart and smiled her calming smile.

"I'm sorry, but we seemed to have missed the introductions. My name is Kristin."

The port agent smiled his best Chicago smile. "Hi, I'm James."

"Okay, James. Can you give me a quick play-by-play of what happened here in the container storage yard between the time the Diaspora docked and now?"

James nodded and leaned against his golf cart.

"It's pretty standard practice, really. The Diaspora docked, on-time. The container cargo was offloaded, which took most of the day. It wasn't so much size, but trucks were already waiting for some of it, so the containers kind of got sorted during offloading."

"Is that a standard practice?" Ben Donewoody broke in.

"Absolutely. The role of the container yard is to transition the cargo containers to either trucks or ships."

"Okay," Kristin said calmly, "let's continue the timeline."

"All the containers were offloaded. All the cranes on the Diaspora were stowed. All of her lines were checked, and the crew that was headed to town cleared Customs. All pretty standard. From there, individual containers have filtered out as trucks have arrived to pick them up."

Kristin twisted the hair around her finger and thought. The answer was here, somewhere.

"James, has the container yard had any problems between then and now? Any break-ins, or suspicious behavior?"

"No, ma'am. Though it is the docks. Shady stuff is pretty much everyday business down here."

"And the crew? They are still accounted for?"

"That's a Customs/Port Authority issue. I do containers."

"But the crew left together and is still out in the city someplace?" Ben Donewoody countered.

"As far as I know."

"And none of them have come back?"

"Just the inventory crew."

Both Kristin and Ben's heads snapped up to look at James, who now was feeling very uneasy.

"Inventory crew," Kristin Hughes said in a police interrogation voice.

"Sure. After the cargo is unloaded, the port agents do an inventory of the cargo. The ship's crew also does an inventory of the offloaded cargo. Any lost containers are added to the inventory and the lists are compared for accuracy. It's a safeguard against ships with multiple drops leaving containers in the wrong ports. It's also Port of Chicago SOP."

"Okay, James. When did the crew inventory the containers?" Kristin could feel it coming to her, slowly.

"They came in the next morning. The three-man crew left early during the offload and came back the next morning to do the inventory."

"Is that a standard thing, too?" Ben Donewoody could also feel something brewing.

"Sometimes. Inventory is up to the captains. Sometimes they give early shore leave, on condition that the men do inventory. Who knows what the motives of the captains are."

"What about the actual inventory men? What did they look like?" Kristin smiled again, sensing that James was getting anxious.

"A white guy, and two black guys."

"Can you define them better, please?"

"White guy was seasoned European. Standard merchant lot. The two black fellows seemed new, like they had never sailed before."

"No, not that way. Were they African, European, Asian?"

"None, really. Light colored, I'd say. They looked more like they were Middle Eastern."

"So, they could have been Arab or Indian?"

"Yeah, I guess so."

"What about Pakistani?"

"Sure, I suppose. They spoke pretty decent English. Usually, when they speak good English they are European. But not always, I guess."

Ben and Kristin stared at each other blankly for a second.

"Rope-A-Dope!" Kristin exclaimed.

"We train all the world's terrorists, didn't you know that?"

Kristin focused on Ben with her all-business look.

"Can you get James the manifest list from Hamburg, with the original container numbers on it?"

"Sure, but I'm gonna need phone service."

Kristin considered the dead cell cover over the port and nodded.

"Use one of the land line phones in the port office. James, can you filter the FBI list against your list when you get it? Find the odd numbers."

"Yes, ma'am. It should take about fifteen or twenty minutes to filter their manifest against ours, once I have it."

"Good. There should be two containers on the original that aren't on yours, and vice versa."

"Yes, ma'am."

Kristin felt like they had a new plan. That was good.

"Okay, search team, fall back to the mobile and hold station. Ben, get James that manifest. James, be ready to do your magic, and please stop calling me ma'am."

Everyone started moving. Kristin drummed her fingers against the side of a cargo container. Something was still funky, she just couldn't put her finger on it. She hoped it would work itself out before one of the bombs decided to go boom.

The NEST team rallied at the mobile command unit in a most professional manner and downshifted into hurry-up-and-wait mode. The military standard loitering made Kristin smile. She could hear her dad in her head complaining about spending all day doing this very thing. Loitering was no way for a soldier to be. Kristin let out a quiet *HOOAH* and headed for the port office.

As Kristin entered the otherwise tiny port office, things were just descending into chaos. It seemed the port man and the Customs agent were having some sort of territorial dispute. Normally, the presence of the FBI solved such issues. Kristin looked around for Ben. She could see the back of his jacket through a semi-opened office door that was off to one side of the room. He was obviously busy doing what he was supposed to be doing. That explained the brewing chaos. Kristin decided to wade into the fight and be done with it all. She headed straight for the two men, who were standing behind a low counter.

"Excuse me, James, can you pull up the yard video of the inventory crew for me, please? Sir, could you please pull up the Customs forms and the TWIC documents for the inventory crew from the Diaspora?"

The Customs agent blinked and instantly started to boil.

"Listen lady, I don't care who you are. The U.S. Customs Office doesn't disperse immigration information to anyone without a court order. It's not gonna happen!"

Kristin took a slow breath to calm herself. She had seen this type of jurisdictional blockade before.

"Not gonna happen? Let me tell you what IS gonna happen. You are going to get me the information that I request, right now, OR I am going to shoot you right in the middle of your damned forehead. Then, I'm going to step over your dead body and get what I want for myself. Once FLYNET was activated, you lost all of your authority."

Kristin pulled a model 20 Glock from a pancake holster at the flat of her back and racked the slide. She stuck the barrel of the weapon flush against the man's forehead and gave it just the slightest push for affect.

"Move or die."

The Customs agent turned white as note paper and began to shake. Ben Donewoody walked into the room and quickly surveyed the situation at hand. He had been listening to the altercation while on the phone in the other room.

"Dude, you wanna get moving. Or, she gonna kill ya, and I'm gonna watch."

The FBI agent's voice broke the magnetic hold that Kristin's semi-automatic had on the Customs agent. The man turned and actually ran to the nearby computer terminal. He tapped the keyboard feverishly as a cold sweat ran down his pasty white forehead. James turned to Ben Donewoody, who was now standing across the counter from him, and smiled.

"That was awesome. He's such a douchebag, most of the time."

The FBI man looked at the floor and smiled.

The old-school fax machine whirled to life about the same time that the Customs agent's printer began to make sound. The man jumped up and snatched the pages out of the printer tray and almost tripped as he handed them off to Kristin. James twisted the computer monitor around so the two government agents could see it. Kristin took a good solid look at the pictures on the immigration sheets and handed the printouts to Ben. Ben looked them over good and then turned his attention to the video monitor.

"Well, they're definitely Middle Eastern," Ben said.

"Yup. I bet they both also have doctorates in nuclear munitions. James, what is the time stamp on the video?"

"Ma'am, oh, sorry, Dr. Hughes, the time stamp is 9:30 a.m. yesterday."

"Kristin, you really think they are both still here?"

Kristin refocused on Ben. He had a questioning look on his face.

"I think that's what's been bothering me this whole time. James, how many containers have left the port already?"

"About two dozen, without checking."

"One of our containers has to be one of those two dozen."

"Why, Ma – Dr. Hughes?"

"Money James, money. Nuclear weapons cost extravagant amounts of money. Way too much money to have two of them go off next to each other. Terrorists don't need redundancy. They need chaos."

"I see."

"Ben, can you send these off to your tech guys. See if they can find these two for us?" Kristin pointed at the immigration printouts and Ben nodded.

"James, could you get started on the inventory list. We need to figure out the container issue right quick." James nodded and headed for the fax machine to retrieve the Hamburg list.

"In the meantime, I need to make a phone call."

Kristin walked into the small adjacent office that Ben had been utilizing. She gave herself a moment to stop shaking. She wasn't naturally aggressive so the adrenaline in her system bothered her and gave her the shakes. Finally calm, she picked up the phone. She dialed her cellphone number and waited for the voicemail prompt. There were no new messages. That was odd. Lou would surely have called by now. She dropped the call and redialed the number. This time, she bypassed the voicemail and went to her text memory. She had received one new text. The phone rattled off Lou Stenson's cellphone number and a two word message: SITREP ASAP.

Kristin set the handset back down in the phone's cradle and stared at it for a moment. What was she going to tell her boss?

CHAPTER 23

Kristin Hughes strolled back out into the port agent's central office space, and this time it was a model of productivity. Everyone was contributing and no one was being disruptive. Still having fifteen or twenty minutes before things with the manifest lists were completed, she decided to go check on her crew.

Emerging out into the bright Chicago sunshine, Kristin squinted to adjust her vision. She quickly retrieved a beat-up pair of Oakleys from her bag and slipped them into place. Her vision readjusted and she could see her whole crew, right where she had left them.

Amanda Fields and Jim Bonner seemed to be engaged in some iteration of rock-paper-scissor-lizard-Spock. From what it had started, she had no idea. The remainder of the team was in varying states of relaxation. David Lessor stood dutifully at his station monitoring the equipment racked in the back of his black Ford command vehicle. Kristin decided that the truck seemed the place where she would proceed.

"David, how are all the meters doing?"

Maj. Lessor smiled as his field ops boss approached. He sat a bottle of blue Powerade into a specialty built beverage holder attached to the door of the truck's rear cover.

"Everything here is fine, I guess. All of the gear is working at peak efficiency and detecting – nothing. Dead cell canopy is solid and holding at the designated boundary."

"Well, it sounds like things are as precise as they can be." She smiled a warm smile at the Army officer to get him to loosen up a bit. He didn't take the bait.

"Do you have any new intelligence on the status of the devices?"

"That would be negative. The FBI and Port Authority are matching up the two port lists to try and figure that out."

"Ma'am, do you really think both nukes are here? It seems like overkill to me."

Kristin turned to look at Glen Adams, who was sitting in the pilot's seat of his fully cooled-down helicopter. His outside foot was stuffed into the jamb of the pilot's door to keep it ajar. She blinked as the sun reflected off the warrant officer III bars attached to his Army-issued soft cap.

"Honestly, Glen, I don't know."

"So, what do you think was the plan?"

"Good question. One medium yield Russian nuke would reduce everything to ash from here to Milwaukee. There's just no need for the second device."

"So, you think there's only one device?" David Lessor added from his station at the command vehicle.

"No David, I think there are two nukes. Every piece of intelligence we have says two nukes. We are missing two containers, which would hold two nukes. I really do think its two nukes."

"So what's the second package all about?" Glen countered, adjusting his foot in the door of the helo.

"That's the $100,000 question, isn't it? Standard playbook says two packages for two targets. One primary target and one secondary target. It's safe to say that the primary target is Chicago."

"No offense, ma'am, but that means that the secondary target could be anything in the greater continental United States," David Lessor added incredulously.

"Yup. Anywhere reachable by a semi-truck."

Everyone in the conversation just looked at each other. The two bomb dogs playing games off to one side had long since quit their distraction so they could focus on the conversation. Everyone seemed to be of the idea that they were chasing a ghost. Kristin Hughes had chased ghosts before. Her blood was still boiling here. She was sure this was no ghost.

The second nuke was on a truck headed somewhere. No matter how many times she ran it around in her head, it came out the same. Unless this was the most elaborate single package con job in history, it was a two nuke deal. It just boiled down to money. Terrorists, even government-sponsored ones, wouldn't, and generally couldn't afford to spend enough money to put two nukes on the same target. It was two bombs and two targets, or one really good hoax and Chicago. She was betting on the first one.

Kristin had been outside with the group long enough to finally realize why everyone, save Maj. Lessor, was hunkered down in the shady spots. It was hot under the Midwestern sun. She didn't think she had been outside very long, but the two beads of sweat migrating down the ridges of her backbone said otherwise. Sensing the sweat beads, she felt instantaneously sticky all-over. It was going to be a long and exasperating day. She hoped she would see the sun come up in the morning. She gave a head nod to Amanda and looked at the cooler where she was sitting. Amanda Fields retrieved a bottle of water from the cooler and pitched it underhand to Kristin. As everyone expected, the wet bottle slid straight through Kristin's hands and went bouncing across the asphalt parking area. Kristin turned and ran after the plastic bottle that was now bouncing to-and-fro across the hot parking lot surface. The entire group laughed at their boss as she collected the beat-up bottle and jogged back to her original spot. Kristin offered up a full curtsy for the crowd, which just made them laugh louder. If nothing, she thought, they would all die in a good mood.

Kristin wrestled off the half-mangled bottle cap and gulped down some of the contents as the laughter subsided. She put the bottle back up to her lips to retrieve the rest of the water when the door to the port office opened. All three men from inside the office came out at a jog and headed straight for the field ops boss. Kristin raised a Dr. Spock-like eyebrow at the new activity and paused on her water retrieval mission. The men from the office covered the distance from the office door to the NEST team in only a second or two. All looked deadly serious. The looks brought every member of the NEST team to full attention. The game was afoot once again.

James, the port agent, came sliding to a stop in front of Kristin, holding each of the ship's manifests in his hands. The Customs agent stopped behind him, and Ben Donewoody pulled up alongside.

"Dr. Hughes, we've figured out the container issue."

"The numbers were changed." Kristin said expectantly.

"Sort of," James said, looking at the FBI man for reassurance.

"What the hell does 'sort-of' mean?" Kristin wanted to glower, but didn't.

"There were two containers on the U.S. list that were not on the Hamburg list, and one on the Hamburg list that was not on the U.S. list."

"Two for one? I don't understand, James. Give me the long version."

At this point, everyone was completely focused on the port agent. The unblinking attention made him extremely uneasy. Kristin could tell that he had not had to deal with extreme individuals very often, so she changed her tack. She smiled at James with her college girl smile and softened her tone away from its previous command-and-control tone, to one a little more feminine.

"All right, James, you originally said that our container numbers weren't in the system. Now, one of them is. Let's start there."

James drew a breath and tried to calm himself down.

"The original scan of the manifest list did not pull up your container numbers, so we ran it a second time to make sure. That was when I came to find you. We actually ran it three times originally, just because the FBI and a bunch of commandos don't really show up here every day."

Kristin smiled at the reference to her group as commandos, and nodded for James to continue.

"I left the original container numbers in the search algorithm, while the two manifests were being compared. When the two numbers from the Diaspora's U.S. manifest fell out of the search engine, so did one of the original numbers from the Hamburg list."

"All three anomalies came out at the same time?"

"Yes, ma'am. The system just expelled every non-matching item."

"Why didn't the system find them the first three times?"

James looked sheepishly at the ground and tried to figure out how he could answer the question.

"Honestly, we can't get money in the budget for new software. The system software wasn't *really* designed to handle 10^{15} magnitude power data base systems like this. The system algorithms compensate for the data load by semi-randomizing the search criteria on bock alpha-numeric sets. In doing so, the system can skip over things that it's actually looking for. Frankly, it's a software issue."

Kristin furrowed her brow and was trying her best not to explode.

"That's pretty common with early '90s algorithms, ma'am. The understanding of data mining symmetry was pretty stone aged. Are you running early Java, or are you back to RAPID?"

James smiled broadly at the military man standing by the black pickup truck.

"I wish it was Java. The outer shell of the system is SELF. The computers are so old that the base logic on the bios is something akin to Python."

David Lessor made his trademarked *"Damn!"* face that only computer guys would understand.

"And it's still kicking?"

"We don't shut the system down. As long as you don't overfeed it, it manages itself pretty well. The older systems are so much more bulletproof. They don't cancer-out, like the new stuff does."

Maj. Lessor nodded at James to show his understanding as a fellow geek. Kristin's head was spinning. She was lost. She turned and focused on her tech chief standing by the pickup truck.

"TECHNO-BABBLE! Digest it and speak English, please."

Dave Lessor was about to speak when James took over.

"Old software has hiccups. The numbers get lost in the hiccups, the same way words get lost in hiccups. Long and short, one of the containers is listed as unloaded and staged here at the facility."

Kristin's head pivoted like it was on a swivel. Ben Donewoody put up a steadying hand in her direction before she exploded on the port agent.

"Okay, fine. Box number one is here, somewhere. That's good. What about mystery box number two?"

James drew a breath and retrieved a piece of paper from a stack on the bottom of the wad in his hands.

"According to inventory, one of the new container numbers is here. The other number left yesterday."

"Left for where?"

"—Port of St. Louis."

"UGH!" Kristin stared at Ben in semi-defeat.

"I know," he said.

"James, get Ben here all of the information for the truck that picked up that container, please."

"He already has it, Dr. Hughes."

"Thank you, James. Now, in what area of the facility are these other two containers?"

"Both containers should be stacked down in Row K."

Ben and Kristin looked at each other with that look that says, *"We're Idiots."*

Kristin spun on her boot heels to find her team fully assembled and awaiting orders. The look of her waiting team washed away her building angst, and gave her hope.

"First things first, let's get back to K and find the two containers in questions."

Everyone broke ranks and headed out without words – all hands to the task. Kristin turned and looked at Glen Adams, who was still sitting in his helicopter. She spun her finger around in a circle, as if to say warm it up because we're leaving.

The second run down Row K, with both ATV teams and the extra port people who had joined, took only a minimum of time to produce the two containers. A funky old red container with the right Hamburg numbers sat directly next to a shiny green container with the right U.S. numbers. Kristin looked up at the two shipping containers and instantly wanted to kill someone. It was definitely a shell game. But, which shell should they pick? She turned and looked around for the port man, James.

"James, could you get us a machine to get the containers down?"

"Yes, ma'am." James turned and jogged off toward the beat up golf cart he had driven out. Kristin walked over to Jim Bonner and paused. He was still looking up at the containers in a semi-inspecting way.

"What do think, Jim? Which one do you want to pop first, numbers or color?"

Jim Bonner, a bomb disposal technician with more experience than anyone else in the U.S. system, just looked at his boss incredulously.

"You mean you're not going to take the lead on the sneak and peek?"

Kristin smiled at her trusted companion. He knew her too well. She really did want to crack open one of them.

"As I see it, one of the nukes is mobile. The other one is sitting up there in one of those boxes. The only bomb tech better than me is you. So, you get the primary container and all the resources here to do the job. Ben and I will go chase down the runner and take care of it. Sound fair to you?"

Jim Bonner gave a single, very proper, military nod.

"Yes, ma'am. Brian and I have this under control. We'll get it done."

"So, numbers or color?"

"I'm leaning toward numbers."

"Me, too. It just seems that numbers get much more attention than colors. They could have thought it was one color when they manifested, and it was another."

"I agree."

"Affirmative. I'll leave you to your task. See you on the other side."

"And you," Jim Bonner said stoically, as he began to take off his pack.

Kristin ran over to the golf cart where Ben and James were explaining the facts of life to the mobile crane operator.

"James, could you get down the red container with the right numbers on it, please. And, gently, please."

"Yes, Dr. Hughes."

James and the crane operator headed off toward the mobile container crane unit. Kristin turned to look at her FBI counterpart.

"Ben, you and I are gonna take a run down to Port of St. Louis and find that other bomb."

Ben nodded.

"Please tell me that you came out here in one of those fast FBI jets."

"Oh, I've got something way better than that standing by."

CHAPTER 24

One-and-a-half days to detonation.

Hafid and his new friend, Bob Russel, had pulled into the cargo transfer terminal at the Port of St. Louis approximately eight hours back. Hafid had thanked the man several times for the ride and all of the conversation. Unless he missed his guess, he wouldn't have very long to get clear of the truck before the authorities came screaming in.

The trip from Port of Chicago to Port of St. Louis had taken a leisurely six hours. Bob and his trusty Kenworth rolled into the container center as they had done so many times. The facility was all business, but much less constrained than the previous port had been. Apparently, Middle America didn't require the security of the Great Lakes. This made Hafid happy.

Hafid thanked Bob for the last time and promised him that he would be careful with his travels. They had said goodbye, and Bob had headed for the terminal office. Hafid turned to head back toward the gate. He walked past several trucks to make sure that Bob made it all the way to the office building, and then he turned a hard right around the next truck in line and made his way back to the parked Kenworth. Walking back along the opposite side of the tractor-trailer, he looked for any yard security cameras that might be pointed his way. He only saw two cameras, both of which were not pointed in the direction of his intended target. He was sure that there were more, but such was his problem at this point. He had to do what he had to do. He had helped to create this situation. He needed to help resolve it. His karma would never let him go forward if he did nothing.

It had continuously surprised him over the course of the last couple weeks that he understood the Americans better than the terrorists seemed to. He really thought this to be odd. They should have studied their prey better before setting out on such a course of action. But, then again, stupidity was the natural state of despots and terrorists. Or so he thought.

The terrorists were working under the assumption that they were dealing with the old, sluggish, Cold War America. A sleeping giant which had one eye firmly fixed upon its untrustworthy neighbor. Not paying attention to others, if they moved quietly and efficiently. But that was the old America. The new America was a little clumsier with its intelligence than others its size, but now they were fleet of foot and keeping both eyes open.

The terrorists, or arms dealers, or whatever, were too aloof. They had too many steps and too many people involved. It was impossible to keep such an enterprise secret for long. Too many countries were now watching and talking. Once one little piece of it was found, the American intelligence/counter terrorism machine would kick into high gear and the result would be problematic for the enemy.

Hafid had considered all of the chatter he had heard on the way to America and decided that the Chicago bomb really wasn't the problem. The Americans would follow the clues to it with little fanfare. The mobile nuke, that was a different issue altogether. They would certainly figure out that one of the nukes had left Chicago. They would also figure out that it came to St. Louis. But would that all happen in time? That bit was the real problem.

There were no guarantees in Hafid's world of calculated probabilities that they would locate the second device before it went off. Actually, the probabilities were quite high that they wouldn't. They would need people that were all at the top of their game for that. He knew that America had such people, but still.

No, Hafid had decided that it would be his responsibility to fix this part of the problem which he had helped to create. It was his act of penance for potentially destroying his newly adopted country. He simply couldn't let such a thing happen.

While it was true that the United States could be seen to be as much a terrorist state, internationally speaking, as others on the planet. It had a haughty moral stance that made everything it did seem self-righteous. It was a country that could be oppressively overbearing. The problem with it all was that a great many times it happened to be on the right side of things. It tended to be on the side of freedom, liberty, and human justice. Much of the time it was all talk. In truth, it most often was secretly after oil, reduction of enemies, and better trade status. To Hafid, that seemed to be the right of any superpower. As it had been with Rome, Macedonia, France, the Ottomans, or a great many others, so it was with America.

Hafid was comfortable with this line of reasoning. More so than most others in his country. Besides, what had America actually done to him? It had accepted him without question. It had educated him. It had given him an outlet to a much larger world of possibilities. Possibilities, which it turns out, were open to all. They had been nothing but good to him. He was not really about to destroy them for that.

It was true that the United States was not as tolerant a country as it had been back in his college days, but that seemed a legitimate response to the current state of the world. Even now, when the Middle East was saying that it would kill all those suspected of foreign pursuits on site, he had still found America to be warm and welcoming. To suggest otherwise was something he saw as one of the great lies that should be abolished.

Hafid had loitered around the large container ship during the journey at sea collecting the tools necessary to deactivate the device once it was offloaded. His list of required tools turned out to be quite minimal. In his coat pocket he had one large paper clip, one set of medical forceps, one number 11 Phillips-tipped screwdriver and two pieces of Juicy Fruit gum.

Where in the movies the gum was usually part of some clever plot piece to foil the plans of the opposition, here it was only half that. One of the pieces would act as a dielectric for the paper clip, but the other was strictly for chewing on. There was also a small pocket knife that he had acquired at a gas station. Not much of a tool kit for performing international espionage, but basics were most always the best way.

Hafid thought back to his days with the Pakistani nuclear program. They had every tool that was known to man in their laboratories. You could build anything in that place. Here and now, he was down to the basics. The basics were mobile and easily discarded. That was important, since this was an in-and-out type of mission. If everything went well, he wouldn't end up in jail as a terrorist. He had heard bad things about the prison in Cuba and its detention facility for terrorists. If he did end up there, well, that was the price that would need to be paid for involvement.

Hafid had made his way back to the blue Kenworth with its shiny green cargo container. He paused to look around. There were no other people visible to him anywhere in the yard. He took a second look around, just to be sure. He saw no cameras facing his way. It was time to get to business.

Hafid approached the rear of the truck. The container had been placed so that the doors were to the rear of the trailer. This made things easier for both him, and the interstate scale house people who checked the security of the loads. Facing the rear of the trailer, he moved to its right side. In the lower right corner of the container was a small square metal plate covering a small square metal box. Looking at the container, it could have covered anything. Hafid knew that it actually covered the arming mechanism.

Hafid laid his tools out on top of one of the trailer's tires and began to extract the screws that secured the cover plate. The eight number eleven machine screws came out without resistance. He placed each one on the edge of the container bottom and pulled the cover free as he extracted the last one.

He paused to look around as he sat down the screwdriver. The lot around the tractor-trailer was still devoid of people. Feeling confident that he was still fine, he retrieved the paper clip from the top of the tire and bent it into a squared-off horseshoe.

The contents of the box behind the cover he just removed included a green LED light, a red LED light, and a nine-pin socket jack. The socket jack was a military design and accepted the controller for the Russian made arming/firing programmer. He had given the firing programmer to Rupert after checking the nukes, hence the need for the tool kit. Looking into the uncovered box, he checked that the green LED light was still illuminated. It was. Everything in the box looked exactly the same as the last time he had inspected it back on the container ship. He noticed no signs of anyone else tampering with the device. That was very good. All the way to St. Louis he had been worried about someone booby-trapping the device after it was armed. It now appeared that his worrying was unfounded. Once again, the terrorists were making the mistake of assuming that the nukes wouldn't be discovered. The terrorist's shortsightedness was good news for Hafid.

Hafid unwrapped the second piece of chewing gum and stuffed it into his mouth. The fresh blast of flavor from the gum made him smile. He rolled the first piece, which he had been chewing since he jumped out of the truck, out on his tongue and stuck it to the middle of the paperclip. A second or two was required to mold it around the paperclip and squeeze it out so that he could hold it between his fingers.

Ready to go, he counted four pins counterclockwise from the twelve o'clock position and lined up the paper clip. As calmly as a man putting change into a vending machine, Hafid inserted the paper clip against the number four pin and the side of the cargo container. A slight metallic crack could be heard from inside the container as the paper clip grounded out against the side of the shipping container and overloaded the fifteen amp fuse inside the firing box. The green LED light faded as the red LED light flared to life. Job done. Nuclear warhead disarmed.

Hafid paused to look around once more. He still seemed to have the yard to himself. One more task to complete and he could disappear.

The fuse he had overloaded controlled the cellular trigger that the terrorists had planned on using to detonate the device. That long range option was out of commission. Still, the device could be detonated by someone stupid enough to plug in the controller and press the button to close the detonator circuit. Hafid really doubted that any of the men he had met held enough conviction to self-detonate the device, but he couldn't afford to take any chances.

He sat down the paperclip and picked up the medical forceps that were lying on the truck tire. He slipped the head end of the forceps into the pin socket and lined up its prongs with the two holes in the back of the plug. Applying gentle pressure with the stainless steel instrument, the spring-loaded pins that held the plug in place released and the plug slid free of its recess in the box. Hafid pulled the plug free of the box approximately three inches to expose the collection of wires on its backside.

Work for the pocket knife came next. Even though he had bought the smallest of the knives for sale at the station, it was still a little bigger than he would have liked. An X-Acto knife would have been much more useful, but he plunged ahead. There was no worrying about details now.

With a deft hand, Hafid peeled back the protective wrapper around the wire bundle and exposed the colored wires that made up the wiring harness. He fished out a blue wire with two yellow stripes on it. It was attached to the second pin counterclockwise from the top position. Sliding the knife blade in, he flicked his wrist and cut the tiny, twenty gauge wire. Now that the manual firing circuit wire was disabled, he placed the blade of the knife against the back of the socket and twisted until the pin snapped off.

Hafid slid the plug back into its holder until the spring-loaded pins snapped back into place. He picked up his small collection of hand tools sitting on the tire and pocketed them along with the screws and cover plate. He considered wiping down the area to get rid of his fingerprints, but that was pointless. His fingerprints would be found all over the interior of the container, along with Hamal's and that Eastern European fellow, Pavel.

Hafid savored an intense sense of satisfaction for one or two moments and then turned toward the yard's exit. Even though the nuke was still live, it would take real work to make it detonate now. Someone would need to physically open the container and unpack half of the shielding just to access the nuke. Then they would need to unattach the junk firing circuit and plug in a good one. All of that surely wasn't going to happen before the bomb was found.

Hafid made his way out of the container offloading area, stopping to talk with the guard for some five minutes. Across the street from the exit was a greasy spoon that seemed as good a place as any to get some information. He made his way inside and found a stool. A strung-out looking, tattooed waitress came by and offered him a cup of coffee. Hafid accepted the cup and quizzed the girl about the best way to get out of town. It turned out that directly across the bridge from where they were sitting was a train station. There was also a freight yard, if he wanted to hobo it. He considered it, but the Amtrak tickets were cheap enough. Hafid thanked the woman for the info as she walked off in her semi-comatose state.

While he attempted to drink the wretched excuse for coffee that she had given him, he surfed the web on the pre-paid phone he had acquired. It took almost two minutes of actual investigative work to find the FBI's terrorist hotline number. He really assumed that the number would be considerably easier to find than it was. It annoyed him.

Hafid left a couple dollars for the waitress and pressed the send button on the phone as he exited the café. The sun was full up and it was starting to get hot as he made his way to the bridge that the zombie waitress had pointed out to him. The phone rang three times before an automated responder picked up. Really, a mechanical connection? What if it was an actual emergency? Hafid pressed 2 on his phone as instructed and waited for the prompt.

"Hello, my name is Hafid. The second nuclear device that you are looking for is in a green cargo container in the Port of St. Louis. I have disabled the firing mechanism, but someone should stop and secure it soon. The other device is still at the Port of Chicago, as far as I know. You don't have much time left to disable the other device, but I can assume your emergency response people know that. That is all. No, wait. You really need to make this phone number easier to find. And add a live person to answer it. Goodbye."

Hafid pressed the end-call button and then powered down the phone. He had talked for 15-seconds. It wasn't nearly long enough to track his location, but the GPS chip in the phone would do their tracking for them once they started looking. That was if he left power to it.

As he walked across the bridge that led toward the train station, he pulled the sim chip out of the phone and snapped it in two. He flicked it out into the air and it was gone. Turning his attention to the phone, a couple hard snaps and pops and he pulled the battery free. With an underhand, side-armed toss he launched both the phone and battery over the side of the bridge and listened for the impact as they bounced off the tracks below. It was now time to go start a new life somewhere else.

CHAPTER 25

Twenty-four hours to detonation.

The two F/A – 18 Hornets that Bob Sloan had borrowed from the Illinois National Guard came down out of the clouds into St. Louis airspace still traveling at supersonic speed. The pilot of the lead aircraft felt the turbulence of the sonic boom created by the air compression on his aircraft's leading edges and just knew there was going to be fallout coming his way. The FBI man sitting in his second seat didn't seem the least bothered by the shockwave that was spreading out over the city. Just the opposite, he seemed a little pensive, like he was late for something.

Where the typical Hornet is a one seater, the D model variant that they were each riding in had two seats. Normally configured for training purposes or giving rides to VIPs, the D variant was still a fully mission capable platform with an operational straight line velocity of 1.8 Mach. Currently, Kristin Hughes was sitting in one Hornet's second seat and Ben Donewoody was flying second in the other. And both screaming over top of the St. Louis outer skyline at a healthy 1.4 Mach.

Both pilots backed down to a milder 0.8 Mach and banked a hard starboard to come around the airport's outer markers so they could lineup with the farthest runway from the tower. The lead aircraft pilot radioed their intent to land, and then without waiting for a response, it was all airbrakes and landing gear.

The two military aircraft shot down the runway, breaking as hard as was allowed by the landing gear, and rolled to a stop at the far end of the runway. The canopies came open and helmet visors were raised. The fleet of police cars that had followed them down the runway was impressive. It looked like one of those '80s movies where a Russian MIG defects and lands at some stray airfield. Kristin Hughes climbed from the cockpit and descended the outer handholds to the tarmac. Two full throttle jet rides inside of one week. *WTH was gonna top this,* Kristin thought, as she sized up the stern-faced men gathering around her.

Not missing a beat, Kristin pulled off her helmet and flipped her long blond hair in a wide arc above her head to loosen it up. The pink strand she had dyed in it for accent went streaking through the air for all to see. It made a distinct impression on her pilot, but not on the gathering crowd. Well, that was usually the way of these things. She was quite used to starting on the wrong foot.

Ben had managed to extricate himself from the cramped second seat and was disrobing from his flight gear when the pilot of Kristin's plane retrieved her backpack from a small storage area under the fuselage. She thanked her pilot for all his assistance and turned to face the tense crowd in front of her.

"Which one of you is in charge here?" Kristin Hughes' voice was all business.

A large Missouri state trooper took a step forward from the group of men and fixed Kristin with an intimidating gaze that had no effect on her.

"I am the responsible authority here. Before we get started, someone needs to explain why you feel you have the right to violate supersonic flight in –"

Kristin was having none of it. She was having no one be uppity, save her. She pointed over her shoulder at Ben as she cut off the trooper in mid-rant. She retrieved a cellphone from her flight suit and punched a speed dial number. Bob Sloan answered on the first ring. She gave him a one sentence request and hung up the phone without ceremony.

"Listen officer. He's FBI. I'm NEST. The pilots are with me. FLYNET is in full effect here, which means that they can do anything that I ask them to. Now, we don't have time for anybody's self-assuming authority, so let's just wait another five seconds for your phone to ring."

Ben had no more than nodded his agreement when the trooper's cellphone rang. The remaining crowd of police and security personnel paused their posturing to watch the phone exchange. There was a solid series of head nods and "yes sirs" as the governor of Missouri explained to the trooper that he was going to assist in any way that he could. Kristin smiled as the large man hung up the phone. Bob Sloan did move fast.

The imposing trooper stared into Kristin Hughes' all-business expression for a long second before detaching.

"What do you need, ma'am?"

"We need a ride to the cargo container area of the Port of St. Louis as fast as humanly possible. Oh, and the pilots could probably use some jet fuel."

"Right this way, ma'am."

The big trooper turned on his heels and started jogging toward a patrol car. As he went, he barked orders into a radio microphone attached to his lapel. Kristin and Ben followed close on his heels and jumped into the back seat of the unmarked black patrol car as the trooper slid behind the wheel. He turned and looked at his passengers as Kristin slammed her door shut.

"Which container yard, ma'am?"

Kristin looked at Ben expectantly.

"How many are there?"

"About four or five."

Kristin looked at Ben again.

"Which one is the most active?"

"The one at the municipal river terminal, ma'am."

"Head there."

"May I ask why, ma'am? Is this an exercise or is there some type of terrorist alert going on?"

Kristin Hughes composed herself and leveled a sturdy gaze at the big state trooper.

"Because there is the very real possibility that a Russian made nuclear warhead, sent to us by some terrorist group, is about to explode there. And, frankly, I'd like to stop the terrorists from winning today."

The trooper turned several shades lighter than his usual dark complexion. Without another word, his head snapped front and he mashed his foot down on the accelerator pedal. Kristin heard the sound of squealing tires as she was forced back into her seat.

The patrol car was in no time at all clearing the airport fencing and rocketing off into metropolitan traffic. Kristin drew a breath and decided that it was time to contact her boss. She grabbed her cell phone and sent a quick and dirty text message to the whole Group. *Landed in St. Louis. Headed to terminal with FBI Ben to find secondary device. Jim Bonner and bomb dogs in Chicago handling primary device. Timeline still unknown.*

Kristin was stowing her cellphone when Ben Donewoody's phone began to ring. Ben answered the call and listened to the person on the other end of the line. He looked instantly perplexed by the situation. He asked to have whoever he was talking to text him the audio file, and then hung up. He turned to face Kristin and paused.

"You are never going to believe this!"

Kristin was about ready to ask what had him so spooked when Ben's phone chimed with an incoming voice text message. He turned on the speaker so that all three of them could hear the text. Everyone in the car stayed quiet and listened to the message that Hafid had left on the FBI Terrorism Hotline. Kristin's expression turned perplexed to mirror Ben's expression. Their trooper counterpart also looked confused.

"What. The. Hell?" Kristin expelled in an exaggerated fashion.

"Do you think it could be legit?" Ben asked with a skeptical tone.

"I certainly hope it is," the trooper responded from behind the wheel.

Kristin Hughes stared at the phone in Ben's hand, all the gears turning in her head at warp speed.

"It could easily be misdirection," Ben said in a concerned voice.

"Play it again," Kristin asked.

Ben played it again.

"Play it again."

Ben played it again.

Kristin poked her chin with her index finger as their driver swayed back and forth across traffic lanes at twice the legal speed limit. *This trooper is a very good driver*, Kristin thought in the midst of everything.

"It sounds legit," Kristin said confidently.

"You think?" Ben questioned.

"I do. The problem is that we still need to treat it like it's live. Booby traps and all, you know? Interesting that it's green."

"Why interesting?"

"Color or number? Jim Bonner is cracking into the red container in Chicago, not the green one."

"You think he's opening the wrong one?"

"Who knows at this point?"

Kristin was about to ask the trooper how much longer they thought they were going to be when he slid the car around a corner to the presence of a closed gate and a big sign proclaiming the place to be the City of St. Louis Port District, Municipal River Terminal. Kristin exhaled.

The trooper pulled the car to an abrupt halt at the gate and lowered the rear window so Kristin could talk to the gate guard. It only took a second and the gate was raised. The patrol car sped off into the terminal headed straight for the yard office.

Ben and Kristin jumped from the car and sprinted for the office door as the trooper skidded it to a stop. The two broke through the door badges in hand and leveled themselves on the man behind the counter. The desk agent took in the badges, and the big state trooper bringing up the rear, and just knew his day was about to go downhill.

"Sir, my name is Dr. Kristin Hughes. I am with the Department of Energy. Your facility received a cargo container not long ago from the Port of Chicago."

Kristin went on to explain the container's color and the numbers on its side. The port agent was just about to start banging away on his keyboard when a voice came from the driver's lounge.

"Ma'am, I can help you with that. The container is still on my truck. I haven't actually unloaded it yet."

Kristin, Ben, and the trooper all spun around to see Bob Russel standing in the doorway, steaming mug of coffee in his hand. Kristin instantly took in the man's stance and mannerism.

"Where is your truck parked?"

"Follow me," Bob Russel said in a nonchalant tone.

The foursome, now joined by the port agent, walked briskly out to the large semi-truck holding area and began to meander through the pack.

About two-thirds of the way through a forest of big trucks sat Bob Russel's blue Kenworth tractor-trailer, loaded with a freshly painted green cargo container. Everyone pulled up from their march at the cab and took in the scene. Ben Donewoody began to explain the sensitive nature of the situation to the group as Kristin pulled off her backpack and sat it on the ground. The lead field agent for NEST operations made a very slow turn around the container, taking in every possible detail. She stopped and surveyed a displaced cover exposing the multi-prong plug in a small box on the container's frame. She slowly produced a sidelong grin as she played back in her mind the message that the man named Hafid had left the FBI.

After her pause, she continued on around the container. Everyone else in the group stood stoic as she completed her cursory inspection. Finally returning to where the group was standing, she stopped.

"Can someone get me a step ladder, tall enough to access the top of the container? Please."

The port man scampered off to retrieve a ladder and Kristin turned her attention to the truck driver.

"I noticed that there is an inspection cover that has been removed since you parked the rig? Was that you?"

Bob Russel took a couple steps forward to see the open box and receptacle plug and shook his head.

"It wasn't me. It might have been Jamal. He might have tinkered with it before he left."

Both Hughes and her FBI counterpart turned to look at Bob Russel square on.

"Who is Jamal?"

"A hitchhiker I picked up in Chicago. Said he had been working out that way, and was now headed back down south. Seemed like a nice man."

"Can you describe him for me?" Kristin said in a way that made it sound like the vapors were coalescing. Bob Russel scratched his chin and considered her question for a second.

"About six feet tall, maybe thirty to thirty five years old. I'd say his family was Middle Eastern, of one country or another. Spoke real good English. His parents probably came over when he was little."

Kristin's eyes went wide as the truck driver spoke. She waved her hands at her FBI counterpart like a crazy lady, and he began rifling through his bag to retrieve the copied TWIC printouts. He handed them over to the truck driver, who didn't look at them for more than a few seconds.

"Yup, that's him." Bob Russel handed the photo of the younger Pakistani back to Kristin. Kristin gave it a good look and turned to look at Ben Donewoody.

"I bet that this fellow here, which Mr. Russel knows as Jamal, is actually Hafid. I also bet that he is one of the two nuclear scientists pulled out of Pakistan. And I'm pretty willing to bet that his phone message is accurate."

"Do you really think it's gonna be that easy?" Ben Donewoody said, playing devil's advocate.

"There are way too many things lining up here for it to be fantasy. Besides, you know what I think about coincidences."

Ben Donewoody shook his head and began to smile. The remainder of the group also started to smile. The port agent came jogging back with an extension ladder and took in the group.

"What did I miss?"

"Nothing. Could you set it up, please, so, I can get up on the roof?"

The port agent did as requested. Kristin returned to the front of the cab and opened her backpack. She pulled out a cellphone and a multi-antennae instrument that resembled a two-way radio. The big trooper eyed the instrument as Kristin climbed the ladder against the side of the truck. She placed the device on the roof of the cargo container and switched it on. She then checked her phone. No service. Pocketing her phone, she descended the ladder.

"That's a signal jammer?" the trooper asked. Kristin nodded and grabbed her open backpack.

"Yes. It's a GM-20. Military grade. It blocks the whole cell canopy, 3G and 4G data signal, Bluetooth and Wi-Fi. It's a bomb girl's best friend."

"I thought it looked familiar. We used to carry a similar model, while doing patrols in Kabul."

Kristin and Ben nodded at the trooper. Bob Russel shook the man's hand without saying a word, in that way that old veterans tend to do. The port agent could tell that he was out of the loop.

"Why do we want to block the cellphones?"

Ben Donewoody smiled at him as Kristin headed back to the multi-prong plug setup.

"About seventy five percent of the planet has access to a cellphone network. It's the perfect way to detonate a bomb these days. The jammer blocks any signals from getting to the container and setting off the bomb."

The man from the port office blanched but made no response. Kristin took a moment to fully study the area around the plug box. The screws and cover were missing. She presumed that Jamal or Hafid had pocketed them when he was finished. Looking inside, the plug looked visually intact. It appeared to be a standard multi-pin type. The kind that snapped into a socket with a couple of spring-loaded clips.

Kristin stepped back two steps and took in a larger view of the scene. Down between the tires of the trailer rested a paperclip that had been bent into a U-shape. She reached down and retrieved the small piece of metal. She studied the affixed chewing gum for several seconds. Holding the gum/paperclip between her fingers, she returned her attention to the glowing red LED light in the plug box. Red light was on. Green light was off. Kristin smiled and tossed the paperclip to her FBI counterpart.

"This guy's clever. Red light's on, so I'm betting that he shunted out the internal fuse by grounding it out against the side of the container."

Ben Donewoody caught the paperclip and gum combination and looked at it in an inspecting way. Kristin retrieved a small pair of needle nose pliers from her backpack and slid them into the slots on the multi-pin plug. A quick push and click, then she pulled the disabled plug from its socket. She inspected the cut wire and broken pin backer, and smiled. She let the plug fall free and reached down to retrieve her backpack. Rummaging around in the bag, she came out with a small metal canister and a one pound ball-peen hammer. The whole group followed as she walked around the back of the container to the locked double doors. Without hesitation, Kristin sprayed the lock on the container door with the metal can from her pack. A thick white frost built up on the lock as she emptied the contents of the can. Letting the can fall to the ground, Kristin Hughes gripped the hammer like a baseball bat and slammed the frost white padlock. The super cold metal of the lock shattered into countless pieces from the hammer's impact. The small pieces of lock went flying in all directions, making the group back up several steps.

With a look of satisfaction, Kristin reached out and pushed the jaw of the lock free from the container's lock opening with the nose of her hammer. Dropping the hammer, Kristin reached up and grabbed the door latches on the container. Then she paused and turned to Ben.

"Without a portable X-Ray machine, I guess we're at the point of no return."

"What does that mean?" the port agent said, again not fully comprehending the situation. Kristin smiled at Ben and then turned to their counterpart from the Port of St. Louis.

"Well, without somehow being able to view inside of it, there is no real way to tell if they booby trapped it before we open it."

"—Oh." The port man started turning white again.

"Well, bomb girl? Think it's booby trapped?" Ben Donewoody sounded confident, but it was definitely a question.

"No. I don't. So far, it has been just as the voicemail message stated. Hafid said that he disabled this nuke, but not the other one. I think he's on the level."

"One way to find out."

And with the words no more than out of Ben's mouth, Kristin Hughes slowly pulled up on the door closures. Once removed from their locking position, she rotated them over to free the closure posts from their upper and lower hold-fasts. Ever so gently she applied force to the door, until it no more than released from its seal. She paused and exhaled.

Kristin retrieved a small flashlight from her pack and inspected every inch of the exposed opening. Finally comfortable with the situation, she stuck the light in her mouth and pulled the door full open. Giving the area a second good inspection, she opened the other door and exposed the container fully. Kristin stepped back and took in the opening, full to the brim with neatly stacked bags of Fancy Cat cat litter. She spit out the flashlight and turned back to the group.

"So far, so good. Somewhere in the middle of this cat litter is a Soviet era nuclear warhead. If the doors weren't booby trapped, then it is unlikely that any of the individual bags will be. It would be too hard to control the booby trap from accidentally setting off the nuke. Still, we need to remove the bags in a calm and controlled fashion. And I could use a hand with that."

The police and FBI men started disrobing out of gun belts and protective vests so they could get to work. The port agent scampered off once again, but returned seconds later with a forklift holding an empty pallet. The ladder was repositioned and the group began removing the bags one by one.

The team worked diligently. Four pallets of bags and thirty minutes later, they had exposed three sides of the nuclear weapon in the middle of the container. Bob Russel helped the port man string out several lengths of extension cord to plug in a large flood light.

With good light and access to the nuke, Dr. Kristin Hughes made short work of disassembling the cellphone trigger and internal antenna connection. Shortly after that she had the firing box pulled and the weapon was effectively dead. It wouldn't be fully inert until the core was separated from the explosive implosion casing surrounding it, but it wasn't going off anytime soon. Kristin set her tools on her backpack and took a seat on the rim of the container opening, letting her legs dangle over the rear trailer frame. She took in each of her compatriots with a warm smile and sighed.

"I don't know about you, but I could use a beer."

CHAPTER 26

Robert Dunn stood in the kitchen of the modest German apartment on the outskirts of Kaiserslautern, and stared at the contents of the refrigerator. Nothing on the shelves really seemed appealing to him. He was a little thirsty, maybe a glass of water instead? Dunn closed the door and moved to the kitchen cupboard by the sink. Letting the water in the tap run for several seconds, he retrieved a glass from the cupboard and filled it to its rim.

Turning to look at the man tied to the chair adjacent to the small kitchen table, Robert Dunn took a drink and smiled. The city of Kaiserslautern had good water. That was nice to know. Some cities had bad water, which was why he usually drank bottled. He sat the glass on the table and took up station in the chair across from the tied up man. So far, the conversation had not gone as well as either man would have liked. And as these things tended to do, it had required a more aggressive approach to bring the other man around.

Robert Dunn had moved into the Port of Hamburg in the shadows of the FBI team to take a nice quiet look around. After assembling the nuts and bolts of the situation, he had zeroed in on the gate man, Klaus. He seemed a good place to start. Klaus was shady enough for Dunn to use the direct approach. Well, that's what he thought at the time. It turned out not to be so. Adrian Beqiri's hold on his personnel was strong, and Klaus had been beaten to unconsciousness before deciding to cooperate.

It was the gate man Klaus who had pointed the CIA assassin south toward Phillip, the truck driver. Robert Dunn had come down from

Hamburg to Kaiserslautern, and found Phillip right where Klaus had said he would. He watched the German come and go for a little while, so he could get a feel for the man. It seemed that Phillip parked his truck in a gated auto park, and spent his downtime equally split between his small apartment and the bar down the street.

In typical fashion, Dunn had let himself into the apartment and waited for Phillip to return home. When the door finally swung opened, Phillip the truck driver was not prepared for the blow that was coming. The German hit the floor with a thud and his Styrofoam takeout container went careening across the living room floor.

Dunn had drug him into the kitchen and sat him in one of the straightbacked chairs. Extension cord worked well enough for rope and a washcloth from the sink made a handy gag. The truck driver was secured to the chair, and Dunn calmly waited for him to regain consciousness.

Once again, the truck driver seemed more scared of Beqiri than he was of whoever his inquisitor was. The conversation between the two men had resulted in the truck driver being beaten to the point of collapse twice. Phillip was sturdy and could absorb a good amount of pain, which the swollen-shut left eye and the draining blood from his broken nose attested to. The fact that his right eye socket was all but shattered at this point had prompted Dunn to switch to the left eye. From the wheezing, it was also pretty evident that there were a couple of broken ribs on the tally sheet.

Robert Dunn lifted off his chair and headed for the cabinets. He opened two before he came across a bottle of white vinegar. He snatched the bottle up and returned to his work station. Yanking the rag from Phillip's mouth shook some resemblance of life back into the man. The CIA man dumped a liberal amount of vinegar onto the rag, and then shoved it back into the truck driver's mouth. It took only a second or two for the vinegar to attack the man's senses, and bring him fully back to consciousness.

Robert Dunn smiled at the man and nodded that he was pleased. He could tell from the fading rage in the man's swollen eyes that his resistance was all but gone. After the first round of passing out, Dunn had wanted to move straight on to more aggressive means of getting his information, but decided against it. He had some small amount of time to spend, and gun shots and screaming would inevitably draw in outsiders. So, it had become the old-school mob approach. You just keep beating them until they tell you what you want to know.

Fortunately, from the look in Phillip's eyes, he was about to transition from the beating stage to the talking stage. Dunn removed the rag from Phillip's mouth and sat it on the table. He retrieved the glass and poured a small amount of water in Phillip's mouth. He waited for the truck driver to calm himself and adjust. He sat the water glass back on the table deliberately. The CIA man pulled a pocket knife out of his pants pocket and laid it on the table, blade facing out. Phillip's eyes went as wide as the broken bones and swelling would allow. Dunn knew that it was always good for the subject to know that the pain could get worse. Dunn adjusted his chair and focused on the man in a professional way.

"So, Phillip, what do you say we talk some more?"

Phillip, for his response, just spit a mouthful of blood at the CIA man. The assassin smiled back at him and reached for the vinegar soaked rag.

"Fine. Fine. What do you want?" The truck driver hung his head in defeat. Robert Dunn sat the rag down and returned his gaze to the German man.

"First, do you, or do you not, transport containers for Vakar Arms?"

The German made to protest, but stopped and nodded his head.

"Say it, Phillip."

"Yes, I do."

Dunn could tell that the man's will was completely gone. For a second, he wondered if the man knew what was coming at the end.

"Do you know a man named Adrian Beqiri?"

"I do."

"Describe him for me."

The German man spit a big wad of bloody spittle onto the floor to clear his throat. He inhaled and Dunn could hear the low whistle of the man's punctured lung.

"Tall – six feet or so. A little bit more than 100 kilos. Dark hair, dark eyes, he's Eastern European of some type."

Dunn ran the description through his mind to compare it to a picture he had pulled off the port's CCTV. The truck driver was giving factual information. Dunn stood and walked back to the sink, where he refilled the water glass. He returned to the table and gave Phillip a large drink of the cool tap water. The truck driver closed his one working eye and swallowed slowly.

"Is he well-spoken?"

"Yes. He speaks good German, good English, and some other languages that I don't understand. Eastern European ones, I think."

Dunn nodded his head in approval.

"Do you know where I can find Mr. Beqiri?"

"No. We never discussed such things."

Dunn scratched his chin for a second. He had the man talking, now he needed to get something useful out of him.

"Okay. How did you two conduct business?"

"They would call when they had a shipment. I would show up and get loaded."

Dunn puzzled over the statement for a second or two and then seemed content.

"Tell me about how and where the shipments were picked up."

The truck driver explained that they would contact him when they needed him, and that he would report to the warehouse in Idar-Oberstien. There, he would pick up whatever needed picking up. Dunn queried, and Phillip explained how to get to the warehouse – that it was on a hill, at the end of a dead-end street. He told the spy about Adrian apparently having an apartment that he used there, but wasn't sure of its actual address. He explained that he would go there and he would wait in the truck as the shipment was loaded and secured. They would give him a bundle of papers for the port people and he would drive the containers straight to the port. At the port, the containers were offloaded. Payment for the work would show up in his bank account the next day. He was just the driver.

"How long have you been driving for them?"

"Maybe five or six years now."

"Do they have any other drivers?"

"I don't know. But I make numerous trips, so I would think not."

Dunn felt like he was about at the end of useful information. He took a moment to mull everything over in his mind.

"The man that contacted you for the shipments, was it Beqiri?"

"Sometimes yes, and sometimes no. A second man would also call. He was also Eastern European, though his English was not as good as his German."

"That's good to know." Dunn reached inside his suit jacket and removed a Sig Sauer P220 automatic. The compact SAS Gen2 handgun only held six rounds, but it was as reliable as they came. It took Phillip a moment to process what was about to happen. He was starting to protest as Dunn pulled a suppressor out from under his suit jacket and began screwing it onto the end of the Sig's barrel.

"But, but, I have answered all of your questions."

"True. But you got into a bad business, Phillip. A bad business, full of bad people."

"And you? What are you?"

"Me? I'm a bad person, too."

As Robert Dunn finished his sentence he pulled the trigger on the handgun two times. Two non-jacketed rounds thudded into Phillip's chest, and it was done. A shocked expression and a couple of twitches, and the truck driver was dead.

Dunn returned the pistol and suppressor to the shoulder holster and took in the room. It wasn't as bad a mess as others had been. He pulled off the pair of surgical gloves he had been wearing and stuffed them into his jacket pocket. He pulled on a sturdy pair on mechanic's gloves and stood. Even with the security of the nitrile gloves, he took time to wipe down all of the surfaces he had touched. Feeling confident that things were acceptable, he set about systematically tossing the apartment. He trashed the place with the style of an artist, to make it look as though burglars had been looking for something of value. He untied Phillip and repositioned his body in a "killed-trying-to-fight-back" position.

The assassin paused in the doorway of the kitchen to take in the whole scene another time. It looked pretty good for short work. It didn't have any of that professional hit look to it. That was exactly what he wanted. A crime scene was to be expected. A professional crime scene was definitely not what he wanted. This scene had the "usual suspects" look to it.

Robert Dunn adjusted his suit jacket and tie. He removed his gloves and placed them in his pocket. Sliding his arm up into his sleeve, he walked to the door and palmed the handle. He gave it a quick twist to wipe it clean and exited the little apartment. The outside knob got the same wipe down, and then he made his way out of the building. He casually gave the main entrance door knobs the same treatment before he turned and ambled down the street.

When Phillip the truck driver's sad and broken body was finally found, no one would be looking for Mr. Dunn. The assassin walked three blocks to where he had left his car and quietly headed out of town.

CHAPTER 27

Eighteen hours to detonation.

Ivan Vakar shuffled some papers on his desk and collected the file folders that represented the last of his immediate business. He had planned the next twenty four hours in his mind numerous times. If everything went to plan, forty eight hours from now the world would be a different place.

That being said, there was still much to be done. Ivan looked up at the painting of Christ hanging on his office wall. *Yes, I am the Roman,* he mused to himself. I am creating the ashes, so that a new empire can be built. A new empire to lead the world. The old guard was too long in the tooth to be useful to this new world. They needed to be put down.

Ivan reached over and snatched up the handset for his phone from its cradle. Hitting the number nine speed dial button, he rang up Hermans and DeVos. Hermans and DeVos, located on the business Street in Antwerp, was one of Europe's premier trading houses. They had handled all of Ivan Vakar's business needs ever since he had come to the EU. The phone rang two times.

"Good day, Herr Vakar. How may we be of service today?"

Alfred Hermans, as the owner of the trading house, knew every person that rang into his private number by both number and name. One had to have a large portfolio to get handed the direct line. And as such, a certain level of service was expected.

"Alfred, my good man, I would like to conduct some trading. Do you have a moment?"

"But, of course, Herr Vakar."

"Excellent. Did you establish the new accounts that I asked about?"

"But, of course. Four new accounts, spread across European manufacturing concerns. They are ready to be utilized. They just need to be populated."

Populated was fancy European talk for putting money in them. As the accounts currently sat, they were just shells.

"Excellent, Alfred. I would like you to liquidate all of my U.S. - associated holdings and transfer the funds evenly across those four new accounts."

There was a pause on the other end of the line. Ivan could see the gears turning in the accountant's head.

"And, the timing of the transactions?"

"Within the next twelve hours, please."

There was a second pause, but less brief this time.

"You will incur a significant penalty for some of those transactions. I would speculate, at least eighteen to twenty percent for the default withdrawals."

Ivan had already calculated the damage for himself and knew that his accountant was hedging. The real damage was much closer to fourteen percent on the transactions. Still, fourteen percent on millions of dollars was nothing to be thrown away lightly.

"I understand, Alfred. Please proceed."

"Very well. The transactions will be handled as you asked within the next twelve hours. You will be able to view the transaction details and new account certificates on our secure server after, say, fifteen hours. That is with the exception of the Asian market transactions. With the timing of the market closings, we will make the transactions, but the certificates most likely will not post until the markets reopen."

Ivan had thought this out as well. As long as the transaction had actually been conducted, the certificates had to be posted, independent of the circumstances involved. Besides, who would really notice with all the chaos that would be unfolding in America?

"That is completely understandable, Alfred. Thank you for your help."

"We are happy to be your representative of choice, Herr Vakar."

"Have a good day, Herr Hermans."

"And you as well, Herr Vakar."

Ivan Vakar hung up the phone and smiled across the room at his favorite painting. It was now all underway. The two devices had been delivered successfully, and were quietly waiting to be detonated. He had now secured his investments from the inevitable stock market collapse to come. Or, secured them as well as was reasonably expected. The world markets would definitely take a hit, but they would rebound. Minus the bothersome Americans and their damned Security Exchange Commission.

For his account, Herr Hermans would definitely be suspicious after the fact. That was fine. With the massive commissions he was about to make, he would keep his mouth shut.

Now, Ivan needed to keep up the charade of going to the G8 Summit. He just needed to be seen as being fashionably late. When the nukes detonated and he was still somewhere over the Atlantic, it would all be seen as accidental providence.

He had officially planned to hold up the travel of the German and Italian representatives, claiming it to be EU business. The French representative got no such saving. He was a weak and impetuous man. The loss of the Russian president was a destabilizing problem, but that damage was calculable. It would all be a tragedy, and the surviving members of the European Union would rally and lead the world out of the disaster.

The only major bit of business left to conduct was cleaning up the Vakar Arms trail that led from the nukes back to him. He was well-insulated from his arms business. Still, that concealment would not stand up to intense scrutiny. And there would definitely be intense scrutiny from every investigative body. The Americans would rally every asset they could to the hunt. The MI6 would definitely be involved, as would INTERPOL. Ivan did not want to leave a trail that could actually see him exposed.

At the end of the day, the loss of Vakar Arms had always been figured into the overall cost of the plan. He would secure all of his buyer contacts and the principle middle personnel, and just let the rest go. It was necessary to give something to get something else. Giving up the people at Vakar Arms would be a loss, but unsavory men were always available. It seemed about time that he talked to Pavel and got moving with the next steps. Everything was in action now.

On the other side of the Atlantic – President Jackson was just finishing up with his late afternoon staff meeting. He had been tying up loose ends all day. He needed to be getting to Air Force One and on his way to the Summit. Knowing the things that were going on, he had been understandably preoccupied all day. Most people on his daily agenda assumed that he had international issues on his mind. Little did they know he was considering the potential end of his nation.

Really, he did have international issues swirling around, they were all the bad kind. How would America explain to the world that it had let the senior world leaders get decimated in a nuclear explosion that punched a crater in the city of Chicago? It was a definite quandary. It was something that couldn't be preplanned for. He just hoped that a shocked and saddened vice president was up to the task. Domestically, what would become of America and the bread basket of the world? He didn't even want to consider that prospect. It seemed that unless something very timely happened, he was well-headed toward being the worst president in history.

President Jackson waited for the group from Congress to exit the Oval Office, and then walked to the door and handed his folio to his secretary, Margery.

"What do you think, Margery, time to go catch a plane?"

"If you say so, Mr. President."

"You sound excited. Well, I have to go pack a bag. Then I have a thing or two to clean up on my desk."

"Just pick the suits you like from what's laid out on the bed, otherwise the first lady has your packing handled."

"I have always said that women secretly run the country."

"Secretly?"

President Jackson laughed at his secretary. He liked her greatly. Margery had been with the family since he was freshly in the political game as Congressman Walker Jackson of Nevada. She was the only person in the whole of the White House to not continuously refer to him as Mr. President. Like any good counselor, she saved the title for when she wanted to press a point home. He was pretty sure that Margery secretly ran the whole place.

"If you would tell the first lady that I have always had great respect for her taste in suits, I will go back to tidying up my desk."

"I'll have your bag delivered to the limousine."

The president nodded and turned back through the doorway of his office. He stopped for a moment to consider the paintings decorating the room. Great leaders had chosen scenes of America to reinforce the greatness of the land. This afternoon it seemed that all of those paintings were looking back at him in judgement. He shook the thought from his mind as Pat Sommers entered the room via the private study entrance. Jackson waved him to one of the couches, and he sat.

"What's the skinny, Pat?"

The president sat down on the couch facing Pat Sommers, and stretched his entire frame.

"Good news first. NEST Field One and Group FBI located the secondary container, in the Port of St. Louis. It is officially out of play."

"St. Louis? How did it get to St. Louis?"

"One of the suspect containers was picked up shortly after offloading and transported via tractor-trailer to Port of St. Louis. After the package was positively ID'd, the team took a hop and intercepted it."

"Define hop."

"Two supersonic F-18 Hornets, borrowed from the Illinois National Guard. We will have some internal politicking to do. Seems Missouri officials weren't happy about supersonic flights in their airspace, or FLYNET being dumped over the whole area without explanation."

"Well, they'll play ball, one way or another. If it takes me giving someone a talking to, then that's what will happen."

Pat Sommers sat quietly, waiting for a question. His pause was short lived.

"Okay, Pat. Now the bad news."

"Port of Chicago device is still unknown. The NEST Team working the package is still under a dead-cell canopy. There isn't really a good way to contact them. FLYNET is in-place, but we had to relax the normal boundary due to all the international flights. We didn't want to spook the G8 members."

"So, the situation on the ground hasn't changed?"

"No, sir."

"You said working the package. That means that they have positively ID'd it?"

"They have two possible containers. They are treating them both as suspect."

"And how do we know this?"

"We received a burst SITREP from Dr. Hughes while on her flight down to St. Louis."

"Flying and texting, oh the horror."

"The flight avionics in the Hornet are hardened against external electronic interference. It shouldn't bother the pilot."

The president looked at his Secret Service man incredulously.

"It was a joke, Pat."

"Sorry, Mr. President."

"Since Dr. Hughes has left the confines of her dead-cell canopy, is it still possible to talk to her?"

Pat Sommers retrieved a cellphone from his pocket and dialed a number from memory. When the connection was established, he gave a quick series of acronyms that the president didn't understand. He was about to ask when Pat Sommers nodded and asked if it was Dr. Hughes on the line.

"Very good, hold for the president."

The phone was handed to the president, who looked at it suspiciously.

"Dr. Hughes."

"Yes."

"This is the president of the United States."

"Good afternoon. You sound different on crypto than you do on TV. But, if Pat says you're you, then I'm good."

"I was wondering if I could get a report on the situation in Chicago, seeing how I'm headed that way when we hang up."

Kristin checked her watch.

"As of six hours ago, the field team was getting ready to start investigating the first of two possible suspect containers. Since they are still under the canopy, I can only assume that they are still working the problem."

"And you believe there is a device in one of those containers?"

"Well, seeing how there was a '60s era Soviet nuclear bomb hooked to a U.S.-made cellular trigger in the St. Louis container, the odds are pretty good."

"Well then, I concur with your assessment. By the way, do you not like me? You seem terse."

"I'm used to dealing with soldiers and spies. They like things to be direct. I haven't had much interaction with politicians."

President Walker Jackson looked down at the presidential seal on the carpet and smiled broadly. Pat Sommers looked at him quizzically.

"You're doing just fine, Dr. Hughes. You continue being as direct as you like."

"Yes, sir."

"Now, I'm getting on my own plane in just a moment. I plan on carrying on with the G8 Summit. That is assuming you and your people can keep us from turning to ash. I would greatly appreciate it if you call me directly upon resolution of the situation on the ground in Chicago. I want to keep everyone calm, if possible. Understand?"

"Yes, Mr. President. How do I go about contacting you directly?"

"You call Pat Sommers. He will be standing right next to me the whole time."

"Very good. I'll call as soon as I have something to say."

"Thank you, Dr. Hughes."

The president handed the phone back to the Secret Service agent. Pat Sommers ended the call and stowed his phone. The president looked at him quizzically.

"She's and interesting individual."

"She can be a free spirit, but she is the absolute best there is."

"So I hear. I think I might like to meet her, if we survive this whole thing."

Pat Sommers did not reply.

"Well, let's get this show on the road, Pat. This thing isn't gonna do itself."

Both men stood and headed toward the door.

CHAPTER 28

Pavel sat in the corner of the Imbisstuben on the quiet section of Ohechaussee and watched the port man eat his sandwich. The town of Norderstedt was just north of the Hamburg airport and a straight run down to the Port of Hamburg. Pavel could understand why he would live here. The tedious pace of the place matched the tedious man. The place seemed a bit too quaint. It seemed that this man Klaus was attempting to live as far up the ladder as possible. A nice house in the suburbs of Hamburg, paid for by a good job at the port, left what? Just enough money to eat sandwiches at the Imbiss? Who knew, maybe he just liked it here? Or, maybe he liked sandwiches? He probably ate a lot of sandwiches at the port.

Pavel caught himself and realized that he didn't care what he thought or what he liked. In a couple of minutes it really wouldn't matter much at all. He finished his glass of Bitburger and sat the empty glass on the counter. He dropped several euro coins on the counter, next to his mess, and walked quietly toward the door.

Outside, the traffic on Ohechaussee was light. He had noticed that it always seemed to be light in European suburb towns. Pavel walked across the Strasse and into a parking area, where he had left his car. The park area had an entry/exit on AM Sood, and the street lined up pretty well with the Imbiss.

The car wasn't actually Pavel's. He had stolen the car from another park area. The park area for the Hamburg airport, to be specific. It had seemed a better choice than a rental car. He didn't want to be attached to the car later on.

As Pavel sat in the stolen car, waiting for the man named Klaus to finish his sandwich, he reflected back on the conversation in the jet. Vakar had said to clean up the loose ends, and that was what he was here to do. He was still concerned about being one of the loose ends that the man had been talking about, but he would deal with that later. He would clean up the loose ends and then deal with whatever or whomever came next. He was certain that if he was, for some reason, on the hit list, Vakar would need to contract that out himself. None of Pavel's men would think about crossing him. Pavel was positive that he was a better killer than any of them. So, he would become a contract hit. If it was to happen at all. Things like avoiding a contract hit couldn't be planned. You just had to react to them as they happened. Pavel was a survivor, and he would fare better than most.

Pavel looked down at his phone, which was lying on the car seat next to him. His contractor back in America had called a couple hours back and stated that the Pakistani scientist was a ghost. It seemed odd to Pavel that someone could hide that well, even in a city as big as Chicago. Pavel had assumed that the man made his way out of town. Running made very good sense, especially in these circumstances. Why would anyone in their right mind hang around an area where people were trying to kill them? Still, the man had ghosted out very well. That, too, was odd. Pavel had asked his contractor to widen the search and track him till he was found.

It was the running and the ghosting of the Pakistani that had given Pavel a second idea of how to handle the pending problem with Vakar. As he had said, maybe the Americans would need a body. Pavel thought that maybe they would be satisfied with a body other than his. The plan was still loose, but it was coming together fast.

Thinking better about everything that was going to happen, he picked up his phone and stuffed it in his jacket pocket. He looked out the windscreen of the auto and noticed the door to the Imbiss open.

Pavel started up the faded blue Opel Omega. It was boxy and smelled like cats, but it was also stolen. The man named Klaus had turned and made it about ten meters down Ohechaussee when Pavel came streaking across the intersection with AM Sood and ran the Opel up on the sidewalk. The Opel's front bumper struck Klaus just below the knee with a thunderous crack, and Klaus' body pendulumed upward from the impact. The port man had no time to react as his head slammed into the passenger side of the windscreen. If Pavel had been paying attention, it would have appeared as if someone had thrown a watermelon at the sidewalk. The massive kinetic energy of the impact shattered Klaus' skull upon impact. Blood exploded across the now spider-webbed windscreen in such a way that made the assassin know his prey was dead. He was quite sure that the man literally never knew what hit him.

Pavel slammed the breaks of the Opel down fully as the man's broken body slid off the side of the car, landing on the curb with the flop of a dead fish. He dropped the car into reverse and pulled back far enough to inspect the scene. The port man Klaus had been reduced to a twisted, lifeless mess. Job done. Surveying the mirrors, Pavel could tell that eyes were gathering in windows on both sides of the Strasse. He dropped the car back into drive and sped off down the 422, back toward the airport.

Pavel was sure that the polizei would give some type of chase. He also knew that they would find the car. But, he was certain that he would be long gone by then. He had been wearing a dark-hooded jacket with a ball cap and dark glasses. He was indescribable, except in the broadest of terms. He looked like a thousand other souls. He would wipe down the car, so there would be no prints to be found. And he wouldn't dump the car at the airport. The Omega would eventually be found at the bahnhof parking area.

Pavel had already researched the parkplatz at the bahnhof to make sure that it had no cameras. The train platform also had no cameras. It was a good spot. Pavel knew to always have the exit figured out before starting.

The East European assassin stuffed his jacket, ball cap, dark glasses, and leather driving gloves into a small backpack and pulled on a rumpled no-iron blazer. When he exited the train, a couple blocks from the Hamburg Airport's private charter terminals, he looked as anonymous as anyone else. Just another body trying to make it to the damned airport on time. He passed several uniformed polizei on the walk from the train to the terminal where his private jet was waiting. None of the men had given him a second look. His subterfuge was complete.

Pavel climbed the steps to the jet and smiled at the captain.

"We can head south whenever you are ready."

"Yes, sir. It will be about fifteen minutes before we can get runway clearance."

Pavel nodded to the captain and took a seat in one of the overstuffed leather chairs. It would only be a quick trip south to find the truck driver. The man should be at his home. That situation would solve itself as quickly as the port man's had. Then, he would deal with other matters. Pavel closed his eyes and exhaled. A quick nap might be nice, just to get rid of the Bitburger.

The nap turned out to be a little longer one than Pavel had planned on, and as he stirred in his seat, the jet was descending into Luxembourg-Findel Airport. The pilot landed the private plane and taxied over to its hangar. Pavel thanked the crew as he went through the doorway. He found his Peugeot 407 coupe right where he had left it. He gave the auto a quick inspection to appease his paranoia and jumped in.

In a well-traveled route, Pavel headed north past the Grand Ducal Golf Club, and hopped onto the E44 east toward the German border. He followed the route toward Trier, and then continued east toward Nohfelden, and on into Kaiserslautern. It was a good day for a drive through the south of the Rhineland and the time passed quickly. Dusk was just coming to the land as Pavel rolled the Peugeot to a stop in a parkplatz about a block from the truck driver's home.

Pavel climbed out of the auto and inspected the area. It had the same suburban feel that the last town had. It was quiet streets and well-kept homes. The quiet nature of the place made him pleased. It would make it easier to do what he was here to do.

Pavel decided to get the lay of the land first. He left the auto and set out to take a stroll about town. The assassin walked a casual two block grid around the truck driver's apartment and surveyed the state of things. All of the directions seemed similar in appearance and makeup. The area to the north had a bit more traffic, due, he suspected, to the intersection-located gasthaus and petrol station. Not bothering to get the map on his phone, he suspected that the direct route to the autobahn was past the petrol station. Petrol stations were usually stationed in traffic corridors.

Pavel made his way back to the truck driver's apartment, and wandered up to the front door as if he were looking for a specific address. He made it about two meters from the front door before noticing the polizei bulletin taped to the door. Instantly, Pavel's sense of dread started to rise. He stopped and inspected the bulletin, attempting to be as unconcerned as possible. His command of the written language was not as good as his spoken German and he had to work on the text for a minute before things started to become clear.

There had been a murder and robbery in the building. All citizens were instructed to be extra vigilant in their activities until the suspected criminals were arrested. Pavel inspected the form further and found what he had feared. The apartment unit where the trouble had occurred was the same unit that he was currently headed to.

Everything in Pavel's being told him to turn and make his way back down the street. Something was wrong with the whole situation. Someone had already been to the truck driver's home and apparently taken care of business. He should go, before anyone saw an unfamiliar face in the area and took a picture of him on some damned camera phone. The problem was, he couldn't leave. He needed to know what happened to the man.

Pavel opened the door and stepped inside. The building's interior space was quiet and properly kept. It appeared as if all was well. Pavel ascended the stairs deliberately and pulled up at the third floor landing. The hallway was quiet and no one seemed to be coming or going. The door to the truck driver's apartment was obvious down the hallway. Yellow police tape crisscrossed it from top to bottom.

The Eastern-European hitman proceeded to the door and gave it a quick inspection. It looked in good repair, but also well used. The natural gap between the door and the frame was a sign of a sloppy locking bolt. Pavel pulled a small blade from his pocket and snapped it open with his thumb. Inserting it into the jamb, it took only a small twist of his wrist to pop the bolt free from its holder. Pushing the door opened, he stepped through the tape and closed the door behind him. He paused a moment to check for noise, but there was none. Still unobserved, he set about inspecting the crime scene.

From the bedroom, to the kitchen, to the living room, it all looked like a toss-and-go. Someone had apparently robbed the place and ran. But, still, they hadn't. The kitchen was where the real story was. Pavel quickly inspected the forensic labeling and tape in the kitchen and was sure that this was no robbery gone wrong. Besides, who would want to rob this poor slob? He was a truck driver. He represented no real opportunity. The wealthy-looking homes could be found only a couple blocks from here. There was nothing to draw anyone this way.

Pavel visually examined the straightback chair, with the two slug holes through its back. He could also see the slug holes in the wall behind the chair. He could see the rub marks on the chair's arms and legs, where some type of cordage had been wrapped. Someone had been tied to the chair and shot. From the look of the blood spray on the floor, they had obviously also been beaten. Nope, this was no robbery gone wrong. Pavel suspected that if the polizei had an inventory of the apartment, they would find that nothing was missing.

Pavel stood in the kitchen doorway and took in the scene for several more minutes. It took him that long to place the lingering smell. The smell of vinegar was still evident in the space. Pavel locked onto the smell fully, and turned to go.

Attempting to stay as natural as possible, he checked for noise at the door and then made his way back out of the apartment. He continued on until he was free of the building. Exiting the building, he had turned in the opposite direction of the parkplatz and wandered up the wide sidewalk. He stopped at a Tobac on the corner and picked up a pack of smokes. He also grabbed a copy of the local newspaper. The picture of the crime scene was still splashed across the front page, and the shop keeper sighed as it hit the counter. Pavel exchanged a bit of small talk and collected his things to continue his evening stroll about town.

After a good twenty minutes of meandering in a wide arc around the neighborhood, Pavel returned to his Peugeot. He fired up the engine and pointed the car back toward the autobahn. Feeling confident that he had not been followed, he grabbed his phone and dialed a number from memory. It rang three times.

"It's Pavel. We have a problem."

CHAPTER 29

Eight Hours to detonation.

At 4 a.m. in the Drake Hotel in Chicago, President Walker Jackson paced back and forth in the middle of the suite's living room. The dark hue under his eyes made it obvious he hadn't slept since the day before. He wasn't worried, per se, he just really wanted to know if he was going to die or not. His conversation with the NEST field agent had left him both worried and reassured. They had apparently already found and handled one of the warheads. It was the other one that was currently bothering him. That particular warhead wasn't terribly far away.

There was little time to do what needed doing, for both him and the NEST people. He thought that maybe he should throw off all of the secrecy and allocate a whole battalion of men to the search. He knew that that wasn't the right course of action. He knew that the group working the nuke problem was the best of the best at what they did. He knew that more people would just muck things up. He just hated waiting. Waiting had never been conducive to a positive outcome. It just never had been. The president was, by his very nature, a doer.

A soft knock came to the outer door. The door opened and Pat Sommers came into the room. He surveyed the room with a quick and thorough efficiency. The president gave him a quick inspection, also. His suit was crisp. His ear piece was as well-hidden, as was his shoulder holster. The suspicion of a long shift was less well-hidden by the Secret Service man.

"Good morning, Mr. President. The threshold lights to the suite were on, so I figured I'd take a quick survey."

"Good morning, Pat. How is everything in and around the Drake?"

"Quiet as a church mouse."

"Well, that's good news. You wouldn't happen to know how things are progressing to the south of us, would you?"

The two men looked hard at each other for a moment. The president was being rhetorical. The Secret Service man still didn't have a good answer for him.

"I'm sure that things are going as quickly as these things can go, sir."

"Always a calm voice in troubled times, aren't you Pat?"

"Well – the United States has the best two nuclear weapons specialists in the world. One is onsite and the other –"

"Yes. The other is streaking across the skies to get there."

"Actually, Dr. Hughes and Special Agent Donewoody just landed at Gary International again. Or, I assume they have, since they disappeared under the dead cell canopy."

"Well, that is something, in and of itself. Let's hope she's as fast with the second one as she was with the first."

"That would be nice, but I think the second will take more work. They had help with the first one."

"Yes, the change-of-heart Pakistani scientist. Kind of makes me not want to kill him. Kind of, but that wouldn't send a very good message, would it?"

"Probably not, sir. But I say we let the field ops guys make the sticky field decisions."

"Sound advice, Pat. As always."

"Sir, if I might ask a few questions outside of my pay grade?"

"Have I talked to the other representatives?"

"Yes, sir."

The president gave his head of personal security an understanding smile. He was *Group*, after all. He had a right to all the information that was available.

"I talked to the Canadian prime minister last night during the hockey game, and the British P.M. over the crypto while on Air Force One. The

Brits aren't talking to anyone. The Canadians are obviously as concerned as we are. It's gonna get them pretty hard, if it detonates. Anyway, they aren't talking, either."

"That's comforting. It can be hard to live in the shadows of another nation, at times."

"Very true. As for Japan, they understand the consequences better than anyone. They're completely onboard. I haven't talked to the Russian president yet. I am going to do that at breakfast. Needless to say, that needs to be a face-to-face talk."

"Agreed. They will be dealing with a lot of pointed questions and political fallout if there is need for a radiation survey."

Pat Sommers thought for a second and smiled.

"The joke was unintentional, Mr. President."

"No worries, Pat. It was well-placed."

"Is there any status update on the arrival of the European G8 members?"

"They are apparently handling some last-minute EU business, but will be along before the summit starts."

Pat Sommers looked at his boss with suspicion.

"I know, Pat. That is exactly what I thought. Ivan Vakar said they would all be a little tardy."

"I don't know about Vakar. He's –"

"Shifty. Untrustworthy. Always seeming to have an alternate agenda."

"Exactly."

"I know. I think the exact same thing. But he is the voice of the European Union. You still think he's the Vakar in Vakar Arms?"

"We haven't completely ruled it out, sir. We don't think so, but there is still a closed-door, black-bag rummage job attempting to confirm that."

"Not that I want to know right now, but if he is?"

"The *Group* has several deniable options available."

"I'm constantly glad you're on our side, Pat."

The Secret Service man nodded without smiling.

"Mr. President, I've taken up enough of your time. I'll head back to my duties. Have a good day, sir."

"Stay safe, Pat."

The Secret Service man nodded and turned for the door. The President turned to look out the windows at the Chicago skyline, which was still shrouded in semi-darkness. Pat Sommers had made it to the door when the president spoke.

"Pat."

"Mr. President?"

"Dr. Hughes, and her team – they are going to handle that second nuke, aren't they?"

"Yes, Mr. President. Yes, they are."

Pat Sommers didn't look back at his boss, but continued on through the door. He turned in the hallway and headed off to make an inspection of the perimeter. The President of the United States of America looked out at the skyline and wondered if the great city of Chicago would exist in another eight hours. Everything around him seemed so permanent. It was starting to seem as if that was just a grand illusion.

A mere four hours after that thought, President Jackson made his way out of the armored limo that was his natural mode of conveyance and into the private executive entrance to the large convention center stately situated on the shore of Lake Michigan. He looked over at the Russian president's car, which was also parked in the high-security basement parking area. He was happy that the Russian was a prompt man. It would give him more time to digest the bad news that was coming.

President Jackson and his security detail made their way up the stairs and through the pre-checked hallways to a posh dining lounge on the third floor of the complex. An even mix of Russian and American security staff were passed along the way. A few British MI5 chaps were noticed in the mix, doing scouting for the British PM's later arrival. President Jackson pulled up to a stop outside the lounge's double doors and turned to his head of security.

"I'm gonna do this one alone, Pat."

"Yes, Mr. President. We'll be standing by."

The president nodded a good solid concurrence and turned back to the door. The big Russian in front of him smiled and opened one of the heavy wooden doors. President Jackson strode in with a purposeful gate that said he owned the room, and smiled at the Russian president. The

Russian president, for his part, was sitting at a table just off center of the room, fanning a cup of coffee.

"Demetri, so happy you could make the trip. You look well. I'm glad things in the East are agreeing with you."

"And you, Walker. Both your weather and hospitality are exceptional, as always."

The American president took a seat at the table with the Russian president and poured himself a cup of coffee from the carafe on the table. The heavy steam that came from the insulated container explained why the Russian was fanning his cup.

"Now that the pleasantries are out of the way, dismiss your staff. The rest of this conversation is one that *YOU* are definitely going to want to keep private."

The Russian president stared at the American president's serious expression, and then nodded.

"ВСе ИЗ!"

The Russian staff, to a man, turned and headed for the door. Mere moments later, the two most powerful men in the world were alone, sitting quietly in the middle of an empty dining room.

"All right, Walker, get to it."

"The direct version. An unknown terrorist or terrorist group, funded a group called Vakar Arms to purchase two Russian nuclear warheads."

The Russian president's eyes narrowed, but he said nothing.

"The Vakar Arms people also bought a couple of Pakistani nuclear scientists from a man called *The Arab* to prime the warheads. The active devices were stuffed into a pair of shipping containers and shipped out of the Port of Hamburg for the Port of Chicago."

The Russian president exhaled and took a sip of his coffee.

"How long ago?"

"Approximately four days. They were split up upon arrival. One was sent to St. Louis. That package has been located and disabled. Since the nuke is yours, we'll be happy to give it back to you if you want."

"I would be much happier if it just disappeared."

"I understand. Consider it done."

"And the second nuclear weapon?"

"Currently, as far as I know, it is somewhere in a pile of shipping containers in the Port of Chicago. That is the reason for the dead cell zone south of here."

"And its status?"

"Live, otherwise unknown. We suspect it is planned for detonation to coincide with the beginning of the G8 Summit. Basically, noon."

"And your plan?" President Demetri Zakharov had gotten steadily paler as the conversation had progressed, but he kept his Russian cool.

"We have the world's two best bomb technicians in the Port of Chicago as we speak. They are going to do what they do. WE are going to act like none of it is happening and continue on with the summit, as if it were any other day."

"Really?"

"It's suck-it-up time, Mr. President. There are times when you have to pay for being powerful. This is one of those times."

The Russian president, a man not averse to using extreme measures to solve problems, thought deeply for a moment and then nodded.

"Who else knows?"

"You, me, the Japanese P.M., the Canadian P.M., and the British P.M. They are all here now, so they deserved to know the stakes. None of the others are going to utter a word. Then there is a very small and select response team, and the terrorists."

"What about the others?"

"The other G8 members?"

"Yes."

"As of right now, no. They all seem to be *delayed* by some sort of mysterious business that Ivan Vakar has going at the EU."

The Russian president thought for a moment.

"That's interesting timing?"

"Agreed. We also find it curious. Though Mr. Vakar did assure me in a phone call that they would all be along before things started."

"Do you think that Vakar and these arms people are the same?"

"It would explain where the funding came from. So far, the spooks can't confirm it. They are saying it's all a series of very strong coincidences."

"I don't believe in coincidences."

"Neither do I. The intelligence people have a black-bag operation going on as we speak."

"So, assuming we don't die today, what's next Walker?"

"Collectively, we are going to act like it never happened. Nobody gains from chaos. Separately, I plan on finding and eliminating whoever is responsible. Preferably in a most painful manner."

The Russian president scratched his chin, which was a sign that he was semi-comfortable with the plan. They both took a drink of the coffee and looked at each other.

"Maybe, you should out-source the cleanup. No offense Walker, but American intelligence security isn't what it used to be. Neither of us really want this sort of thing in the world press."

The Russian president looked at the American president thoughtfully. They both had seen bad security issues in the past decades, and felt the pain from it. He considered that the American president's expression was as resolute as he had ever seen it.

"Don't worry, Demetri. We plan on handling this *the old way.*"

The Russian president smiled a very cold smile.

"In that case, when the time comes, if Russian Intelligence can assist you, the old phone lines are still in good repair."

"I appreciate that."

The two world leaders nodded at each other in understanding that there were still ways to get things accomplished in an overly connected world. Things that would never come to light.

"Now, you hungry? I hear the omelets in this place are excellent."

CHAPTER 30

The two F/A-18 Hornets that Kristin and Ben Donewoody had been using as their primary means of travel were receiving massive radio chatter from Midway tower as they descended toward the outer markers of the Gary International Airport. The chatter stemmed from the fact that they were still traveling at a respectable Mach 1.5 when they appeared on Midway's radar. The blast of radio traffic was met with a single response; *FLYNET is in effect and NEST will be landing in Gary.* And that, as they say, was that.

Kristin knew that any fast moving jet, headed straight for the G8 Summit, would definitely freak people out. She also knew that either Lou or the president would make the problem go away. And, if for some reason they failed at the port, well then it didn't really matter.

The pilots, who must have been ex-Navy, performed two of the best carrier landings Kristin had ever experienced. They rolled up a negligible section of runway before bringing the attack aircraft to a stop and pivoting them on a dime toward a taxiway. The two jets rolled back down the taxiway and pulled to a stop next to the patiently waiting C17B Globemaster.

As the cockpit canopies raised to the open position, Kristin took in the sight of her next transport and raised a single eyebrow. Warmed up and idling next to the Globemaster was a jet black, FBI issue, A/MX-6X mission enhanced "Little Bird" helicopter. The Boeing designed gunship was a favorite choice of Hollywood for the obligatory air battle sequences. Its size and external gun pods made it perfect for the Hollywood set.

The fact that it was, by design, a two-seat aircraft was not perfect for this particular situation.

Kristin climbed down the side of the Hornet's airframe and gave the pilot a large and extra-long hug to say thank you. Ben shook hands with his pilot. The two turned and ran over to the helicopter. Ben gave the pilot a big shrug as they both inspected the single seat. The pilot cupped his hands around his mouth to project his voice out over the rotor wash.

"I was the only available bird outside the dead zone. They only said one passenger, ma'am."

Kristin made a face and then slapped Ben on the shoulder. He jumped into the empty seat and then Kristin jumped in on his lap. A ground man attached to the C17B crew tossed in her backpack and gave the pilot a thumbs-up while retreating from the rotor wash. Kristin cupped her hands around her mouth the same way the pilot had and looked at the ready man holding onto the sticks.

"Compensate."

Without much hesitation, the pilot ramped up the rotor speed and the helicopter lifted off the runway apron with a sideways lurch. Their pilot trimmed the rotors all the way over to compensate for the shift in center of gravity and headed north toward the port. Off to the east, a slim line of light slowly rose over Lake Michigan.

Both Kristin and Ben were impressed with the way the FBI man adjusted his mission and moved on. Kristin assumed from the no-nonsense manner that he was ex-military. Mainly because that's the way ex-military men were. The mission was whatever it was at that moment, not what was written on some piece of paper.

The helicopter screamed north, operating just at the edge of its flight envelope, and came in hot and fast over the Port of Chicago. As they streaked over the NEST crew operating on the ground, they could instantly tell that things were not going very well. The pilot flared the machine and made a hard skid landing about 10 feet off the rotors of the stationary NEST helicopter. Kristin jumped out, putting extra energy into her launch so she could clear the helo's gun pods, and landed heels down on the tarmac. Ben jumped down and turned to face the pilot. They exchanged a thumbs up and the FBI pilot began to idle down the rotors. Warrant

Officer Glen Adams climbed out of his pilot seat and came over to inspect the newly arrived helicopter. He was starting to circle the machine with an ever-widening smile as Kristin and Ben headed off toward the group out in the container stacks.

The sprint out to where the original two containers were located took half the time that it had the first time they had done it. When they turned the corner on container row and headed down the lane that held their targets, the scene that met them was chaos. Numerous portable light plants had been set up to broadcast light onto the night work area. In the gloom of morning, they were just starting to become redundant. The light of day showed that there were wooden machine crates scattered everywhere. About two-thirds of the crates were spray painted with a large orange X, to indicate that they had been checked and cleared.

Amanda Fields was in the process of going over a large wooden crate with a portable imaging device similar to a portable X-ray machine. She was moving over the crate with slow and deft precision. Watching Amanda helped the scene slowly coalesce in Kristin's mind from one of chaos to one of individuals performing specific tasks.

A scraping and grunting sound came from the door of the red shipping container and two dock hands emerged, along with Brian Johnson, pulling a pallet jack holding a large wooden crate. She noticed a two-inch black X in the upper right corner of the crate, signifying that Jim Bonner had noticed *something interesting* while doing the primary inspection. The crate was dragged over to a much smaller pile, where Brian Smith was giving the crates a gentle, and much more thorough, second inspection. Kristin watched the scene from the edge of the container row for a good minute to take it all in.

"They're working on the wrong container."

Ben Donewoody nodded in agreement. As a member of the FBI's Hazardous Device Operations Section, and sometimes instructor at the school, he was a natural at sizing up explosive situations. He had seen this ruse many times over his career. Some of them had almost gotten him killed.

"I agree. It sure doesn't look like the situation we just left in St. Louis."

Kristin waded into the situation at a moderate, but cadenced, pace. The numerous bomb dogs scattered about the stacks of boxes instantly noticed the cadenced pace, but did not respond to it. The deliberate cadenced pace that all members of the NEST operation's team utilized on site was meant to portray calm to those around them. They all knew that panicked people ran, and calm people walked. Besides, no one could outrun a nuclear blast. For those two reasons, there was no reason to run on an active bomb site. Cadenced pacing was the professional standard.

Kristin walked to the door of the red container with Ben at her four o'clock. Reaching the opening, she found Jim Bonner on all fours inspecting the intersection of two crates. It seemed that he was looking for booby traps and pressure plates. Kristin stepped slowly into the container and approached Jim's field of view. Knowing she was where he could make out her image, she paused. The second-in-command finished his inspection and rocked back onto his knees.

"Jim, have you found anything that makes you sure you're in the right container?"

Kristin's voice was measured, but direct. Everyone in the group responded better to direct tones. Jim turned to look at Kristin and wiped the sweat from his forehead.

"Negative. Nothing for certain."

"I think that's because you're in the wrong container."

"Why?"

"Because this looks nothing like the one that we unloaded down in St. Louis. That container was full of bagged kitty litter, save for a big-ass Russian nuke buried in the middle. It was also bright green."

Jim Bonner drew a measured breath and stood. The two walked out of the container and looked up at the top of the adjacent stack of containers.

"That color green?"

"Yup. That exact color green."

"Bastards."

Kristin nodded in agreement and took a hard look around the scene. The terrorists had picked one hell of a decoy. Jim looked at Kristin with his all-business look.

"Describe the package."

Kristin took another look around at all the crate scattered down the container row.

"The container was clean, and in good repair. Interior wise, it was also clean, except for the package. No boobytraps or alternative devices. The surrounding space was completely filled with uniformly packed bags of kitty litter. The kitty litter fully encased the package."

Jim Bonner looked around and nodded his head.

"No secondary triggers. What was the primary trigger?"

"U.S. military spec cellular detonator attached to a high-gain antenna. The antenna was mounted to the inside top of the container."

"Cellular-only detonator?"

"Yes, sir. Cellular-only detonator."

"How good was the antenna? Could someone hit it with a focused burst?"

"Punch a hole through the dead-cell? They would need to be close. And it would need to be a fully focused microwave beam, or some such thing. Seriously, why would they want to? Makes more sense that they never planned on the packages being discovered."

"Still?"

"Okay, Jim. Fine. Hook a microwave burst transmitter to an oscilloscope so you can modulate a single frequency, and feed it to a large-diameter focused-field cone. That would punch a working hole in the net. It would probably also fry all of our gear."

Jim Bonner scratched his chin for a moment.

"It does sound like a bit much. But finding a fully functioning nuke is also a bit much."

"I say we switch packages."

"Are you sure, Kristin?"

"Give me thirty seconds to check one more thing."

Kristin dropped her pack on the ground and moved in between the two stacks of containers. Nimble like a cat, the NEST field leader scaled the tower of metal containers. Reaching the top, she placed her back square against one container and began inspecting the shiny green container before her. Upon initial inspection, it looked the same as any other in the stacks. She moved slowly down the side of the container until, at the other end next to the door framing, she came to what she was looking for. In the corner, same location as the St. Louis package, was a small receptacle box covered by an eight screw inspection cover. Kristin smiled at the metal cover plate and began to make her way back down to the ground. She went to her backpack, where she retrieved a screwdriver and some pliers.

"Same box, bomb girl?" Ben Donewoody watched her, half sure.

"Sure looks that way. I'm gonna pull the cover and see if the light is red or green before saying for sure."

Jim Bonner could tell he was a little out of the loop, but he said nothing. Kristin scampered back up the stack of shipping containers and wedged herself into a good spot to do her work. With deft, but cautious precision she removed the screws, one by one. Starting at the upper left corner, she extracted the screws one at a time. Proceeding to the right, she worked her way clockwise around the face plate. The screws were extracted and placed into her pocket. Knowing that the St. Louis face plate was smooth, she backed off pressure on the last screw, but didn't extract it. She sat her screwdriver down on the container edge and slowly rotated the face plate of the box out of the way. The internal configuration of the box was the same as the St. Louis device, except this time she was looking at a glowing green LED.

Dr. Kristin Hughes expelled a half-exasperated, half-excited breath and retrieved her screwdriver. She rotated the cover plate to its original position and tightened the screw. She replaced a screw in the opposing corner to hold the plate secure. Feeling it would make its way to the ground okay, she pocketed the screwdriver and descended to the ground. This time, her two counterparts both held expectant expressions.

"Well, that's the second package. The voicemail was spot on. This one is still live. Big bright green light in the box."

"OK, that definitely sucks," Ben said without levity.

"Well, what do you think, boss? You're already geared up." Jim Bonner was the type of individual that had no ego to bruise. He was the top of the heap. There was only one person who was better, and she was standing right in front of him.

"I say we clear all of this mess out of the way as fast as we can. Then we set that container down on the ground and go to work on it."

"Sounds good."

"Collect your tools and I'll start clearing the junk."

"Roger that."

Jim Bonner headed back into the red shipping container to collect his things. Kristin drew a deep breath and spoke in a loud and clear voice.

"All NEST personnel. Full stop. We are switching containers. Stop what you're doing and clear your work area so we can move the other container to the ground."

Without objection, all members of the NEST team stopped what they were doing and began to assemble their tool kits. With rapid precision, all tools and equipment were mustered and laid out for inventory. All items accounted for, several men disappeared to retrieve pallet jacks and dolly equipment to start moving the crates. One of the dock hands helping the crew turned and ran off in a different direction.

The bomb disposal men returned with a couple of pallet jacks and began to position them under the bigger crates. One by one, the larger crates on the outside of the piles slowly began to move off, out of the way. Kristin knew that if the second nuke was like the first, she could disarm it fairly quickly. Still, she wasn't sure that they had time to move at the glacially slow pace of the pallet jacks.

The crew returned with the pallet jacks to get the next set of boxes, when around the corner of the container row the port hand reappeared driving a rusted-out old pickup truck with a snow plow affixed to the front. The man lowered the snow plow to the ground and moved ahead slowly until he was against the crate pile. He stomped on the gas pedal, black smoke poured from the tail pipe, and the whole pile of crates began to slide down the container row. Two or three quick passes later and the port man had cleared out about half of the container row. He pulled the rattling truck up, out of the way, and killed the engine. Jumping from the pickup truck, he jogged over to the mobile crawler crane and began to ascend the ladder to the operator's cab. Kristin turned and looked at Ben and Jim.

"When this is over Ben, buy them a new truck!"

"Definitely."

With an everyday precision, the port man, who had now universally become known as Javier, rolled the mobile crane over to the row and secured the green container. The cargo container was lifted, maneuvered, and lowered to the ground without so much as a bump along the way. Javier detached from the cargo container and rolled the mobile crane back where it had been parked. He scampered down the ladder and jogged back to where the NEST crew was waiting. Kristin smiled at Javier with an illumination that could not have been faked.

"That was outstanding. Good thinking."

"We get busted containers in here all the time. It's the best way to clean up the mess."

Brian Smith slapped Javier on the back and nodded his head in approval.

"Okay, people," Kristin said with authority, "let's get to business."

CHAPTER 31

Sitting on a rooftop on the west side of Mackinaw Avenue, watching the on-goings at the port through a high power spotting scope, Alex Leka started to get anxious. It appeared from the activity in the container area that the Americans had figured out where the nuclear device was. They were earlier than planned. That was no good.

Ivan Vakar had known that there was a chance the Americans would not be so easily faked by his ruse. If any cracks were found in his plan, it would quickly come unraveled. To keep it from doing so, certain extra precautions had been taken. The biggest one of those precautions was Alex Leka.

Alex Leka, or John Smith, according to his French passport, was an Eastern European veteran of the genocides that tore apart the old Soviet bloc. He was educated, smart, savvy, brutal, and without a moral compass. Fortunately for Ivan Vakar, he was also dying. Advanced pancreatic cancer and a rare form of blood cancer gave the man mere weeks left on earth. This lack of a future had made Alex very amenable to Ivan Vakar's request.

The bargain was as such. Ivan Vakar showered Alex Leka with cash so he might live his remaining months in whatever fashion he so chose. When done, Leka made his way to Chicago to babysit the nuke. He was to observe the run up to detonation, and if the Americans got too close, take the steps to detonate the device himself.

Sure, the nuclear device was supposed to go off at the start of the G8 Summit, but did it really matter if it went off a couple hours early? Not as far as Vakar was concerned. What mattered was that it went off. Alex Leka was there to make sure that happened. True, he was literally going to blow himself up, but his death was inevitable. He was a dead man either way things played out. It seemed that causing a little chaos on the way out the door sat good with Alex.

To the greater plan, it would be fine with Vakar if either outcome transpired. He was actually planning on setting off the two warheads if Adrian was unable to do it on time. The trail was supposed to lead back to Adrian, and the Americans would get their man. If Alex Leka needed to detonate them early, then all signs of his involvement would be erased in the blast. If all else failed, Ivan Vakar himself was the third option. He would deal with that if it came to be. The bombs would go off, whether the timeline was accelerated or not. And if Alex ended up pushing the button, all of the breadcrumbs from the sale of the weapons and the acquisition of manpower still led back to Adrian. Ivan Vakar won, one way or another.

Alex Leka watched the men and women down at the port complex moving crates out of the way so they could clear a space. A man had run off and retrieved a truck with a plow in its front. He was pushing stacks of crates out of the way in such a way as had not been done before.

A young woman with blond hair stood center stage pointing at the green shipping container on top of the stack and talking to the truck driver. The intriguing Dr. Kristin Hughes, he assumed. She was pretty. If he had more time, and was still back in Serbia, he might consider binding her to a bedframe. Sadly, this was business and the doctor seemed to be doing hers. The truck driver moved off and came back with a mobile container crane. That was the sign to Alex that he needed to get moving. The operator grappled onto the container and sat it on the ground without any real shaking or banging.

Alex Leka stood and walked back to the doorway which led down off the building's roof. Several military grade shipping containers had been stacked next to the stairwell wall. He reached down and retrieved a green box, approximately one-foot cubed, and sat it on the adjacent cement block ledge. Unsnapping a half-dozen twist lock closures, he removed the box top and punched the power button inside it. He pressed scan and watched the meter cycle through its preset series of frequencies. The meter in the middle of the cluster of buttons and knobs didn't as much as twitch as the numerous frequencies were scanned. A quick look at the cellphone sitting in the box next to the meter showed no bars and no signal. Alex Leka walked back to the spotting scope and peered down at the team's commo truck. Whatever equipment set they were running out of the back of the black Ford pickup truck, it was very good. The American dead cell zone around the port was complete. No one was going to remote detonate the nuclear device while they were on site. Alex had assumed that this would be the case. Fortunately for Alex, all of this nonsense was taking place in Chicago. He really couldn't have asked for a better location to operate than Chicago.

Alex Leka knew that once you stripped away all of the tourist hoopla, Chicago was actually one of the most violent cities in America. It was definitely the deadliest. The deep-seated crime and corruption in Chicago made places like Beirut and Tel Aviv look pretty provincial.

Alex knew some people that knew some people that made getting weapons and other restricted items rather simple. He had established some contacts upon arrival, and procured the items he had wanted within days. Graft, corruption, and the liberal application of money made anything possible.

He looked through the spotting scope and watched Hughes give some type of pep talk to the group assembled around her. He pulled a pack of cigarettes out of his shirt pocket and lit up a smoke. He pulled a long drag off of the American smoke and inhaled it all the way deep into the bottom of his lungs. The American cigarette was milder than the European ones he was used to, but he still found the taste to be enjoyable. He rolled the cigarette around in his fingers as he exhaled. He placed it to his lips and repeated the process a second time. It felt like this cigarette was going to be Alex Leka's last. He savored the smoke as he exhaled a second time. For a last smoke, it was a good smoke. He thought that a bottle of beer would be nice, but that was not going to happen. Besides, the alcohol made his pancreas ache in a deep and painful way. He had actually sworn off alcohol right after the cancer prognosis just because of this.

Expelling another lungful of smoke, Alex Leka looked down at the group of American personnel and then shifted his gaze over to the commo truck. From the way the truck and other vehicles and helicopters were spread out across the parking area, he considered that he may have a chance at maximum damage if done correctly. Of course, all he really needed was a good thirty seconds of clear cellphone signal and it would all be academic.

It appeared through the high power scope that the young doctor had finished with her pep-talk. Her people started moving off in various directions. That seemed the sign that it was time to go for Alex Leka. Alex flicked his half-smoked cigarette across the flat rooftop and turned back to the stack of military crates.

Alex flipped the releases on the top crate one by one, moving in a star-shaped path around the container, until all the latches were cleared. He pressed the bright red detent button on its side to equalize the pressure inside and outside of the seal and then raised the lid. Alex looked into the foam packed fiberglass container and smiled. Reaching in, he retrieved a FGM-148 Javelin anti-tank missile from its foam cradle and hoisted it onto his shoulder. Walking back to the edge of the rooftop, he stood next to the spotting scope and looked down on the port action. He flipped switches and the electronics of the weapon came to life. Alex focused the missile's guidance system on the communication truck until the target locked in and the onboard infrared targeting system signaled an image lock by bracketing the truck in a red LED box.

Feeling comfortable with the status of the weapon system and its target lock, Alex Leka took a deep, slow breath and fingered the activation trigger. The rocket ejected from the end of the launch tube in what was known as a soft launch. It slid through the air cleanly for a proper distance before the main solid rocket motor fired. Staying tuned on the pickup truck, the focal plane array on Raytheon's $250,000 weapons system kept the warhead locked on target.

Though the Javelin was designed as a fire-and-forget weapon and its seeker system located in the missile's transparent nose cone kept it locked on its designated target, Alex stayed with his eye to the view finder. He was at the outer limits of the missile's 2,500-meter range. He wanted to make sure that it hit what he had aimed it at. He wasn't actually worried. He had used the Javelin numerous times and it had always worked flawlessly. He was sure that this time would be no different.

The screaming missile dipped and weaved as it adjusted its angle of attack on its designated target. As it streaked through the air of South Chicago, Capt. David Lessor only had time enough to turn his head and wonder what the new sound was before the Javelin's warhead slammed into the body of the Ford pickup truck at a descending angle. Since the warhead on the Javelin was designed primarily as an anti-tank weapon, its detonation came from its kinetic impact with the target. The Ford pickup truck was not nearly as robust as tank armor, and the Javelin's warhead plowed straight through the pickup truck and impacted the asphalt beneath it before finally exploding.

Upon impact with the earth under the truck, the warhead on the FGM-148 Javelin anti-tank missile did exactly what it was designed to do. The initial shaped charge made a clearing pusher charge, actually designed to clear explosive tank armor, and the main shaped charge excavated a crater out of the parking area in a massive release of energy. Capt. Lessor no more than realized there was a problem before everything vaporized around him. The Ford pickup truck and a significant section of the parking area under it instantly transformed into super-hot ejecta. The chassis of the vehicle was launched a good fifteen feet straight up into the air in a ball of flaming debris before shredding from the force and turning into projectiles.

Due to the attack angle of the missile and the cratering effects of the warhead on the parking area, the exterior blast wave propagated itself in a semi-circular arc out away from the point of impact. To this end, the customs building took the worst of the secondary blast. The ejecta from the crater and the numerous pieces of pickup truck tore through the masonry block building with little resistance. The building basically collapsed in its own footprint, surely killing everyone inside.

The blast wave had blown both Glen Adams and his new FBI pilot companion, who were standing just outside of the blast area, off their feet. The tumble across the asphalt left both men in a scarred and bloody oozing mess. A large piece of metal from the pickup truck's cargo box slammed into the tail rotor assembly of the NEST helicopter. The impact all but tore the rear rotor off the helicopter.

Smoke rolled up all around and the raining debris and noise became unrecognizable. The sheer volume of the explosion left both pilots nearly deaf from the concussive force. The large walls of containers that formed the container rows kept the remainder of the group from the ferocity of the attack. As the shockwave washed over the container holding area, the crew working the device was shocked into inaction. As the rubble from the explosion began to rain down, all of the military individuals in the NEST group, and their FBI counterpart, turned and ran toward the source of the explosion. Clearing the end of the container row, they were ill prepared for the scene that greeted them. The entire area of the parking lot and the Customs building was reduced to smoldering rubble. Debris was scattered out completely in an arc from the point of impact. The Customs building was all but erased from the Earth. Some of the men and women spread out toward the fire extinguishing equipment that remained intact. Others ran toward their downed comrades who were attempting to regain their feet.

Alex Leka sat the launcher tube nose down on the rooftop and smiled in supreme satisfaction. The Javelin had been the right choice for the job. There was a warzone shot spread out before him that could replay on CNN for days. *Or, no, it wouldn't,* he thought. In a minute or two more, there wouldn't be any Chicago for CNN to take videos of. The thought of the mushroom cloud that the old Soviet era nuclear bomb was about to make made him smile even wider. It turned out that the chaos raining down at present was just a warmup for the main show.

Alex reached down and picked up the pack of American cigarettes that he had sat on the roof ledge. Another smoke would be enjoyable. He retrieved a smoke from the pack and the lighter from his pocket. Firing the end of the cigarette into a bright red cherry, he looked over the flame at the carnage down below. He thought it was kind of sad that no one else was going to see the sight he was seeing. It really was a thing of beauty.

Alex Leka turned and casually walked back to the stairwell door. Looking into his small equipment container, all of the meters on the signal tracking equipment were registering a full signal. Alex reached down and grabbed the cellphone. Looking at the display, he now saw four out of five signal bars and a 4G signal. It seemed that his little maneuver with the Javelin had returned cell service to the area, just as he had planned. Alex Leka smiled and took a long pull off his cigarette.

CHAPTER 32

R obert Dunn stood next to a tree in a little wooded section of Idar-Oberstein and watched the comings and goings of the small German town. Some 800 yards away and uphill from his current position, sat a rental apartment that was the occasional residence of one Adrian Beqiri. The international arms dealer sat on his patio and talked on his cellphone. He seemed quite content in the setting the quaint German town provided.

Dunn knew that Beqiri was Albanian, and that his actual residence was in the Fourth Arrondissement of Paris. The reports all said that Beqiri was an accomplished killer. He supposedly had a strong moral compass, but little resistance to violence. That probably explained the arms trade. He got to keep his hands clean and still facilitate the action. The idea seemed hypocritical to Dunn, but at the end of the day, who was he to throw stones. He was an assassin by trade.

Robert Dunn had been watching Adrian Beqiri for some time and he was as regimented as one would expect. He rose early and conducted business. He checked on different proceedings and conducted more business. Dinner was usually light, at a little place down the street from his apartment. Midday was exercise and evening was quiet. There had been one woman during his observations, but she appeared to be a stray. Beqiri seemed the untrusting bachelor type.

That last little bit of info was good news for Robert Dunn. He need have little worry of anybody walking in during the combat, or looking for him after it was over. He could secure the package and be on his way. Dunn really didn't like the idea of leaving the arms dealer alive. He really wanted to kill him. And, kill him slowly. Dunn's moral ambiguity had bottomless depths, but his patriotism was a different matter. He didn't like people taking shots at his homeland, especially with nuclear bombs.

The CIA assassin finished off a cup of service station style coffee he had procured from a shop down the street. He crushed the half-soaked-through paper cup in his hand and placed the crumpled cup in his suit jacket pocket. He had reached the interval in the day where his quarry was heading out to acquire his dinner. This seemed the best time to act.

Dunn turned and walked a short distance to a nondescript Volkswagen transporter van he had found parked at the bahnhof and jumped in. The old utility van was almost perfect for his operation tonight. It was as close to anonymous around these parts as anything could get. He fiddled with the wires under the dash and the old four cylinder engine came to life. It sputtered a touch and then smoothed itself out and ran without worry.

Dunn dropped the van into gear and pulled away from his parking spot. He made a long casual left, a right, then a left around town. Finally, the van came in below Adrian's terrace, where Robert Dunn pulled off the side of the road and activated his four-way blinkers. He stepped out of the van and opened the gas filler door. He removed the gas cap and let it hang free against the side of the van by its plastic strap. If the polizei happened by, they would naturally think he ran out of petrol and was off to find a service station. So, if they returned later and it was gone, they would think nothing of it. Of course, that was if they stopped at all. The small town was quiet and saw little patrolling by the local authorities.

Dunn grabbed a small duffle off the van's rear floor panel and closed the sliding side door. A quick look about showed that no one was watching, so he headed off up the hill toward the arms dealer's apartment. The hill was short, but steep, and made Dunn huff a little by the time he topped out. He stopped outside the apartment door to consider his exercise routine for a moment. Maybe it was time to get a little more active? Screw that, he had just jogged up an eighty degree incline. He was in good enough shape. Well, good enough for killing people anyway.

The standard lock package favored by European builders gave Dunn no fight, as he popped it and let himself into the apartment. A quick scouting session revealed no alarm pad to be disabled. Dunn considered this for a split second. Would an international arms dealer actually live in a place with no alarm system or armed guards? It seemed very unlikely that he would. Dunn took a second pass around, but still saw no alarm system to worry about. Apparently, the Albanian thought himself anonymous. That was good for Dunn and bad for Beqiri. A lack of paranoia seemed a poor quality for a man such as Beqiri. It might even be his undoing.

Robert Dunn sat his duffle down and relaxed to take in the layout of the small apartment when he finally saw it. The alarm system was there all right. Above the painting on the far wall, hung a small, wide-angle camera. It was looking right at him. The iris of the camera looked passive, but the ring around its edge made it look night-capable. Damn!

Had he tripped a passive sensor? He must have. He had wandered all around the front room. He had to have tripped the motion sensor for the camera. He walked up to where the camera was mounted and took a good hard look at it. The device seemed to be immobile, like it might have been shut off. It seemed odd to Dunn that his luck would be this good. At this point Robert Dunn stopped and made a complete inspection of the apartment. Three more such cameras and a laser tripwire were discovered in discreet locations. All of the cameras seemed to be non-functional. The laser tripwire appeared to be operating fine. He disabled the tripwire. He also disabled a passive door alarm found on the terrace door, before opening it fully. Then, he found a place in the darkness and settled in.

As expected, Robert Dunn didn't have to wait long before Adrian Beqiri returned home from his dinner. He opened and closed the main door. He locked the door and secured the bolt on the door for the evening. He was halfway to the kitchen when he noticed the terrace door was ajar. Beqiri paused. He removed a Sig Saur P323 stainless from under his suit jacket. The slide on the stainless .380 caliber handgun glinted in the light that was coming through the terrace door. Beqiri released the safety on the weapon and started slowly for the terrace door. He was now moving as quiet as a jungle cat, which made Robert Dunn reconsider his quarry. He needed to not screw up the takedown, or he was in for a major altercation.

Beqiri stepped through the door onto the terrace and took a good hard look around. Nothing seemed out of place. Maybe he had left the door open? No, he never left the door open. It was odd. Beqiri relaxed his jungle cat stance and lowered his weapon to the forty five degree position. As the handgun stopped moving, Dunn, who was crouched in the shadows of the apartment's coat closet, pulled the triggers on two M26C Tasers simultaneously. The probes from both weapons were all but at their fifteen-foot maximums when they slammed into Adrian Beqiri's back. Some 50,000 volts, times two, pulsed through the man's body at twenty pulses per second, and dropped the big Albanian immediately. Dunn let both weapons run through their five second cycle times before moving an inch. Adrian lay on the tiled floor of the terrace twitching, but otherwise completely incapacitated.

Robert Dunn slowly approached the big man and waited out of reach for a second or two, just to see if he was playing possum. Dunn bent down and retrieved the pistol from Beqiri's hand. He pocketed the weapon and gave the Taser leads a quick yank. He spooled up the leads and tossed the Tasers on top of the terrace table. Dunn removed an auto injector from his pocket and planted it against the back of Beqiri's neck with little concern. A small metallic click could be heard as the needle plunged into Beqiri's neck. The cocktail of chemicals that rushed into Adrian Beqiri was a company favorite for incapacitating people. It would put him down without doing any lasting damage. Dunn didn't want the cocktail doing the arms dealer any harm. He wanted to do that himself.

He placed the auto injector back in his pocket, retrieved a length of rope from the duffle, and set to work. Only moments later and Adrian Beqiri, international arms dealer for Vakar Arms, was trussed up like a Thanksgiving turkey and being lowered over the side of the terrace. Dunn let Adrian's body hit the hillside with a thud and start its rolling decent down the grass-covered hill toward the van. Loosing the rope from his grasp, he quickly retraced his steps and collected all of his gear back into the duffle. Walking back out onto the terrace, he tossed the duffle over the railing and jumped over after it. A quick tuck and roll and Robert Dunn was coming up on his feet at an angle to stabilize his movement on the eighty degree descending grade. He grabbed the duffle and scurried down the incline to find Adrian laying in pile by the edge of the ditch. Dunn reached down and secured a good grip on Adrian's restraints and unceremoniously dragged him to the Volkswagen van. In went Adrian, and then in went the duffle. The gas cap was replaced and the four-way signals shut off. Wires were twisted and the van quietly pulled away from the road's edge and out onto the quiet street.

Across the roadway in a darkened piece of woods, Pavel watched as his boss was ungraciously handled by the CIA man. He watched it all take place with a small smile on his face. He had thought that, under different circumstances, he might like to do work with this CIA man.

Robert Dunn drove the van back through the middle of town, as if he weren't in a hurry to get anywhere particular. The fake license plates on the van meant that the polizei may give him a passing glance, but they wouldn't bother stopping him. It was one of the first rules in escape and evasion in the spy business, slow is fast. Move as though you belong, and everyone will assume that you do.

Dunn threw a casual glance in his mirrors now and again to check the conditions of the traffic. It was quiet and light. Cars came and went behind him, but none stayed for a length of time that might be considered excessive.

The van rumbled through the streets of the town as easy as if it were any other day. Dunn turned the van north and kept going to the roundabout. Merging and exiting northeast, the van continued on until it passed by the local hospital. The van turned off onto a residential drive and continued. Pulling up at a four-way intersection, Dunn turned right onto Wolfsacker. About halfway down the residential street Dunn pulled into a single family home. He pressed a button on the van's remote control and the house's garage door started to open. The CIA assassin pulled the stolen van into the garage and let the door close behind him. Checking the street outside through one of the garage door's small widows, it seemed that his entrance had not made any of the neighbors notice.

Dunn had found the house while driving around the area when he first arrived. The look of it said that it might work well for his plans. The sign on the side of the house announced that it was for rent. He had managed to retrieve the keys for the property from the rental company's office that evening. Considering his timeline in the town, the house was chosen because it was disposable, just like the van.

Robert Dunn retrieved the immobile Adrian Beqiri from the van and dragged him into the living room. Adrian was placed in a straight back chair and a black pillowcase was pulled over his head. None of the restraints were loosened. Dunn didn't care if he was comfortable. In reality, his state was about to get a whole lot worse.

Dunn returned to the van and retrieved the duffle. Back in the living room he rifled around in the duffle until he came out with a second auto injector. This one was bright orange, differing from the original's olive drab color. It seemed evident to Dunn that green meant attack, and orange meant help. Most everything in the world that was orange was a safety device. In this particular case, it was also true of the injector. Where the green injector contained the disabling agent, the orange one he held in his hand contained the reversing agent.

The CIA assassin slammed the auto injector into the side of the arms dealer's neck and dumped the contents into his circulatory system. He exchanged the spent injector for a bottle of water that was in his duffle. Robert Dunn drank several swallows of water as he waited for Adrian's body to respond to the second drug cocktail. It didn't take long and the arms dealer was beginning to shuffle around in his chair.

"Mr. Beqiri, you would do good not to struggle too much, as you are restrained."

"Whoever you are, you're a dead man." The words came out in a groggy, almost untethered fashion.

"Idle threats will only prolong the conversation we are going to have. That won't be good for you."

"You should leave now. Before I see your face. Once I see your face, you're a dead man."

Robert Dunn stood and took one long step toward Adrian. When his foot landed on the floor, his fist landed squarely on Adrian's check bone. The big man's head rocked back and he grunted loudly, but didn't cry out. Dunn tilted his own head to one side, in semi-admiration, and returned to his chair.

"We have the entire night to have this conversation, Mr. Beqiri. Now, tell me about the nuclear weapons."

It was in the pause between Dunn talking and Beqiri returning an insult that Robert Dunn heard the pop of the front window breaking. At the same time as the pop became audible, Adrian's head exploded in a fountain of blood and brain.

The same sub-sonic 7.62x39 mm NATO round that punctured the window pane punched a hole in the side of Adrian's head and turned its contents into Jell-O. As the bullet exited, it extracted his brains out the other side. Adrian's head rocked fully to one side and a fountain of blood and grey matter sprayed from the exit tear in the pillowcase.

Robert Dunn dove from his own chair and landed prone on the living room carpet. He waited, flat as writing paper, on the carpet for a second shot to come screaming into the room. He listened for exterior noise of any kind. Maybe the sound of men approaching the house, or the sound of neighbors coming to life? The sound of polizei sirens in the distance? There was nothing. He stayed prone on the carpet by the kitchen for a good 30 seconds. No noises came at him from any direction.

It was now decision time. Was this a one shot affair, or was the shooter waiting him out. He looked over at Adrian, still sitting in his chair. A large pool of crimson was collecting on the white carpet under his chair. Only one shot. No one coming to open up the house. Seemed to be a conversation stopping deal. Time to move.

CIA assassin Robert Dunn low crawled over to the duffle and zipped it closed. Turning ninety degrees on his stomach, he low crawled out into the kitchen. He continued on to the garage. He quickly removed the fake plates from the van and stuffed them into the duffle. He stayed low and frog stepped to the door at the rear of the garage. Looking out into the night, he saw no movement in his direct field of view. Feeling fifty percent sure that the back of the house was safe, he stepped out into the dark. Wasting no time, he hustled off away from the scene as fast as his limited night vision would allow.

Parked partway down the residential block, where he could see both the front and rear of the house that the CIA man had pulled into, Pavel sat and watched as the CIA man scurried out the back door. He could tell from the punch that the CIA man had landed, his boss was being uncooperative. He figured it was time to end the conversation before something important came out instead.

Pavel pulled his eye from the scope on his 556xi assault rifle and flipped the selector switch back to the safe position. He placed the matte black weapon on the seat of the Mercedes sedan he was driving and stepped out of the auto. Walking casually along the quiet residential street, Pavel made his way around the back of the house to the rear garage door. He walked to the front of the van the CIA man had been using. Reaching under the front bumper, he retrieved a small metal gadget from its reverse side. He switched off the tracking device and pocketed it. Slowly, he made his way into the living room. Adrian's life force had expelled all the blood it was going to expel, and the pool under his chair was the size of a small pond. Pavel reached inside Adrian's jacket and removed a cellphone from his pocket. The device sat odd in his hand and upon inspection he realized that it had become damaged in Adrian's abduction. The big crack across its back plate and its spider webbed front screen meant it was probably unusable. Pavel shrugged and stuffed it in his pocket.

The new head of Vakar Arms backtracked out of the house the way he had come. Walking back to the car, he stuck his hand into the pocket of his trousers and pulled out four small batteries. He looked at the batteries from Adrian's security cameras, smiled, and tossed them sidearm down the street. They needed a body. They now had a body. Pavel climbed back into the sedan and drove off, as if he'd never been there.

CHAPTER 33

President Walker Jackson sat on a chaise lounge in the corner of the executive meeting room where the G8 Summit was scheduled to take place. He studied a few cards he had made the previous evening. Lately, he had been having short-term memory issues. It usually came on when he was stressed. He was stressed now. Anyway, he wasn't a young man anymore. At sixty one, he figured he was allowed a crutch or two.

The president's moment of quiet went as fast as it had come to him. The Japanese prime minister came through the decorated wooden double doors of the meeting room and walked straight to him. The prime minister had that upright and proper posture that Japanese dignitaries tend to have. Before the doors could close behind the Japanese delegate, the Russian head of security came in as well, but headed off toward Pat Sommers.

"Good morning Prime Minister Higashi." The president presented a warm tone out of courtesy.

"Mr. President, good morning."

"You seem to be on a mission this morning."

"I would like to question you regarding the large explosion at the Port of Chicago. My security team just informed me as to such an event happening."

President Jackson raised an eyebrow at the statement and turned his vision to Pat Sommers. His head of security was just finishing a quick conversation with the Russian which appeared to be along the same lines. The Secret Service man looked at his boss and gave him a very commando-like nod of the head. The president wasn't sure what it meant, but it obviously wasn't a nuke going off.

"Prime Minister, I don't know as I'd get too worried about any port activity. I'm sure that the response teams are doing whatever needs to be done."

"But, Mr. President, you don't find this all to be somewhat suspect?"

"I know that if it was the explosion that everyone here is worrying about, we wouldn't be having this conversation right now. Using that as my yard stick, I think I'm less worried than I normally would be. But, yes, it is suspect."

"I think you should send some people to investigate the situation, just to make sure."

"They have already been dispatched, Mr. Prime Minister."

The Japanese prime minister visually calmed at the mention of a response team. The president hadn't actually sent any people to the port. He was referring to the original team. He was really wishing that he could talk to the NEST operative, Dr. Hughes. The tension between the delegates was only going to build until the situation was resolved. He was hoping that that resolution was not a detonation.

"I hear that the tea is especially good here, not that I'm often a tea drinker. Maybe a cup of tea, Mr. Prime Minister?"

"Yes. Tea sounds like a reasonable idea."

The Japanese prime minister headed off toward the coffee service at the far end of the meeting room. President Jackson looked at his security man and gave him the *"get over here"* nod.

"What's going on at the port, Pat?"

"That's a good question, Mr. President. The news sounds like something from downtown Kabul. The Russian security team was just asking the same question."

"Pat, be more specific."

"According to the Russians, someone launched a surface-to-surface missile at something in the port. Since we're still talking, that probably wasn't the device."

"True. Is there any way to find out what's really going on?"

"I peeled a chopper off detail, put a Secret Service sniper in it, and sent it in that direction."

"Good job, Pat. Let me know what they find, as soon as they find it."

The Secret Service man was starting to respond when the president's cellphone rang. Pat Sommers paused as the president removed the crypto-level cellphone from his pocket. The screen read, Eugene Taggart, CIA.

"Hold that thought, Pat."

The president punched the pickup button on the phone and waited a second for the three little clicks that let him know the line was secure.

"Didn't expect to hear from you today, Eugene. What's up?"

"It's been a tense bunch of hours, Mr. President. I don't know if I'm going to make it better or worse."

"Go on."

"We are almost completely positive that Ivan Vakar is the owner of Vakar Arms."

"And? –"

"And the individual behind what's transpiring at the Port of Chicago."

"All right, with as crappy as my morning has already been, go ahead and give me the long version."

"Originally, all we had to go on was circumstance. He seemed to be in the know, but that could have been easily written off to his position. His financial status has always been curious. Some deep source investigation by other members of the group have shown a net worth that isn't able to be accounted for by either his paper businesses or his stock trading. And it was the later that sealed the deal. Our tech experts over at the NSA have been keeping an eye on everything that Vakar has been doing since this whole thing started. Approximately fifteen hours ago, Vakar had his investment people at Hermans and Devos, Antwerp, pull all of his money out of the US stock system."

"He liquidated his whole portfolio?"

"Yes, Mr. President. The bankers were careful to do it in small pieces, as not to draw SEC attention. But he divested completely. This isn't speculation trading, it's a card-tip."

"I completely agree."

"So, the next question is what do we do with the information?"

The president paused. He looked at Pat Sommers, and pondered on his conversation with the Russian president earlier in the morning. Absolute deniability was what he had promised. Absolute deniability was what was required.

"For the immediate future, we do nothing with it. Nobody is going to breathe a word of it to anyone. Nobody is going to lift a finger in that direction. We will hope that Dr. Hughes and her team do what is required of them, and then we will consider this new aspect."

"Deniability."

"Exactly, Gene. I already made Demetri Zakharov that guarantee. Complete and utter bullet-proof deniability. The old way."

"Not to worry, Mr. President. We still have that capability."

"That's what I like about you, Gene. You need to teach the new kids how to think this way."

"I'm not sure that's possible, sir. Weak Congress, everybody is our friend, brave new world and all that."

The president stifled a laugh.

"Fair to say that not everyone is our friend these days. What else do you have?"

"The secondary device has been located and neutralized. There seems to be a situation developing around Port of Chicago. We're waiting for confirmation from the ground, sir."

"Yes. I've already talked to Dr. Hughes about the St. Louis affair. Very good work. As for Port of Chicago, everyone's security team here seems to know more about it than I do."

"I understand, Mr. President. As long as it's gunfire and the odd missile, it's not a detonation. Back up for the NEST team is on the way."

"It would seem from multiple avenues." The president looked at Pat Sommers, who was scanning the room for anything anomalous.

"Mr. President?"

"No worries, Gene. Just keep me up to speed. Thanks."

"Yes, Mr. President," and the line went dead. The CIA director was direct. He could see how young Dr. Hughes had developed her response to authority.

"Pat, anything from Dr. Hughes?"

"No, Mr. President. No word from there in general."

"Let's go see if we can find our Russian counterparts."

"Yes, sir."

The president and his head of security were turning to leave the conference room when the Russian delegation came flowing in. The Russian security team dispersed evenly into the room, taking up station at the approximate location of everyone else's security teams. Demetri Zakharov walked directly to the president and smiled diplomatically.

"It would seem that things to the south have turned into the Wild West?"

"That's what I hear, too. The Japanese prime minister seems freaked out by people blowing things up."

The Russian president did everything in his power to suppress a smile, but his stoic exterior cracked. President Jackson looked at the carpet for a second, so the Russian could save face.

"Regarding our earlier conversation –"

President Zakharov raised an eyebrow and waited for the American president to continue.

"—it turns out that what we had been considering about our EU counterpart is true."

The Russian rubbed his chin in understanding – A sign that made all of his security team tense.

"And?"

"And nothing – immediately. Though I suspect it will have an influence on my attitude toward the EU trade discussion."

"And mine as well."

"Yes. Otherwise, other items will be handled other ways, as previously discussed."

"Very good, Mr. President. In that case, I suggest that we start on time, and not wait for the others'."

"I agree, Demetri. If they show, they show. And if not, then not."

"Agreed." The Russian president pointed toward the coffee service.

The American president pointed toward his cup on the chaise lounge. The Russian president nodded and turned toward the table at the far end of the meeting room. President Walker Jackson checked his wrist watch and thought that Dr. Hughes was running out of time.

CHAPTER 34

Four hours until the start of the Summit.

Glen Adams stood as steadfast as would be allowed by the beating from the explosion. He was scuffed and bloody, but otherwise no worse off than his new comrade. He assessed the shockingly loud ringing in his ears and decided that his equilibrium was intact enough to allow him to fly. He turned to look at the FBI pilot. He was performing the same self-assessment. Glen spun his fingers around in a circle, the universal signal among helicopter pilots for "get your rotors spinning," and was immediately understood. The FBI man turned and headed toward his gunship.

Glen Adams made his way to the NEST helicopter and was greeted by a sad sight. The tail section of his aircraft had been all but torn off by the blast debris. Everything from the back of the cabin was a twisted mass of metal and wiring. Glen took in the sight of his machine and had an expression that was equal parts sad and maddening. It was a bad death for a machine that had been born for flight.

Brought back to reality by a person running by with a fire extinguisher, Glen turned back around and saw that the FBI man had his machine up and running. The blades of the AH-6 Little Bird were almost up to proper speed. Glen Adams mustered some resolve and ran to the passenger door of the other helicopter. He hopped in the second seat as the FBI pilot pulled back on the collective and sent the machine skyward.

Kristin Hughes was halfway across the smoldering scene when the

FBI gunship lifted off the tarmac. She skidded to a stop and inspected the mayhem in her field of view. There were clouds of black and grey smoke emanating from piles of smoldering rubble that obscured the area around her, but she was pretty sure that the Customs building no longer existed. She swung her head in an arc and suddenly realized that the communication truck was also missing. A hulking pit had been excavated out of the parking area where the F350 pickup truck once sat.

It took a moment for the world's preeminent nuclear weapons technician to fully process that the pickup truck no longer existed. As the realization that it was gone sank in, she reached into her pocket and pulled out her cellphone. The image of five full bars of signal strength on the phone's screen brought everything that was transpiring into crystal clear focus.

Without yelling to her crew, Kristin spun on her boot heals and sprinted at top speed back toward the green shipping container. She zigzagged her way back through the people and debris piles as she went. The scene at the port was descending into chaos so quickly that no one even noticed her running by.

Kristin ran as fast as her legs would allow. She knew that the hours that they all thought they had were now reduced to minutes or seconds. Eliminating the equipment that deadened the cell signal meant that there was someone within view of the port getting ready to remotely detonate the bomb. The thought of some terrorist standing on a rooftop with a cellphone just made her run faster. She turned the corner back into the container row with such velocity that she actually skidded sideways in an arc around the corner. Pulling a long runners breath, she put on more speed. Planting her boot heels into the concrete, Kristin ground to a stop in front of the green shipping container. She ripped off her backpack and went for the zippers.

The FBI helicopter pilot turned the nimble gunship in an incredibly tight arc only some twenty feet off the ground and got the bird moving. Glen Adams was holding himself steady with one hand and warming up the weapon's system with the other. He had utilized similar systems during his early Gulf War years, and later on more obscure loan outs. For once, he was not going to complain about arming non-military aircraft.

The FBI pilot pulled the helicopter up to a more respectable 100-feet off the deck and leveled off to take in the scene. From the higher elevation, it was easy to take it all in at once. A teardrop-shaped, semi-circular crater had been augured out of the ground directly under where the communication truck had been parked. The wash from the excavated crater had all but decimated the Customs building and surrounding area. All the vehicles in the immediate area of the crater had been rendered unusable. Smoke and random fires gave the scene a Hollywood quality.

The FBI pilot turned his helmet to look at his new gunner. Glen Adams locked eyes with him and gave him a big thumbs-up in return. Adams looked down at the crater and pointed his finger along the obvious back azimuth. The FBI pilot nodded once, and then banked the gunship over to pick up speed.

Ben Donewoody and Jim Bonner took a turn through the rubble of the Customs building. They both knew that the explosion was a diversion, but they were already at the pile of rubble. If someone was alive in the rubble and could be saved, they should try.

A quick recon of the area showed no one left alive. It was all demolition debris. The F350 pickup truck and all of its super sensitive equipment had been reduced to ripped pieces of metal no larger than a fist. Ben cleared numerous pieces of pickup truck out of his section of search area before he even realized that the bits of metal had once been the commo truck. He paused his searching as the realization sank in. No truck meant that they had no cellphone cover net. He quickly dug around in the pocket of his FBI windbreaker for his phone. Five full bars came up on the top of the phone's display and Ben gasped. He yelled at Jim Bonner and then tossed him the cellphone underhand. Jim Bonner looked at the screen and then back at his FBI counterpart. Ben cupped his hands around his mouth to focus his voice.

"Do you have a backup cell jammer with you?"

"NO. The rig covers the scene."

"What are we going to do now?"

The NEST operative thought for what could not have been a full second before responding.

"Kristin has one in her backpack."

"That's right! We used it in St. Louis."

Both men abandoned their searches in favor of what was now a much more important mission. They needed to reestablish some type of a cell canopy over the port of Chicago or a bunch of the free world's most influential leaders were about to become ash.

About the same time the rest of the team on the ground was realizing that the commo truck was missing and they were without RF cover, the two men in the helicopter were finally starting to get their hearing back. Glen Adams was sure that he was hearing tower traffic out of both Midway and O'Hare airports.

"Hey, you hear radio traffic?" He turned and looked at the FBI man who was just starting to focus in on the radio chatter.

"Yeah, I do."

"That means that the dead-cell canopy is down."

"Well, that's not good." The FBI pilot twisted the sticks of the gunship's flight controls to make it pick up speed.

Kristin Hughes pulled the small cell jammer from her backpack and went to flip the switch on. The jammer came to life and immediately started flashing low battery. The NEST operative swore at the device, which in no way helped her situation. The flashing light on the signal jammer meant that it wasn't putting out a full signal. It also meant that it could stop working at any moment. The specific jammer that she used was a good unit, but notoriously fickle when it came to battery life.

Kristin made an assumption that both bombs had been built with the same configuration, which meant that the antenna for the cellphone trigger was attached to the inside of the container's roof. She scurried around to find something tall enough to put against the side of the metal box. It seemed that everything tall enough had been moved out of the way with the snow plow. Taking a second look at the area, it seemed to Kristin that the bomb container was only about ten feet from the big container stack it had come off of.

Kristin snapped the cell jammer to her belt and started scaling the stack of shipping containers for what seemed like the eleventh time in two days. The large metal clip from the signal jammer dug into her waist and made her think that she wasn't in good enough shape for her new urban mountain climbing lifestyle. Her container wall was only three containers tall now, but she needed to get to the top before it would provide her with a flat surface. Oh well, she had no time to make the situation any better.

At the top, Kristin rolled over the edge and onto her back. She stood and moved to the back of the top container's roof. She visually lined up her target from the edge of the other containers around her and took off sprinting down the length of the container's roof. At the ledge, she propelled herself into free air. Bicycling her legs while in the air, as she had learned in her high school track and field years, she covered the open airspace in a low descending arc. Kristin's right foot landed flat on top of the roof's corrugated surface. Her left foot landed with its heel in the void space of the corrugation. Her ankle immediately folded up under the velocity of the landing and Kristin slammed into the container's metal roof. Her newly broken ankle swelled as blood poured into the bone's surrounding tissue. The pain from the impact shot the full length of her body and assaulted her brain.

Hughes pulled herself onto her good foot and made it to her knees. In the quiet space of her middle ear, her father was talking to her, as he always had throughout her life during times of extreme stress. *Suck it up, kid. You can do it if you really want to.* The words ran through the semi-conscious part of her mind and gave her strength. Her father had always known her to be a strong child. To be a fighter. She was the daughter of a warrior. She could overcome.

Kristin unsnapped the signal jammer and placed it dead center in the middle of the shipping container's metal roof. She checked to make sure that it was still working, and then, without ceremony, she rolled off the roof to the concrete ground below. Several expletives were immediately expelled after her impact with the concrete. Taking no time to collect herself, she rolled up onto her knees and surveyed the side of the green metal container. There was no box. She had rolled off the wrong side of the container. Several more expletives came out as she made it to her feet and began hopping around the outside of the large metal box. Kristin was collapsing in front of her backpack when Ben Donewoody and Jim Bonner came charging up from the rear.

"Are you okay?" Ben appeared shocked as he looked at her.

"What? Oh. The battery on the cell jammer is about dead. We need to get this thing unplugged, NOW."

Jim Bonner dropped to his knees in front of the small metal box on the side of the container that Kristin pointed at and began extracting the remaining machine screws with a multi-tool that he carried in his utility vest. While Jim was releasing the inspection cover from the box, Kristin was dumping her backpack out on the ground to find what she was looking for. Out of the mess on the ground came a set of needle-nose pliers and a pair of wire cutters.

Kristin drug herself, with some assistance from Ben, over to Jim Bonner as he was extracting the last screw. Looking inside the box, the green LED light was glowing brightly. Ben Donewoody dug for his phone. He had one bar and a capital E looking back at him from the cellphone screen.

Glen Adams pointed a steady finger through the gunship's canopy at a rooftop more than 1,000 meters away, and then set a big pair of spotter's binoculars in his lap.

"He's set up on the rooftop. You can't miss the OD green military containers."

The FBI pilot nodded in understanding and flipped the switch to free the weapons on the Little Bird. Fortunately for the two men in the helicopter, the Little Bird had been designed to have an ambidextrous firing platform. That meant that Glen Adams could fire the weapons while the FBI man concentrated on flying. Glen grabbed the firing stick located in front of him and flipped on the target overlay. A sighting box appeared as a 3D image projected onto the inside of the flight helmet he was wearing. The upper right corner of the helmet display showed a bright red number five, which told Glen that the two 12.7 mm GAU-19 chain guns were set to cross firing streams at 500 meters. He could also see from the helmet display that the two LAU-66D launchers were both full of the standard Hydra 70 rocket projectiles.

Alex Leka watched the helicopter closing in on his position and knew that his time had finally run out. The East European militant dropped down below the roof's brick knee wall and grabbed his cellphone. He had three bars and 3G. That would do nicely. The cell tower he was using was located on the roof of the adjacent building, so the signal had no travel time. They couldn't stop him at this point. As calmly as a man calling a cab, Alex Leka pressed the send button on the phone and smiled. With the short distance to the tower in both directions, it wouldn't take more than about another ten seconds and the city would be lit up in crimson. Alex looked up at the cell tower that he was now envisioning as the silver sword of destiny when a full pack of Hydra 70 rocket projectiles slammed into it. The spread barrage punched several holes in the building's roof before ripping the tower from its mounts. The metal spire twisted and fell off the back of the building in a rush of smoke and noise.

Alex Leka sighed and put his palm down on the roof surface to push himself to his feet. He was almost to his knees when the 12.7 mm rounds from the two chain guns tore through the knee wall. The east European mercenary- turned-terrorist, was reduced to a pink mist as the machine gun fire decimated his body.

Kristin Hughes shoved the needle-nose of the pliers into the holes in the multi-prong plug socket and popped it free. Pulling the plug several inches out to expose the wires behind the plug, she counted over two prongs and clipped the wire free. She counted over another four prongs and clipped that wire free as well. Pushing the end of the last wire against the side of the container, a small metallic glassy click could be heard as the green LED faded to be replaced in brightness by the red LED light. All three people staring into the small box took a collective breath.

Kristin rolled onto her back and raised her broken ankle up against the side of the shipping container. Jim Bonner started about the remaining tasks of completely disarming the nuke. Ben Donewoody looked at his phone again. The phone showed four bars and 4G. The signal jammer battery was dead. He dropped the phone onto Kristin's stomach and moved off to help Jim Bonner.

Kristin could hear the helicopter they had borrowed from the FBI coming in to land at the port, as several other members of the NEST team appeared to help with the unloading of the kitty litter. The FBI pilot brought the gunship down right on top of the row of containers to her 4 o'clock and started to let the rotors wind down. Looking up at the gunship, Dr. Kristin Hughes knew that there was going to be a lot of explaining to do. Right now, she just didn't care.

CHAPTER 35

Ivan Vakar looked out the window of the EU's corporate jet and wondered what in the world was happening in Chicago. Sliding up the cuff of his suit jacket, he checked his watch. The gold Rolex told him what he already knew: two hours until the G8 Summit started; two hours until detonation. Two hours until the world was a different place.

He was pretty sure that his unease was unfounded. It was a simple case of nervous jitters. It had to be. Everything had gone to plan. Every step had been accounted for. All the variables had come and gone. If there was a last one to present itself, that would be Alex's problem.

The jet pushed off of the Greenland coast and continued west. Ivan took a deep breath to calm his mind. He exhaled slowly. His phone rang. He dug out the device and checked the screen. The incoming call was from Pavel. He silenced it on the third ring.

"Yes."

"Mr. Vakar. Reporting in. Adrian won't be able to detonate the device."

Ivan Vakar literally pulled the phone away from his face and starred at the screen, as if it would change the statement.

"What exactly do you mean?"

"It seems that the Americans weren't as slow on the uptake as we had assumed they would be. The CIA found the trail and tracked down Adrian. They took him at his apartment in Germany."

"And?"

"And the CIA man took him to a safe house across town to interrogate him."

"Is he still there?"

"His corpse probably is."

Ivan Vakar began to fume. He couldn't make any sense out of what the East European hitman was trying to tell him. He wanted to scream into the phone, but collected himself instead.

"Pavel. Please tell me what happened between the CIA and Adrian. Start at the beginning."

Pavel drew a breath and thought about it all for a moment.

"The CIA man followed the trail from the port man, to the truck driver, to the warehouse in Idar-Oberstein. Fortunately, we made it to the warehouse before he did. There wasn't any part of our operation left to find. There may have been a slight background radiation hit, but no physical evidence. Unfortunately, what was left to find was Adrian."

"I understand – continue."

"The CIA man spent a little time observing Adrian. I spent a little time observing the CIA man. He did a sneak-and-peak on Adrian's apartment, and when the boss came home he Tased him and tossed him over the side of the balcony. Pretty effective, all in all."

"Go on."

"The man took the boss to a house across town, and gave him the black site treatment. He was just getting ready to get aggressive with him when I decided to call it off."

"Call it off how?"

"I put a bullet in him."

"I see. Go on."

"I popped Adrian from across the street. I couldn't get a clean shot at the CIA man. I didn't want to get into a gun fight in a residential area. The CIA man did an escape and evade out the back door into a semi-wooded area. I did a quick check of the place. Adrian was definitely done. I retrieved his cellphone before I left, but it won't be much good."

"What do you mean by that?"

"The cellphone took a big hit, either from the tumble down out of the apartment or during one of the throws around when he was tied up. It's in multiple pieces. It won't be much good to anyone at this point. I handed it off to a tech guy I do business with. He's trying to resurrect the memory."

Ivan looked at his Rolex again. Two hours until detonation, except no Adrian to detonate it. He pounded the arm of his seat with his free hand and cursed in his native tongue. Pavel heard and understood the cursing, and waited for the man to compose himself.

"Are you sure that Adrian didn't tell the other man anything useful?"

"Adrian is a tough one. It would take more of a beating than he sustained to make him talk. He didn't say anything."

"I understand. Where are you now?"

"I'm on the move."

Pavel certainly wasn't going to tell Vakar where he was or where he was headed. That would be stupid.

"Good. Stay that way. I'll get back to you."

"Very good, Mr. Vakar."

Ivan Vakar disconnected the call. Adrian was out of play. He wasn't going to activate the Chicago nuke, or the St. Louis one either. Alex could do it, but if there was nothing going on in Chicago, he would simply wait it out. If things had already proceeded, then Alex would have already done his bit.

Ivan looked out the window of the jet at the clouds below and thought it was a nice view. He opened the web browser on his phone and looked up a breaking news website. The international news website had some articles on horrors going on in Central Africa, but nothing about anything in the Americas. Apparently, the nukes hadn't gone off yet. So, no Adrian and no action from Alex Leka. He checked his watch again. One hour and forty one minutes until the planned detonation time. Should he wait it out? Should he handle it himself? It was obviously not going to be the Vakar Arms front man handling it, as was planned.

Ivan Vakar drew a long, slow breath and steadied himself. It was all falling to him. He had started it all, and now it would seem that it was all falling to him to finish. Looking at the clouds one more time, he pulled up a pre-saved number out of his contacts and pressed send. The signal went out from his phone at the speed of light, bouncing off satellites and cell towers until it came to the area of the globe where it could make contact with the U.S.-made cellular trigger. Ivan looked down at the returned screen prompt. *The number you have dialed cannot be found.*

Ivan Vakar exhaled, pressed the red disconnect button, and then the green send button. A second time the call went out and found nothing. The second attempt returned the same screen message as the first attempt had.

Ivan sat the disconnected phone in his lap and put his head in his hands. His temples were beginning to pound. If the U.S. dead-cell canopy was still active, the message would have said that the call couldn't be connected at this time. The message he had gotten back was a responder message. It actually meant that the trigger was no longer active, and hence, couldn't be found. That message only had one possible explanation. Ivan put his phone back in his pocket and decided that a drink might be in order.

In Chicago, President Jackson paced from the chaise lounge to the coffee service on the far side of the room and back. The other delegates in attendance did the same in differing areas of the meeting room. Numerous members of the individual security teams stood about conspicuously and watched the men pace. Everyone in the room was waiting. They all just happened to go about it in different ways. The U.S. president checked his watch and then glanced at Pat Sommers. The Secret Service man just shrugged his beefy shoulders at the leader of the free world. There was no news. And today, no news was troubling news. The president looked over at the Russian president, who was distracting himself with some papers in a manila folder. Jackson assumed it was probably plans to take over some ex-soviet bloc country and drag them back to the motherland of the oligarchy. Well, if he survived, he could do whatever he wanted.

Pat Sommers stuffed his hand into the inner pocket of his suit jacket and extracted his phone with deft speed. He muttered something that seemed like a password challenge, and then visibly relaxed. The president watched the security man begin the initial contractions that led to muscle movement, and turned completely to face his head of security. Pat Sommers closed the distance to the president with three quick strides. He handed the president his phone with a clear and audibly loud statement.

"Dr. Hughes is on the line."

Every person in the room, delegate and security man alike, stopped what they were doing and focused their attention on the cellphone in the

American president's hand. President Walker Jackson drew a breath and put the phone to his ear.

"Dr. Hughes, it's good to hear your voice. I hope this is a good news call."

"Both packages are inactive and stable. Your immediate problem has been handled."

The president pulled the phone from his ear and swung his head around to look at each of the men and women in the room.

"We're all good. Dr. Hughes and her team have handled the problem."

Everyone in the room released a collectively held breath. Each of them expressed congratulations in one form or another toward the cellphone. President Jackson put the phone back to his ear.

"You said immediate?"

"Yes, sir. Someone blew a crater in the Port of Chicago parking lot and reduced the Customs building to a pile of rubble. They also destroyed our commo truck and killed a member of our team."

"Go on."

"Shortly after that, NEST and the FBI pretty much shot the top floor off of a nearby building to terminate the situation."

"Anything else?"

"Your Secret Service chopper backup showed up just as the gunfight was finishing. They're here helping with stuff. We pulled the trigger out of the Chicago package, but someone needs to secure it soon. I'm going to need to get someone in here to do that. Someone is going to need to do damage control. It looks like the outskirts of Beirut around here."

"I see, doctor. I'll tell you what – you continue to do what you need to do and I will take care of all the damage control."

"Thank you, Mr. President."

"No, thank you." The president paused in consideration for a moment.

"One more thing, Dr. Hughes. Next week some time, when you have a moment, swing by my office."

"Sir?"

"Don't bother making an appointment. Stop at the gate and ask for Pat. He'll take care of the rest."

"Okay." Kristin hung up the phone. The president looked at the phone and its *End Call* icon and realized that he had just been dismissed by the young scientist. He smiled. She did have some brass. President Jackson turned and looked at his head of security.

"Pat, get me a list of all the casualties down there. Do it before the day's out. We'll need to properly recognize them, in some discreet fashion."

"Yes, Mr. President."

President Walker Jackson looked over at the other dignitaries, who were now collected and conversing over by the meeting area. He returned his attention to the phone in his hand and smiled at the thought of being dismissed by the NEST agent. He pulled his own phone out of his pocket and programmed Dr. Hughes's cell number into his personal phone. When done, he tossed the other phone back to Pat Sommers.

President Jackson scrolled down through his contacts until he landed on an international number, and pressed send. Numerous clicks came through, routing the call around the NSA's secure crypto signal processors before the line made connection and began to ring. It rang seven times.

"Ivan? President Walker Jackson."

The pause on the other end of the line was long and distinct.

"Mr. President. Good to hear from you."

"And you, Ivan. Are you and the other G8 members on schedule to make Chicago or should we postpone things for a couple hours?"

There was a second long pause.

"I would think that we will make Chicago on time. There shouldn't be any problem starting everything on time. Why do you ask?"

"No real reason. I was just checking. If you could, tell the other *actual* G8 members that we are going to talk out some issues while we're waiting. That way we can get straight to business."

"I will be happy to, Mr. President."

"That's good, Ivan. The Russian president and I both have conflicting plans, so I'll be heading straight back to Washington after. If you still have anything that you feel needs discussing, maybe you can swing by Pennsylvania Avenue sometime next week. If you're still in town, and I have time."

"I see. I'll need to check my schedule."

"Thought so, Ivan. It's a busy world out there. Probably should talk, at some point. Wouldn't want smoldering issues to explode, would we?"

There was a third noticeable pause.

"No, Mr. President."

"Good." And with that, President Walker Jackson hung up on the European Union High Representative and stuck the phone back in his pocket. The president casually strolled, if that was the right definition for his gate, over to the seating area. He pulled out the seat behind the marker denoting the space as that reserved for the delegate of the United States. He adjusted himself in his seat and smiled at the other G8 members.

"What do you say, boys? We maybe can get a little alliance building done while we're waiting on the others?"

All of the other G8 members in attendance focused on the president and smiled or nodded. He nodded back and then looked over at his head of security.

"I think we're all good here, Pat."

Pat Sommers, Secret Service head of personal security details, nodded and turned on his heels in the direction of the door. Some other instructions were given about the room and the other security personnel made their way out. The G8 members from the representing countries took up seats and readied themselves for the summit business.

CHAPTER 36

Fifty-six hours after failed detonation

Ed Crowley's standard issue bulletproof black Chevy Suburban pulled into the gravel drive of *The Group's* secured gathering place outside Washington, D.C., and positioned itself in its standard parking space. Ed looked out of the rear passenger window at a robin's egg blue Kia Rio, and made a face. No one he knew drove a Kia. Also, no one who would intentionally park here would drive a Kia.

It could be a drop car from some situation that transpired in the neighborhood? Kids drove cars like that, and were always looking for a place to drop park. On the other hand, it could easily be an improvised explosive device. Every person that congregated at this location could easily be the target of a car bomb.

As if sensing that there was trouble in the ether, Ed's phone chirped with a text. He extracted the device from his suit pocket and looked at the screen. The text was direct. *It's not a car bomb. Just come inside.* Ed Crowley made a face at his phone. The number was Lou Stenson's. But why would the NEST operations chief be driving around in a Kia Rio?

"Sir, do you want us to give it the once-over, and then get rid of it?" The protective service agent in the front passenger's seat of the black bulletproof Suburban had seen numerous expressions play out across the senior spy's face as he took in the auto.

"Nope. I don't think the guy driving it would appreciate that at all."

The protective service agent made a face. Ed Crowley shrugged and exited the back of the Suburban. He made his way to the front door, paused for the retina scanner, and let himself in. He trudged up the stairs to the fully secure second floor game room as his security detail took up their customary positions in what would later be the shadows.

Letting himself into the heavily secured room that *The Group* used as its meeting place, Ed Crowley, senior NSA man and customary first arriver, took in the sight of Lou Stenson sitting on the leather sofa surrounded by empty beer bottles and paused.

"What the hell, Lou?"

"Don't worry, I'll clean up before everybody gets here."

"Are you in any shape to?"

The big ex-SEAL laughed at the comment, and then surveyed the scene around his feet.

"It's not as bad as it looks. I needed someplace to hangout off the grid for a couple hours. I spent the last forty eight hours detailing, and re-detailing congressional subcommittees and DOE senior chiefs. Frankly, I hate this town."

This time Ed Crowley laughed. He dropped his items in the holder spot marked NSA on the table, and retrieved a beer of his own.

"Lou, I know exactly what you mean. I think that thought almost every single day."

Lou Stenson jumped to his feet like he was going off on a road march and began policing up the empty beer bottles. He was tossing the last of the empties into the trash when Nathanial Baker came strolling in.

"What happened Lou? They take away your vehicle allowance?" The judge dropped his phone into the holder spot marked for the justice and retrieved a bottle of mineral water from the beverage cart.

"It's a rental. I didn't feel right having Pat's men chauffer me around everywhere. They have better things to do than babysit me. Besides, I can take care of myself, most days."

Nathanial Baker gave the NEST operations chief a fatherly look.

"I have no doubt."

"Okay, I get the rental, but a sub-compact? You're a little big for that, aren't you?" Ed was having trouble concealing the smile that came from the image of Lou Stenson dressed like a clown and stuffed into a tiny car.

"It was all that they had,"

Both Ed and Nathanial laughed at the big ex-SEAL. Paul Spencer came trudging through the door with that *who's got the rental car* look on his face.

"Yes, Paul, it's mine." Lou raised his hand with a self-imposed look of defeat on his face.

Paul Spencer wanted to ask questions, but took in the scene and thought better of it. Lou took the pause to change the topic.

"By the way Ed, who handles the housekeeping in this place?"

"What do you mean?" The senior NSA man looked confused by the question. Secretly, it was a ruse.

"I mean, you show up, out of the blue, and the beer is stocked and cold. The place is dress-right-dress. Hell, there's even full ice in the ice bucket. Does the invisible man live downstairs or something?"

"You're not too far off the mark." Eugene Taggart strode in as if he owned the place. It was his customary entrance.

"What do you mean?"

"It's not the invisible man. It's actually the woman next door. Pat Sommers has a Secret Service agent that lives next door. She handles the game room, amongst other things. Don't worry, she's cleared top secret plus. And she has a little extra company oversight."

"Secret Service?" Lou Stenson was rolling the idea over in his mind to give it merit.

"Yes, sir. It's efficient."

"I have no doubt."

Bob Sloan came trudging through the door with a beaten-down look that attested to his last forty eight hours of grilling by congressional subcommittees. He nodded at each of the men as he walked to the corner table to deposit his weapon and phone in the holder spot marked FBI.

"Pepper, you look like hell. You just extract yourself from the sublevels of the Capital Building?"

Lou Stenson could completely sympathize with his FBI compatriot. The last forty eight hours had been a hornet's nest of finger pointing and blame avoidance. For his part, Lou knew that the president had stood right out in front of his men and absorbed all of the onslaught that he could on their behalf. Nevertheless, there were pissed off congressmen, senators, TSA personnel, DHS personnel, military leaders, and one fuming mad DNI.

"Nope. I've been playing political hot potato with the DNI for the last three hours. That, on top of two subcommittees and the joint chiefs."

"Nothing in that sounds like fun." Lou was instantly happy that he didn't have to deal with the headaches Pepper had to deal with.

"Let's just wait until we're all assembled, so I only have to do stuff one time."

Everyone nodded in agreement and slowly began to meander toward the poker table. Lou walked to the beverage tray and grabbed a bottle of water and a bag of trail mix. It was time to go back to work. Nathanial Baker made a comment and Lou grabbed a second bag of trail mix, which he tossed to the chief justice. The group conversed quietly, killing time until all had arrived. Once Pat Sommers took his seat, the meeting was unofficially called to order.

"Seeing how it's technically the FBI's case, what say we let Pepper go first?" Lou Stenson was inhaling trail mix and speaking at the same time. Ed Crowley wondered if this was something that was actually taught in operator school, as several other elite fighters he had known tended to do it as well. More likely it was just a learned time-saving tool – but still.

"Thanks Lou, you're a pal"." Bob "Pepper" Sloan looked worn out. Except for his eyes. His eyes were alive and sharp. Lou Stenson shrugged his buff shoulders and inhaled more trail mix.

"Okay, might as well start at the top. According to our man Pat, POTUS is in good shape. He has been fully briefed on the affair. NEST Field One gave him a personal SITREP and he seems good with it all. He has taken all of the individual states' representatives in hand, and they are calming down. He said he'd get to the joint chiefs next. Sound about right, Pat?"

Pat Sommers nodded in agreement.

"While we're on this topic, I want to thank Pat for the backdoor service at the White House. I would like to keep Kristin as far from the worldwide press people as I can." Lou nodded at the Secret Service man with respect.

"It was the least I could do. The president enjoyed the encounter more than Dr. Hughes did, I think. Anyway, you guys are on the leading edge next year, budget wise."

Everyone at the table laughed. It was the standard Washington thank you. You do a good job, and you get more budget money.

"By the way," Pat threw in, "a bright pink cast?"

Lou shrugged, "she is a girl."

"That she is. A bright pink cast and an almost non-existent sun dress. Interesting fashion choices."

"Well, she is a free spirit."

"There's no doubt about that."

Everyone laughed a second time. Considering the usual tone of world events that the men seated in the game room dealt with, it was definitely odd to hear this much laughter emitting from around the card table.

"All right, that being taken into account, how are things on The Hill? How is the mood in Congress?" Nathanial Baker already knew the answer, but always enjoyed a spy's interpretation of it.

"Seething." Both Lou Stenson and Bob Sloan spoke in unison.

Gene Taggart raised an interested eyebrow upon hearing both men utter the same word.

"They're going to be some time calming down. Especially the boys and girls on the Domestic Terrorism Subcommittee." Bob Sloan's voice carried the sound of long days talking, saying things no one wanted to hear.

"I spent a little time up on The Hill, myself. I'd say they're all just scared. They're reacting like they're scared." Gene Taggart's tone was measured.

"You going to tell them that?" Nathanial Baker sounded like the skeptical voice of reason.

"I already did. They didn't like it."

Everyone at the table nodded.

"Now, let's do the big one. What is someone telling the DNI? Right now, our esteemed John Hudgens is out looking for scalps. He's well beyond pissed off."

The director of national intelligence, a post created after 9/11 to focus and coordinate the myriad U.S. intelligence agencies, was currently held by Sen. John Hudgens. He was a weak and non-motivated fourth term senator who had just enough friends to get control of a director's chair. He was universally disliked by every man at the card table and by their boss, the president.

Nathanial Baker ran a hand through his hair and took his glasses off to clean them on his shirt sleeve. It was the sign from the Supreme Court justice that he had something he would like to say. His current company waited patiently for him to collect himself.

"Everyone on The Hill knows that the different intelligence interests still really answer to their respective subcommittee. In every essence, the DNI is a political puppet. The FBI will need to deal with him, since they deal with domestic terrorism. The DOE will need to deal with him, since they deal with the whole nuclear issue. Otherwise, I say we don't tell him anything. As for FBI and DOE, you both have already done your due diligence with the subcommittees. I say you send him the redacted subcommittee briefs and let him stew. We can just let POTUS keep him in check."

Everyone processed the thoughts in their own time and then nodded their approval. The justice placed his glasses back on his face and smiled.

"Both of us, respectively, have already given the DNI our debrief packages," Bob Sloan said matter-of-factly, "so, that should be that."

Lou Stenson nodded in agreement.

"Next topic, Terrorism SITREP. Or should I say, post-terrorism SITREP?" The CIA boss actually sounded casual as he spoke. He never sounded casual.

"I say that you keep right on talking," Bob Sloan had made the transition from one beer to a second, and seemed to be slowly coming out of his post-congressional haze.

"The word out of Europe goes like this – the Vakar Arms network from the port man to the warehouse where the nukes were processed has been dismantled. Personnel in those positions have all been expunged."

Everyone nodded in understanding.

"The front man, Beqiri, was apprehended by Mr. Dunn, but terminated before he could provide any useful information."

"By Dunn?" Paul Spencer, Senior Systems Director at the NRO, asked suspiciously.

"Negative. He was headshot, from range, by a rifle. Best guess is that he was shot by the new front man for Vakar Arms."

Everyone at the table nodded a second time.

"Realistically, Vakar Arms is now a non-player. They are so high up on the international radar that no one would dare do business with them for some time. We'll make sure that they die of starvation."

"And the mystery cash man?" Pat Sommers had been silent up till this point, just kind of taking it all in.

"Good question. I would say with eighty percent certainty that Ivan Vakar is both the owner and cash man. All the solid intelligence so far points to him. We still need something to make it 100 percent before proceeding further."

"I have a whole floor of people working on nothing but Mr. Vakar as we speak. If it's there to be found, we'll find it." Ed Crowley sounded as confident as he ever had about such things.

"So, until Ed's done, we all just wait on Vakar."

"And when Ed's done?" Bob Sloan added curiously.

"The CIA will do what the CIA does about such things. And it will be done cleanly." Gene Taggart's tone was solid and authoritarian. No one raised an objection.

"Okay, moving on. What about all of the kites?" Pat Sommers could tell that the topic needed changing.

Gene Taggart scratched his chin for a second and summarized things inside his head.

"The Farooqi woman is alive and off our scope. As far as we know, she is continuing her normal career path. Her contact, The Arab, should be alive for about another twelve hours or so."

The CIA director did some math in his head after checking his watch. No one commented.

"He has ceased to be of use to anyone. Now, the older Pakistani scientist has completely fallen off the scope after making landfall in the port. He is presumed dead, at the hands of his employer. The younger scientist is at large. We think he's making his way south, toward the coast."

"What do you see as being his final disposition?" Pat Sommers asked the question everyone else was thinking.

"That seems to be a popular topic of conversation these days. Speaking as a spy, I'd would like to make a friend out of an enemy. You get better information that way. Speaking as a patriot, we don't negotiate with terrorists. We kill terrorists. Frankly, the CIA could be persuaded to go either way on this one."

"FBI field ops has some thoughts they would like us to consider." Bob Sloan said calmly.

"So does NEST Field One," Lou Stenson said in a level tone.

"So does POTUS," Pat Sommers put in, a little bit more quietly.

Everyone's gaze shifted over to Pat Sommers, but no one said a word for several seconds.

"In light of the numerous individual concerns, I say that we let the field ops people converse and make a determination for themselves." Nathanial Baker employed his fatherly tone, which was normally saved for the reading of court decisions.

"That sounds practical. CIA field ops will be back in country in a couple of days. I will have him get with the others."

Everyone nodded in agreement. It seemed that they had covered all of the big talking points. The remainder could easily be handled over cards. Gene Taggart picked up the deck of cards and showed them to the group. Everyone began to reach for their money. Lou Stenson eyed his empty bag of trail mix and made a face. For some reason, he really wanted a pizza.

CHAPTER 37

Two weeks after failed detonation

Hafid walked out the front door of the coffee shop and made his way through the throng of sidewalk tables with a small tray of coffees. It was a bright and sunny day in South Beach, and already on its way to being a perfect beach day. Hafid paused at the table farthest from the door and smiled warmly at the three people seated there. A half-caf latte for the gentleman, an espresso with a shot of chocolate for the lady, and a double espresso straight up for the other gentleman. All three shifted their drinks, orienting them toward their preferred hand. The three seemed to Hafid as if they were ex-military or maybe current military. It was hard to tell in this town. South Beach attracted all sorts of people, and a lot of them were military.

"Can I get anybody anything else?"

"No, thank you. This is excellent." The young lady spoke casually, as if she was talking to someone she had known for years.

"All right. Just flag me down if you decide on a refill. My name is Omar. Enjoy."

Robert Dunn watched Hafid walk away with the small tray efficiently tucked under his arm, and then tilted his gaze down to inspect his double espresso. He didn't dislike Hafid, which was odd. He was naturally inclined toward dislike and distrust. Normally, he could sense bad deeds and they instantly affected his judgement. In this case, he already knew what the bad deeds were and still couldn't get to the dislike stage. He found it a little harder to pull the trigger if he didn't dislike a target. He picked up his coffee and put half of it down his throat.

"I don't know. He seems the decent sort. You know, for a terrorist."

Ben Donewoody poked at the foam on his half-caf and made a frown. He was obviously unhappy with the presentation of his beverage.

"I agree with Robert. He was as much of a help as a hindrance. That should count for something, shouldn't it?"

"I agree." Kristin threw the chocolate espresso down in one go and sat the coffee cup back down on the grated metal tabletop. She looked neutral and composed, which was not one of her natural states.

"He should get a pass. I don't mean a free pass. We should definitely keep tabs on him, just for national security and all that. But I don't think we need to exercise any hostility here."

Both men listened to Kristin as she talked. Ben Donewoody was looking at some girls a couple of tables over. Robert Dunn was looking at a black Audi parked across the street that seemed suspicious. Kristin was looking through the large glass storefront at Omar. Omar went about his work with a smile and a pleasant manner. He seemed as American as anyone transplanted into the South Beach scene.

Robert Dunn pulled out his phone and began typing on the screen. Kristin rolled her eyes in his direction and waited. Robert scrolled down his screen and drank the remainder of his espresso.

"Well, apparently we aren't the only ones interested in our boy Omar. The car across the street is attached to a free-lance guy out of Chicago. He does a lot of wet work for the groups in Europe and farther East."

"You think that Vakar Arms is cleaning up the rest of their mess?" Ben Donewoody commented without emotion.

"It would seem that way."

"That puts a new knot in it, doesn't it?" Kristin Hughes still seemed neutral, but it was fading fast.

"All right, first thing's first. Omar, give him a pass or not? I say pass."

Kristin nodded in agreement, "pass."

"Yup. Pass." Ben Donewoody wiped the foam off the top of his half-caf with a napkin and smiled.

"Okay, that's that, I guess. Now, for the sake of all of our individual jurisdictional issues, I'll be happy to take care of Audi man."

"You mean permanently?" Kristin's voice had grown quiet.

"Yes."

"OK."

Ben Donewoody finished his coffee and looked at Dunn. He nodded his approval of the upcoming unsanctioned hit.

"I'm good with it."

"So, another coffee?" Robert picked up his empty coffee cup and inspected it.

"I have time for another. I was thinking about the beach before I head back west. There's a pretty decent break not far from here."

"I could use some work on my tan. I'm in." Kristin smiled at both men.

"Isn't the cast on your foot going to cause a compromising tan line?" Robert smiled at his compatriot.

"By the time the cast gets removed the tan line will have faded."

"Well, you have paled a little since Italy. Sadly, I'm not a beach guy. If you were nightclubbing, I'd be there. It's more my natural setting."

"It just so happens that I know a good one of those down here, as well. What do you say, we meet at Club 47, say, 8 p.m. or so. It's down the main drag, about halfway. Easy to find. That will give everyone time to do – whatever." Ben smiled at Robert in a conspiratorial way.

"I like it. Count me in," Kristin said.

Robert nodded with a genuinely warm smile.

"Sounds like a plan. Now all we have to do is flag down our buddy, Omar."

At the same time a little father to the north, in the Oval Office, President Walker Jackson looked down at the carpet under his chair and smiled. He didn't exactly know how this day was going to turn out, but he had expected a little more concession out of the man in his office. Apparently, when you have gone too far, you just keep trucking on down that road. Understandable, he guessed.

"Ivan, I can appreciate that the EU has economic issues of its own. I mean, I imagine that Greece is consuming more of your time than we are.

That being said, I don't feel that a concession of import goods fees would be good for the American worker."

He studied Ivan Vakar as he digested the news. The man actually looked put-out by the rejection. No, repugnant was a better word.

"Mr. President, the European Union has no trouble handling its internal problems. Our trade inequity with the U.S. is not one of those things. The EU feels that the inequity is such that we may need to find new markets for our goods, if a more realistic agreement cannot be reached."

The president looked down at the carpet again. This pain in the ass really didn't know when to quit, did he?

"All right, Ivan, who?"

"Pardon?"

"I said, who? Who are you going to exploit if you decide to move to your alternate markets? Who?"

"We have numerous options for our exports. We don't have to ship our goods to the United States."

"Yes. You really do need to ship them here."

"I assure you that we have many outlets in the global economy."

"Well, let's take a moment and analyze your options. The Caribbean, South America, and Africa are taking all of the goods they can afford to take, so they're out. Eastern Europe has either been absorbed by the Union or is still emerging, so they're out. South Asia doesn't want anything you have to offer. Australia is a solid trading partner, so they may be able to handle a couple percent increase in trade. That leaves the U.S., Russia, and China. You're coming here and trying to strong arm us because you're scared to begin serious talks with China. They will certainly tell you to go pound salt, just like the Russians already have."

The president just starred at Ivan Vakar with his college professor look, until the man finally broke. Ivan's shoulders slumped and Jackson knew it was all but done.

"Let's face it Ivan, unless you can figure out how to conjure up some market with the penguins in Antarctica, you're pretty well screwed."

Ivan Vakar started a rebut to the president's comments, but stopped. President Jackson smiled broadly. The multi-line phone on the president's desk buzzed with an incoming call. The president looked at the phone, and then at his guest.

"Looks like other matters need tending to, so I guess our time is up for today. Never a dull moment being leader of the free world. Maybe next time we can discuss something more satisfying."

The door opened, and it was the cue that Ivan Vakar was being officially dismissed. He stood and said that they would continue their conversations later. President Jackson gave him the political version of the *whatever* response, as Maggie showed him out.

Once the outer door was closed, and President Jackson was alone, he stood and walked across the Oval Office to the door of his private study. Going into the study and closing the door behind him, he found Eugene Taggart patiently waiting for him.

"Well, Gene, what do you think?"

Eugene Taggart, CIA DCI, pointed in the general direction of the Oval Office and cast a spy-like gaze at the president.

"Vakar, I'm 100 percent sure that he's the one we're looking for."

"What's the final piece of the puzzle?"

"NSA picked up three calls to the trigger number for the detonator in Chicago. One came from the Chicago tower that the FBI chopper destroyed. The other two came from a cellphone, geo-located over the mid-Atlantic. Time stamped to the time that Vakar's plane was there."

"Are you sure it was him? It could have been someone on the plane with him."

"Did you call Vakar from the Summit, after talking to Dr. Hughes?"

"Yes."

"Then I'm sure. The outgoing call number was the same as the one you dialed from Chicago."

The president of the United States exhaled slowly.

"We should have had this sooner. It took the NSA boys and girls a little longer than normal to sift out the information, given all the chatter that blew up directly after the incident at the port."

"I understand. Job well done, by all."

"Agree, though there is one last smoldering issue to resolve." Eugene Taggart pointed toward the empty Oval Office."

"You mean Vakar."

"Yes, I do."

"I have to admit that all the time he was in there, I wanted to reach across the desk and choke the life out of him."

"I completely understand."

"Now, it's time to handle retribution."

"I've been waiting for that sentence."

"Gene, again, this needs to be handled extremely delicately. I promised the Russians that there would be complete deniability. No repercussions, understand?"

Eugene Taggart looked at the president and smiled another spy-like smile.

"Don't lose a second's sleep, Mr. President. I have exactly the right option for this situation. Zero blowback, and complete deniability."

"Good."

President Walker Jackson and Eugene Taggart shook hands and turned to walk in opposite directions.

Printed in the United States
By Bookmasters